Pigeons on the Grass

A Portico Paperback

Pigeons on the Grass

WOLFGANG KOEPPEN

Translated by David Ward

HM

HOLMES & MEIER
New York   London

Published in the United States of America by
Holmes & Meier Publishers, Inc.
30 Irving Place
New York, NY 10003

Great Britain:
IBS
International Book Services Ltd.
Perth Street West
Hull HU5 3UA

Originally published under the title *Tauben im Gras* copyright © 1951
by Scherz & Goverts Verlag GmbH., Stuttgart. Copyright © 1972 by
Suhrkamp Verlag, Frankfurt am Main, as one of three Koeppen novels
collected in a volume entitled *Drei Romane*. All rights reserved by
Suhrkamp Verlag, Frankfurt am Main.

This book has been printed on acid-free paper.

Library of Congress Cataloging-in-Publication Data

Koeppen, Wolfgang, 1906–
    Pigeons on the grass.

    Translation of: Tauben im Gras.
    I. Title.
    PT2621.046T313   1988   833!912   88-11043
    ISBN 0-8419-1291-2 (acid-free paper)

Manufactured in the United States of America

PIGEONS ON THE GRASS ALAS
Gertrude Stein

Author's Foreword to the Second Edition (1953)

Pigeons on the Grass was written shortly after the currency reform, when the German economic miracle was rising in the West, when the first new movie theaters, the first new insurance palaces towered above the rubble and the makeshift shops, in the glory years of the occupation forces, when Korea and Persia troubled the world and the sun of the economic miracle could have set again quickly, and bloodily, in the East. It was the time in which the newly rich still felt unsure of themselves, in which the black marketeers looked for ways to invest their profits, and those who had had savings paid for the war. The new German paper money looked like good dollars, but still people had more faith in tangible goods, and there was much lost time to make up for and stomachs to be filled at last; heads were still a bit muddled from hunger and bomb blasts, and all the senses sought gratification before maybe World War III broke out. I depicted this time, the root of our Today, and I suppose I gave a generally valid description of it, for people believed they saw in the novel *Pigeons on the Grass* a mirror in which many, whom I had not thought of while writing, thought they recognized their own image, and several others, whom I had never associated with the circumstances and depressed states such as this book portrays, felt—to my dismay—that I had affronted them, I who had acted only as an author and, as Georges Bernanos writes, "filtered life through my heart in order to draw off its secret essence, full of balm and poison."

Translator's Note and Acknowledgments

Several sources of information related to *Pigeons on the Grass* are available in English. On Koeppen and postwar German writing, two books by Peter Demetz are particularly useful: *Postwar German Literature* (1970) and *After the Fires* (1987). In *The Inability to Mourn* (1975), Alexander and Margarete Mitscherlich offer psychoanalytical insights regarding the society and the behavior Koeppen portrays. And for a political, social, and cultural survey of the first postwar decade, Alfred Grosser's *Western Germany: From Defeat to Rearmament* (1955) remains helpful.

The only Koeppen texts available in English are *Death in Rome* (1956; *Der Tod in Rom*, 1954), translated by Mervyn Savill, and "Angst-Anxiety," a passage from an uncompleted novel, published in German with the English translation by Christian Seiler and Richard Kalfus on the facing page, in volume 11 (1978) of *Dimension: Contemporary German Arts and Letters*.

As always, I am deeply indebted to my wife, Judith Ward, for her never-failing support and encouragement. I have also benefited from the opportunity to visit and consult with the author. A. Leslie Willson, who presided over my apprenticeship as a translator, and the late Ralph R. Read were the first of many readers whose suggestions and comments contributed substantially to my efforts at reproducing the complexity and fluidity of Koeppen's prose.

Introduction

Pigeons on the Grass was unique in its day. At a time when most other German authors were avoiding the here and now, when many were struggling to produce even simple narrative forms, Wolfgang Koeppen composed a complex and socially critical novel in the tradition of Joyce's *Ulysses* and Alfred Döblin's *Berlin Alexanderplatz*. It portrays West Germans just as they were about to turn the corner from postwar despair and self-doubt to the new, forward-looking self-assurance of the *Wirtschaftswunder*, the German economic miracle.

Yet readers initially reacted coolly to this novel, which first appeared in 1951—they did not want to face the disturbing questions it raised. Germans were blocked by the enormity of the Nazis' crimes from working through the grief process that normally follows any loss. They expended much energy keeping acceptable memories separate from unacceptable ones, and this diminished their capacity to cope with the present. In the early 1950s Koeppen was virtually the only literary writer to insist on describing the kinds of self-deception he had observed and on posing questions about the continuing impact of the recent past upon the present.

Koeppen's novel appeared nearly a decade before Günter Grass's *Tin Drum* heralded the rise of West German writing to international prominence. But while the sudden burst of mature and no less critical novels and plays that marked the late fifties and early sixties brought Grass, Martin Walser, Peter Weiss, and several others critical acclaim and a large, enthusiastic readership, Koeppen remained a solitary, unappreciated figure in the first postwar decade. The contrasting reception accorded these similar literary voices reflects two distinct phases in West Germany's recovery from the effects of National Socialism.

At the war's end, Germany lay in ruins—spiritually as well as physically. The systems around which people ordered their lives had not survived the war intact. Universities, schools, the press, the Church, philosophy, art, literature, and even the German language itself had been corrupted by twelve years of Nazi rule and by the inability of any of these institutions to resist its barbarity effectively. To speak of a "zero hour," as many did, was to ignore the wreckage that had to be cleared away before there could be a new beginning. But 1945 did mark a watershed, and the choices each author made in response to its challenges permanently marked his or her literary identity. Three fundamentally different responses brought about three distinct literary cultures in the immediate postwar years.

Throughout 1945 and 1946, writing was dominated by the authors of the so-called inner emigration—Werner Bergengruen, Ernst Wiechert, Hans Carossa, Hermann Kasack, and others. These were established, conservative writers who had remained in Germany during the years of National-Socialist rule. Some had continued to publish in the Third Reich. Yet they claimed émigré status because they had parted company with the regime in spirit. These were the first writers to publish books in the western occupation zones. Their main aim was to bring back the "other Germany," the intellectual and spiritual Germany of lofty ideals and timeless values that they clung to as their real homeland, the Germany that Madame de Staël had called the land of poets and thinkers. Most of them avoided addressing specific political issues, reasserting the claim of earlier German intellectuals that they stood—or should stand—above politics. As a result, writing in the first score of postwar months had little to do with the concrete realities of life in war-ravaged Europe.

By the beginning of 1947, a second group had begun to make its presence felt—in print, if not in person. These were the émigrés. They, like the first group, represented an older generation; most had been established writers before the Nazi takeover forced them to leave. Among them were most of the outstanding authors of the 1920s.

Of the politically committed exiles who returned to Germany (among them were Anna Seghers, Johannes R. Becher, Theodor Plievier, and—after some delay—Bertolt Brecht), most chose the Soviet occupation zone as the one in which the fundamental Socialist restructuring of German society that they regarded as imperative was most likely to be achieved. Once the Cold War polarized East and West, the already small impact of their writing in the West was choked off.

Others were hesitant about returning to the land that had driven them away a dozen years earlier. Thomas Mann, for example, became embroiled in a year-long controversy when he rejected public appeals by writers of the inner emigration that he return from California in 1946 to help them lead Germany's spiritual reconstruction. Paradoxically, though, the appearance in 1947 of Mann's novel *Doctor Faustus,* along with *The Glass Bead Game* by 1946 Nobel Prize winner and fellow German expatriate Hermann Hesse, contributed substantially to the restoration of conservative Germany's self-esteem—and set the aesthetic standard by which literature would be measured until well into the 1950s.

Novelist Alfred Döblin was one of the few exiled writers who did return quickly to the western zones and participate in the rebuilding effort. In an article published in February 1946, three months after his return, Döblin drew clear distinctions between exile and domestic writing; in fact, he called them "two German literatures." The great and varying challenges of exile had kept exile writers sharp and alert, Döblin asserted, while those still in Gemany, forced to write harmlessly, had produced anodyne "belles lettres." They could not, he acknowledged, shed those habits overnight. "When they emerge into the present freedom, which of course is not complete, they bring . . . their old cowering and fretting attitude with them." Döblin concluded that the Germans needed

> a new, realistic literature that clears away the backlog of the old literature of falsehood and repression, a literature that formulates clearly and without bombast, that criticizes and is not shackled by party politics. It must be artistically daring and not least: it must open wide the gates to other countries. (*Neue Zeitung*, Munich, 8 Feb. 1946)

Gradually, a third group began to be heard from—writers who were very much in sympathy with Döblin's call for a new literature. They were men in their twenties and early thirties for whom the end of the war, the collapse of Nazi power and ideology, meant the end of all they had known during their adult lives. They had been soldiers. During 1946 and 1947, they returned to Germany from military hospitals and POW camps across Europe and North America. Most were self-taught writers. And they knew little about twentieth-century literature, most of which had been banned in the Third Reich.

In fact, access to literature was a serious problem in occupied Germany as well. Many modern authors were still missing from library shelves. New publication to fill the gaps depended on the publisher securing a license and a paper allotment from the occupation authorities. And, until the currency reform of 1948, most books were available only under the counter.

Meanwhile, magazines sprang up in response to the general hunger for ideas and literature. One particularly influential magazine, *Der Ruf* (The Call), was established in 1946 for the "young generation" by Hans Werner Richter and Alfred Andersch. The previous year, as prisoners-of-war in Fort Kearney, Rhode Island, the two had helped edit a bi-monthly newspaper bearing the same title for distribution to all other American POW camps. They dismissed the writing of the older generation as decorative, insubstantial "calligraphy;" in its place they endorsed Döblin's appeal for a new, realistic literature.

When pressure from the American military government forced Richter and Andersch to leave *Der Ruf* in 1947, they formed a circle of writers who met to read their unpublished texts aloud and criticize each other's work. Named after the year of its origin, the *Gruppe 47* (Group 47) would become the premier critical forum for young talent; it provided probably the single greatest impetus to the spectacular flowering of German letters a dozen years later.

The first obstacle these writers faced lay in the German language itself. The one means of expression available to them was the same German language that Hitler and Goebbels had spent twelve years forging into an instrument of monumental lies and obfuscation. Authors who participated in early *Gruppe 47* meetings would later recall having to teach themselves to write and speak German all over again. Heinrich Böll remembers the early atmosphere of linguistic uncertainty, the groping for valid, untainted forms of expression: "It was incredibly difficult shortly after 1945 to write even a half page of prose."

Their distrust of abstraction and the widespread availability of American short stories in translation led many young writers to imitate Ernest Hemingway's concise, concrete, journalistic prose. Two aims—reduction of language and reduction of form—comprised their position, which Wolfgang Weyrauch later dubbed *Kahlschlag,* chopping away underbrush to clear the land.

The terse, unadorned realism of *Kahlschlag* is best realized in the short prose of Heinrich Böll and Wolfdietrich Schnurre, and in Hans Werner Richter's 1949 novel, *Die Geschlagenen* (The Defeated). But these were the exceptions, and many novels and stories written in this style became increasingly superficial and banal. Most of the authors who had written in this vein fell silent by 1950, acknowledging the need to broaden their repertoire in order to move beyond *Kahlschlag*. They immersed themselves in the foreign and émigré works that were just now appearing in quantity on the German market in 1950 and 1951. Perhaps only Heinrich Böll, whose first novel, *Der Zug war pünktlich* (The Train Was on Time), appeared in 1949, was able to find a durable personal style within the narrow limits of *Kahlschlag*.

The first author even to approach Döblin's standard for a new literature stood apart from each of the groups outlined above. In 1951, Wolfgang Koeppen was a singular phenomenon: a keen observer who had been witness to both the fascist dictatorship and the emerging Federal Republic, and who had both the literary skills and the sense of commitment to confront those realities in a major work of fiction.

He did not share the conservative, inner-emigration view that granted the writer a privileged status. In his speech accepting the 1962 Georg Büchner Prize, the Federal Republic's most prestigious literary award, Koeppen discussed the sense of intense moral commitment he had always associated with the writing vocation: "I saw the writer among society's outsiders, I saw him as a sufferer, as a sympathizer, . . . The writer is committed to oppose authority, power, the constraints of the majority, the mass, the great numbers, to oppose convention grown rigid and rotten; he belongs to the persecuted, the expelled. . . ."

Unlike the émigré authors, he had firsthand knowledge of his readers' past and present experiences. And unlike the writers in the *Kahlschlag* vein, he also had the skills of a mature writer conversant with the broad range of European modernist tradition.

Born in 1906, Koeppen grew up in rural East Prussia in the home of a civil servant uncle who loved art and literature and who missed city life: he subscribed to several Berlin newspapers and kept his large personal library up to date. The young Koeppen ignored school and spent all his time reading. As a teenager, Koeppen was an outsider and a loner who enjoyed the indignation provoked by his long hair and nonconformism. Meanwhile, he had begun writing, and his articles were being published. During several vagabond years in and out of work, the theater, and university studies, Koeppen kept reading. He tells the story of how, one Friday in 1926, he spent the month's rent for James Joyce's *Ulysses*, which had just appeared in German, devoured it over the weekend, and returned the book the following Monday for a refund.

In the late 1920s Koeppen arrived in Berlin, the dazzling cultural capital of Europe, center of the frantic activity and fertile innovation in all the arts that accompanied the final years of the Weimar Republic. There he wrote free-lance articles for several papers and magazines, read, studied, attended the theater, and in 1930 caught the attention of Herbert Ihering, who hired him as drama critic—second to Ihering himself—for the liberal, urbane feuilleton section of the *Berliner Börsen-Courier*.

In January 1933 Hitler was named chancellor; within a few months, Weimar Germany's creative ferment was driven underground or into exile. The Nazis closed the *Börsen-Courier* within a year. Max Tau, editor of the prestigious Cassirer publishing house, gave Koeppen an advance to write a novel. That first novel, *Eine unglückliche Liebe* (An Unhappy Love), is a sensitive study of an unequal and unfulfilling yet lasting relationship of mutual dependence between an introverted young man and an émigré actress. By the time it appeared, in 1934, Koeppen was living in The Hague. There he wrote a second novel, modeled on his uncle's study abroad and subsequent adjustment to life in the provinces: *Die Mauer schwankt* (The Wall is Tottering). In 1935 it was one of the last books the embattled Bruno Cassirer was able to publish.

Both novels are marked by a sense of imminent danger: a precarious imbalance that cannot be sustained but is never resolved, hints at the impossible position of the artist in Hitler's Germany.

Yet neither addresses recent political developments directly. Nor is there more than a flirtation with the techniques of montage and interior monologue that Joyce, Alfred Döblin, and John Dos Passos had been developing. The new regime's hostility to modernism in any form precluded such unconventional prose. Thus, any experimentation in the modern vein, which Koeppen recalls having been eager to carry out, had to be deferred.

Lacking the papers to obtain work in The Netherlands and unable to survive without it, in the late 1930s Koeppen smuggled himself back into Germany, where a friend found him a marginal but draft-exempted job reading scripts in the film industry. Only after he had had to drop the attitude of conspicuous outsider/provocateur ("I went underground, I made myself small," he recalls) in order to survive in Nazi Germany did Koeppen discover the opportunities that lay in his outsider role—opportunities to quietly observe his surroundings with a critical eye—which he exploited so successfully in the postwar novels and three travel books. In 1943 he went underground literally as well, spending the last year and a half of the war in hiding.

Pigeons on the Grass was the first in Koeppen's trio of postwar novels, each in turn presenting an increasingly acerbic view of German reconstruction. The second was *Das Treibhaus* (The Hothouse), published in 1953. Its central figure is a sensitive poet-turned-politician who becomes so disillusioned with Bonn politics and with his role in it that he takes his own life. Similarities between Koeppen's characters and some prominent politicians caused a scandal, which briefly made *The Hothouse* Koeppen's only bestseller.

Der Tod in Rom (*Death in Rome*, trans. Mervyn Savill, 1956) appeared in the following year. In this scathing indictment of recrudescent fascism and middle-class opportunism, Koeppen depicts German sons trying to put together the pieces of their ruined lives while their unrepentant parents negotiate and then celebrate the completion of their return to the positions of power they enjoyed in the Third Reich. *Death in Rome* is the last novel Koeppen has published.

Koeppen recalls both *Pigeons on the Grass* and *The Hothouse* meeting with general incomprehension among reviewers. Only by 1954, with *Death in Rome,* did his writing no longer seem to critics to be, in Koeppen's words, "from the moon"; by that time, critics had assembled a sufficient frame of reference for assessing Koeppen's formal and thematic innovations. In fact, while the reviewers found plenty of details to praise or damn, they all managed to circumvent the main thrust of all three novels: that the recent German past is a reality still at work in the present.

Two hypotheses have been advanced to explain why Koeppen stopped writing novels in 1954. Critic Marcel Reich-Ranicki claims that the uncomprehending response accorded his three novels in the early 1950s presented Koeppen with a choice similar to the one he had faced in the mid-1930s: either to conform or to stop writing. Reich-Ranicki declares it shameful for West Germany and for the West German literary public that this could have come to pass. Others took the view that Koeppen had reached a crisis in his writing that had more to do with specifically literary problems than with societal and political ones. In a recent interview, Koeppen acknowledged that he found some truth in each view.

The new generation of authors, who by the 1960s were producing the sort of literature the original *Gruppe 47* had called for, embraced Koeppen as their only predecessor in the Federal Republic who was both aesthetically challenging and socially committed. In a 1958 article, the essayist and poet Hans Magnus Enzensberger praises Koeppen's keen sensitivity and his courage in writing what he sees around him, even when that means making enemies. He also calls Koeppen's novels "the most delicate and pliant prose that our impoverished literature now possesses." Günter Grass, who refers to Alfred Döblin as "my teacher," said in a recent interview that Koeppen is one of only two writers who preceded him in learning from Döblin and who then established their own distinctive voices while continuing to share Döblin's combination of formal innovation and uncompromising moral commitment.

Meanwhile, Koeppen's insistence on maintaining his privacy, and his unwillingness to participate in the public demands of the book trade, have contributed to the continued high respect he commands, but also to his books' less high (yet steady) sales figures. Nearly four decades later, his three novels are still an inside tip passed by word of mouth among writers, scholars, teachers and students.

Koeppen did not stop writing altogether. Three volumes of essays about his travels throughout Europe and in the United States again reflect Koeppen as the sensitive observer and mature stylist. He visited seven countries for several weeks each and composed the essays as a series of radio broadcasts. The books are *Nach Rußland und anderswohin* (To Russia and Elsewhere, 1958), *Amerika-Fahrt* (America Trip, 1959), and *Reisen nach Frankreich* (Journeys to France, 1962).

In 1976 Koeppen published *Jugend* (Youth), a loose collection of fragments in poetic prose based on his childhood memories. He also returned to writing about literature after 1951; a selection of his essays on authors past and present appeared in 1981 under the title *Die elenden Skribenten* (The Miserable Scribblers), followed in 1987 by *Morgenrot* (The Red of Dawn), three opening chapters of novels Koeppen never finished. Wolfgang Koeppen lives in Munich.

An essence distilled from the "root of our today," the stuff out of which our present situation has evolved, is what Wolfgang Koeppen promises his readers in a foreword to the second printing of *Pigeons on the Grass*. That claim still holds true to a remarkable extent for both German and American readers.

By 1951, the year in which the novel's action is set, the decisions that continue to define superpower politics today had been made.

The United States had decided to use the atomic bomb in war and to base world peace on the threat of its further use. The emphasis of American policy had shifted by 1947 from anti-fascism and democratization to cold-war anti-Communism; the best defense against the Communist threat was to foster an economically strong and politically stable Western Europe, including Germany.

This meant that the two halves of Germany would not be reunited. The currency reform of June 1948 had opened the way for the West German economic miracle. It had also provoked the Soviet blockade of Berlin, locking in the cold war boundaries and perceptions that have been in place ever since. The permanence of the split had been formally acknowledged in 1949, when the two German states were founded.

Finally, fighting in Iran and the outbreak of war in Korea in 1950 fueled fears of a superpower confrontation and accelerated the process of West German integration into the Western alliance, culminating in the rearmament of Germany, which would be accomplished in 1955.

The global issues Koeppen summarizes in 1951 have not changed: "Eastern world, western world, broken world, two world halves, alien and enemy to each other, Germany lives on the seam, where the seam splits open, . . ."

The first pages introduce a cluster of themes and images that will dominate the entire novel. Koeppen first sets an acoustic backdrop—the endless drone of Allied war planes above the city. He associates the planes with ominous birds and with the ancient practice of auguring the future by examining the entrails of birds. The bomb bays are empty: the augurs smile.

Typically, Koeppen makes his point—that the present moment is but a temporary, fragile respite from the omnipresent threat of war—by way of a metaphor that links present technology with ancient rites and rituals. He will go on to draw images and associations from the Bible and Christian lore, both Greek and Germanic myths, fairy tales, Persian poets, a Sanskrit epic, Italian Renaissance painting, folk and classical music, the jingles of popular songs and advertisements, baseball, vintage jazz, nuclear physics, and the works of an astonishing array of modern European and American authors. Koeppen is not just showing off: he is inviting his German readers, whose cultural heritage was so badly shaken by the twelve years of fascism, to explore all facets of past and present culture critically—to see what each can contribute to an understanding of the present.

The first segment also introduces a central motif: the constant thundering of the bombers is so familiar that no one takes notice of it. The overwhelming shadow of war with all its consequences is still upon the Germans, no matter how they try to ignore it. This motif has two crucial aspects: first is the pervasive noise, which interferes with communication. Its effect is summarized later in the novel: "Time had condemned this place. It had condemned it to noise and muteness." Again and again, human communication fails. Cries for help are drowned out by church bells, sirens, or automobile horns. When a distinguished poet begins his lecture on the Western humanist tradition, a malfunctioning loudspeaker system fills the hall with static.

Critic Klaus Scherpe observes that where Koeppen's narrative technique causes characters' paths to cross, those intersections are marked by misunderstanding. From Alexander's call to his daughter, which gets muffled and lost in his bath towel, to Edwin's unanswered call for help, there are dozens of encounters where communication either does not take place or is badly distorted. And the result is either speech without communication (noise) or no speech (muteness).

The other important aspect of that introductory passage is that everyone is ignoring the din, the constant reminder of past and potential future war: they are trying to carry on their lives as usual. On one level, the novel is a look at how—and at what cost—

Germans in the 1950s turned their backs on problems emerging from the years of war and Nazi dictatorship. *Pigeons on the Grass* was prophetic of the malaise that would accompany West Germany's headlong flight into affluence and go virtually unaddressed until the 1960s, when a new generation, too young to have experienced Nazism directly, would lash out at their parents' failure to face up to the unresolved issues of Germany's past.

Koeppen remarks in one of his travel books that the key to understanding a society is to know what people fear. Here, he distills the fears of a nation and those of its individuals—and the responses of both to their fears—by means of a remarkable amalgam of montage and interior monologue.

Koeppen employs a montage technique reminiscent of Dos Passos's trilogy, *USA*, inserting a headline or a snatch of song lyrics into his characters' trains of thought. While none of the headlines are taken verbatim from the postwar German press—Koeppen's aim is to distill and interpret rather than merely to document—they do sum up the issues of the day. The first three pages of *Pigeons on the Grass* are peppered with headlines that catalog global fears: WAR OVER OIL . . . RUSSIANS BEHIND THE SCENES . . . ATOM TESTS IN NEW MEXICO, ATOM FACTORIES IN THE URALS . . . CONFERENCE REACHES DEAD END. Headlines appear again in the following pages to highlight and summarize national worries, past and present.

While headlines reflect fears, music evokes pleasure—or the illusion of pleasure. Dozens of popular songs, jazz tunes, spirituals, sentimental folk songs and military marches make their appearance. They seldom pass without comment. In a chilling moment at the *Bräuhaus*, for example, American GIs and former German soldiers, full of beer and *Gemütlichkeit*, happily clink their steins and pound their feet to the beat of an oom-pah band; the GIs hear just another lively tune, but every German present recognizes it as the Badenweiler March, favorite of the dead *Führer*.

The action of the novel takes place in the American zone of occupation. What did Germans associate with the United States? There was America the powerful, which had defeated Germany and now kept its troops in German cities as a protective force. There was the generous America of CARE packages and Marshall Plan aid, Amerika-Haus cultural centers with their donated public libraries, and GIs who gave candy bars and gum to German children. America was also an entire mass culture the GIs had brought with them and replenished daily at the central exchange—Coca-Cola and big cars, popular songs and hot jazz, glossy magazines whose advertisements promised a world of push-button luxury, AFN radio and exotic sports like baseball. And finally, America was the home of flawed idealists crusading for democracy and justice in the world, while in their own society the races were segregated and unequal.

Koeppen includes all these Americas, using a total of nine "Amis" as foils by which to illuminate their German counterparts, and vice versa. Former German soldiers, for example, had frequently associated their arduous journey home at war's end with that of Odysseus after the fall of Troy. In *Pigeons on the Grass*, Koeppen recalls this by now hackneyed association, giving the name Odysseus Cotton to a black GI, who, like Homer's hero, must survive by his wits in a hostile land; but unlike his German counterparts, this Odysseus has no homeland to return to that will be any less hostile.

While the Amis come in for their own share of revealing scrutiny, most of the unflattering associations with animals are reserved for German characters. The novel's title is taken from a Gertrude Stein play entitled *Four Saints in Three Acts*. Koeppen takes Stein's lament "pigeons on the grass alas" to mourn—and not, as some have suggested, to indict—a society in short supply of everything that raises human life above the vulnerable, directionless, and dirty existence of those unlovely urban birds. Hence the endless references to herds, to predatory animals or vulnerable birds, to the hunt, alarm, flight, and death. Hasty patching could not conceal the deep scars that war left on the city's structures as well as on the lives and identities of its inhabitants. The more they cling to their damaged identities and systems of belief, the more they behave like the animals of Koeppen's bestiary.

David Ward

Pigeons on the Grass

Fliers were over the city, ominous birds. The noise of their motors was thunder, was hail, was storm. Storm, hail, and thunder, daily and nightly, flying in and flying out, exercises of death, a hollow din, a quaking, a remembering in the ruins. The bomb bays of the airplanes were empty for now. The augurs smiled. No one looked up at the sky.

Oil from the arteries of the earth, crude oil, polyp blood, fat of the saurians, armor of lizards, the green of fern woodlands, the giant rushes, sunken nature, time before man, buried legacy guarded by dwarfs, stingy, skilled in magic, and evil, the legends, the fairy tales, the devil's treasure: it was hauled up into the light, it was harnessed. What did the newspapers say? WAR OVER OIL, CONFLICT ESCALATES, THE WILL OF THE PEOPLE, OIL TO THE NATIVES, THE FLEET WITHOUT OIL, PIPELINE ATTACKED, TROOPS GUARD DERRICKS, THE SHAH MARRIES, INTRIGUES SURROUND PEACOCK THRONE, RUS-SIANS BEHIND THE SCENES, CARRIERS IN PERSIAN GULF. The oil kept the fliers in the sky, it kept the press occupied, it worried the people and, with lesser detonations, it propelled the light motorcycles of the newspaper carriers. With numb fingers, irritable, cursing, wind-buffeted, raindrenched, beerdull, tobaccostained, unrested, night-mareplagued, the smell of a nightfellow, a spouse, still on their skin, stiffness in the shoulder, rheumatism in the knee, the vendors

1

received their freshly printed wares. It was a cold spring. The latest didn't make it warmer. TENSION, CONFLICT, you lived in a field of tension, eastern world, western world, you lived on the seam, perhaps just where the seam would split open, time was precious, it was a breathing spell on the battlefield, and not enough to quite catch your breath, and again armament had begun, armament made living more costly, armament curtailed happiness, here and there they were hoarding the powder to blow the planet Earth to bits, ATOM TESTS IN NEW MEXICO, ATOM FACTORIES IN URALS, they were drilling blast chambers into the hastily patched masonry of the bridges, they talked about construction and made ready for demolition, what had begun to crack they allowed to go on crumbling: Germany was split into two parts. The newsprint smelled of machines running hot, of reports of misfortune, violent death, unjust rulings, cynical bankruptcies, of deceit, chains, and filth. The pages smeared, stuck together as if damp with fear. The headlines cried out: EISENHOWER INSPECTS TROOPS IN FEDERAL REPUBLIC, DEFENSE CONTRIBUTION DEMANDED, ADENAUER OPPOSES NEUTRALIZATION, CONFERENCE AT DEAD END, REFUGEES FILE SUIT, MILLIONS AT HARD LABOR, GERMANY: GREATEST INFANTRY POTENTIAL. The popular magazines lived on the reminiscences of the fliers and field marshals, the confessions of the stalwart men who had only nominally been party members, the memoirs of the brave, the upright, innocent, surprised, duped. Atop collars with oak leaf clusters and crosses they glared down from the walls of the newsstands. Were they there to sell advertising space for the magazines, or were they recruiting an army? The fliers that rumbled in the sky were the others' fliers.

The archduke was being dressed, he was being assembled. A medal here, a ribbon there, a cross, a shining star, aiguillettes of fate, chains of might, the shimmering epaulettes, the silver sash, the Golden Fleece, Orden del toisón de oro, Aureum Vellus, the sheepskin on the flint, dedicated to the greater glory of the Savior, the Virgin Mary, and Saint Andrew, to the defense and to the promotion of the Christian faith and the Holy Church, to virtue and the increase of morality. Alexander was sweating. Nausea plagued him. The tin, the Christmastree glitter, the embroidered uniform collar, it all cramped and confined him. The wardrobe man fumbled around at his feet. He was fastening on the archduke's spurs. What was the wardrobe man before the smartly polished dress boots of the archduke? An ant, an ant in the dust. The electric light in the dressing cubicle, this shack they had had the nerve to give Alexander, competed with the first morning light. Another one of those mornings! Alexander's face was pasty beneath the makeup; it was a face like curdled milk. Schnapps and wine and lack of sleep seethed and boiled in Alexander's blood; they pounded against the inside of his skull. Alexander had been brought here very early. Her Hugeness still lay in bed, Messalina, his wife, the ballrus, as they called her in the bars. Alexander loved his woman; whenever he thought about his love for Messalina, then the marriage he had with her was beautiful. Messalina was asleep, her face puffy, her mascara smudged, her eyelids looking like they had taken a beating, her coarsepored skin, a complexion like a hack driver's ravaged by drink. What a personality! Alexander bowed before this personality. He sank to his knees, bent over the sleeping Gorgon, kissed the crooked mouth, breathed in the vapors that now rose from her lips like pure distilled spirits: "What is it? You going? Cut it out! Oh, I feel sick!" That was what she was to him. On the way to the bathroom, his foot trod on broken glass. Asleep on the sofa lay Alfredo the painter, small disheveled crumpled delicate, exhaustion and disappointment in her face, crow's-feet at the corners of her closed eyes, pitiful. Alfredo was amusing when she was awake, a fast-burning torch; she sparkled, bantered, told stories, cooed, sharp-tongued, astonishing. The only person you could laugh about. What did the Mexicans call lesbians? It was something like

corn pancakes, tortilleras, probably a flat, dried cake. Alexander
had forgotten the word. Too bad! He could have used it. In the
bathroom stood the girl he had picked up, the girl he had lured with
his fame, with that wry smile that everybody knew. Headlines in the
movie magazines: ALEXANDER PLAYS ARCHDUKE, THE GERMAN SU-
PERFILM, THE ARCHDUKE AND THE FISHERMAIDEN, he had fished for
her, fished her out, served her up. What was her name again?
Susanne! Susanne at her bath. She was already dressed. Cheap
department store dress. Was rubbing soap over the run in her
stocking. Had doused herself with his wife's Guerlain. Was irritable.
Sulky. They always were afterwards. "Well, enjoy yourself?" He
didn't know what to say. Actually, he was embarrassed. "Bastard!"
That's what it was. They wanted him. Alexander, the great lover!
Fat chance! He had to shower. The car below was honking like
mad. They needed him. What still drew full houses? He still did.
ALEXANDER, THE AMOURS OF THE ARCHDUKE. People had had it;
they had had enough of the time, enough of the rubble; people
didn't want to see their cares, their fear, their everyday life, they
didn't want to see their sad state reflected. Alexander slipped off his
pajamas. The girl Susanne looked, curious, disappointed, and angry, at all of Alexander that hung slack. He thought: 'Go ahead and
look, and say whatever you want, they won't believe you, I'm their
idol.' He spluttered. The cold stream of the shower struck his
sagging skin like a whip. Downstairs they were honking again. They
were in a hurry, they needed their archduke. In the apartment a
child cried out, Hillegonda, Alexander's little girl. The child cried:
"Emmi!" Was the child calling for help? Fear, despair, loneliness lay
in the child's cry. Alexander thought, 'I ought to show her some
attention, I ought to have the time, she looks pale.' He called:
"Hille, are you up already?" Why was she up so early? He spluttered
the question into his towel. The question was smothered in the
towel. The child's voice fell silent, or it was lost in the furious
honking from the waiting car. Alexander rode to the studio. He was

4

dressed. He was booted and spurred. He stood before the camera. All the spotlights lit up. The medals sparkled in the light of the thousand candlepower bulbs. The idol drew himself up. They were filming the archduke A GERMAN SUPERPRODUCTION.

The bells tolled for early mass. Do-you-hear-the-bell-sounding? Teddy bears listened, dolls listened, an elephant made of wool and on red wheels listened, Snow White and Ferdinand the Bull on the bright wallpaper heard the mournful song that Emmi the nursemaid sang, droning and dirgelike, while she scrubbed the little girl's frail body with a coarse brush. Hillegonda was thinking, 'Emmi you're hurting me, Emmi you're scratching me, Emmi you're pulling my hair, Emmi your nail file is sticking me,' but she didn't dare tell the nursemaid, a robust country woman in whose broad face the simple piety of the peasants had frozen into an evil mask, that it hurt and that she was suffering. The nursemaid's song, do-you-hear-the-bell-sounding, was a constant warning that meant: don't complain, don't ask questions, don't be happy, don't laugh, don't play, don't fool around, use your time, for we are doomed to die. Hillegonda would rather have gone on sleeping. She would rather have gone on dreaming. She would have liked to play with her dolls, too, but Emmi said: "How can you play when God is calling you!" Hillegonda's parents were evil people. Emmi said so. You had to atone for the sins of your parents. That's how the day began. They went to church. A streetcar braked for a young dog. The dog was scraggly and collarless, a homeless stray dog. The nursemaid squeezed Hillegonda's little hand. It was no friendly, supportive squeeze; it was the firm, implacable grip of a prison guard. Hillegonda watched the little homeless dog go. She would rather have run after the dog than go to church with the nursemaid. Hillegonda pressed her knees together, fear of Emmi, fear of the church, fear of God weighed on her little heart; she hung on Emmi's hand, she let herself be pulled along, to put off their arrival, but the guard's hand dragged her on.

It was still so early. It was still so cold. So early and Hillegonda was on her way to God. Churches have portals of thick planks, heavy wood, iron fittings, and copper bolts. Is God afraid, too? Or is God, too, a prisoner? The nursemaid turned the wrought iron door handle and opened the door a crack. You could just barely slip into God's house. God's house smelled of sparklers, of miracle candles, like on Christmas Day. Was the miracle being prepared here, the awesome miracle she was told would come, the forgiveness of sins, the absolution of her parents? 'Show business child,' thought the nursemaid. Her thin, bloodless lips, the lips of an ascetic in a peasant face, were like a sharp line drawn for eternity. 'Emmi I'm afraid,' thought the child. 'Emmi the church is so big, Emmi the walls are going to fall in, Emmi I don't like you any more, Emmi dear Emmi, Emmi I hate you!' The nursemaid sprinkled holy water over the shivering child. A man pushed through the crack of the door. Fifty years of strain, toil, and cares lay behind him, and now he had the face of a hunted rat. He had lived through two wars. Two yellow teeth rotted behind his constantly murmuring lips; he was caught up in an endless conversation; he spoke to himself: who else would have listened to him? Hillegonda tiptoed after the nurse-maid. The pillars were dark and gloomy, the masonry showed wounds from bomb fragments. The child felt a cold draft like the chill of a grave. 'Emmi don't leave me, Emmi Hillegonda scared, good Emmi, bad Emmi, dear Emmi,' the child prayed. 'Leading the child to God, God punishes even unto the third and fourth genera-tion,' thought the nursemaid. The faithful knelt. In the tall room they looked like careworn mice. The priest read from the canon. The transubstantiation of the elements. The bell sounded. Lord-forgive-us. The priest was cold. Transubstantiation of the elements! Power, granted to the Church and its servants. Futile dream of the alchemists. Visionaries and frauds. Scholars. Inventors. Laborato-ries in England, in America, also in Russia. Wreckage. Einstein. A look into God's kitchen. The wise men of Göttingen. The atom photographed: enlarged ten thousand million times. The priest's rationality caused him to suffer. The murmuring of the praying mice sifted over him like sand. Sand of the grave, not sand of the Holy Sepulcher, sand of the wilderness, the mass in the wilderness, the sermon in the wilderness. Holy-Mary-intercede-for-us. The mice crossed themselves.

Philipp left the hotel, in which he had spent the night but hardly slept, the Hotel zum Lamm, on an alley in the old quarter of the city. He had lain awake on the hard mattress, the bed of traveling salesmen, the flowerless meadow of copulation. Philipp had given himself over to despair, to a sin. Fate had backed him into a corner. The wings of the Erinyes beat with the wind and the rain against his window. The hotel was new; the furnishings were factory fresh, varnished wood, clean, sanitary, shabby, and sparse. A curtain, too short, too narrow, and too thin to afford protection against the noise and light of the street, was printed in a Bauhaus wallpaper pattern. The glow of an electric sign meant to attract customers for the écarté club across the way flared at regular intervals: a clover spread its four leaves above Philipp and then slipped away. Beneath the window, gamblers who had lost their money cursed. Drunks staggered out of the Bräuhaus. They pissed against the houses and sang the-infantry-the-infantry, discharged, defeated conquerors. On the stairs there was a continual coming and going. The hotel was a devil's beehive, and everyone in this hell seemed cursed with insomnia. Behind the flimsy walls there was shouting, belching, and filth being flushed away. Later the moon had broken through the clouds, gentle Luna, rigor mortis.

The manager asked him: "Are you staying on?" He asked the question rudely, and his cold eyes, deathly bitter in the smooth, rancid fat of gluttony sated, thirst satisfied, lust gone sour under the connubial bedcovers, looked at Philipp suspiciously. Philipp had arrived at the hotel in the evening with no luggage. It had been raining. His umbrella had been wet, and aside from the umbrella he had had nothing with him. Would he stay on? He didn't know. He said: "Um, yes." "I'll pay for two nights," he said. The cold, deathly bitter eyes let him go. "You live right here on Fuchsstrasse," said the manager. He was looking at Philipp's registration slip. 'What does he care,' thought Philipp, 'what does he care, as long as he gets his money.' He said: "My apartment is being painted." It was a ridiculous excuse. Anyone could tell it was an excuse. 'He'll think I'm hiding, he'll figure out just what's going on, he'll think someone's looking for me.'

The rain had stopped. Philipp stepped out of Bräuhausgasse onto Böttcherplatz. He hesitated in front of the main entrance of the Bräuhaus, in the morning hours a closed maw that smelled of vomit. On the other side of the square lay Café Schön, the American Negro soldiers' club. The curtains behind the large plate glass windows were pulled to one side. The chairs stood on the tables. Two women rinsed the night's trash out onto the street. Two old men were sweeping the square. They stirred up eddies of beer coasters, paper streamers, drinkers' dunce caps, crumpled cigarette packs, burst balloons. It was a filthy tide, which came closer to Philipp with every push of the men's brooms. The night's breath and dust, the stale, dead refuse of merrymaking engulfed Philipp.

Frau Behrend had made herself comfortable. A piece of wood crackled in the stove. The janitor's daughter brought the milk. The daughter was sleepy and hungry. She was hungry for life as she saw it in the movies, she was a princess under a spell, forced to do menial tasks. She was waiting for her messiah, the honking horn of the prince come to her rescue, the millionaire's son in a sports car, the dinnerjacketed dancer at the cocktail lounge, the technical genius, the farsighted engineer, the winner by a knockout over the backward, over the enemies of progress, young Siegfried. She had a narrow chest, rickets in her joints, a scar on her stomach, and a pinched mouth. She felt she was being used. Her pinched mouth whispered: "The milk, Frau Obermusikmeister."

Whispered or shouted: that title conjured up the image of glorious days. The Musikmeister strode proudly through the city at the head of his regiment. The march resounded from hide and brass. Bells jingled. The colors high. Legs high. Arms high. Herr Behrend's muscles strained against the fabric of his tight uniform. Open air concert at the forest pavilion! The Meister conducted Der Freischütz. At the command of his raised baton, Carl Maria von Weber's romantic strains ascended in a muted pianissimo to the treetops. Frau Behrend's breast rose and fell like ocean swells at her garden table by the restaurant. Her hands lay inside net gloves on the brightly checkered linen of the table where the ladies sipped coffee. For this cultural hour Frau Behrend saw herself accepted into the circle of the ladies of the regiment. Lyre and sword, Orpheus and Mars fraternized. The major's wife graciously served what she had brought along, her own homemade layer cake with three kinds of jam, slipped into the oven while the major sat on his horse, commanding the parade grounds, forward-march, accompanied by the drum roll of the Wolfsschlucht.

Couldn't they leave us in peace? Frau Behrend hadn't wanted the war. The war poisoned the men. Beethoven's death mask, pale and stern, surveyed the narrow attic room. A bronzebearded and bereted Wagner balanced forlornly atop a sheaf of classical piano excerpts, the yellowing legacy of the Musikmeister who, in one or the other part of Europe occupied by the Führer and then lost again, had latched onto a painted hussy and now played, in God knows what kinds of coffee houses, music for Negroes and their Veronicas, things like Well-I'm-goin'-to-Alabama.

He didn't get to Alabama. He didn't give them the slip. The time of lawlessness was over, the time that reported SS SQUAD LEADER POSES AS RABBI IN PALESTINE, BARBER DIRECTOR OF GYNECOLOGICAL CLINIC. The impostors were captured; they were sitting, sitting out

9

behind bars their new, far too lenient sentences: concentration camp inmates, the persecuted, deserters, phony MDs. There were judges again in Germany. The Musikmeister paid for the attic room, he paid for the wood in the stove, the milk in the bottle, the coffee in the pot. He paid for it with the wages of his Alabama sins. A tribute to respectability! What good was it? Everything is getting more expensive, and once again it's covert routes that lead to the amenities of life. Frau Behrend drank Maxwell House coffee. She bought the coffee from the Jew. The Jews—those were blackhaired people who spoke broken German, undesirables, foreigners, drifters who looked at you accusingly through darkly glistening, nightspun eyes, likely wanted to speak of gas and gravedigging and of execution sites in the gray of dawn, the faithful, rescuees who could think of nothing else to do with their rescued lives than to stand on rubble tracts in the bombed-out city (why a target for bombs? my God, why beaten? in punishment for what sin? the five rooms in Würzburg, home on a southerly slope, view out over the city, view out over the valley, the Main glistening, the morning sun on the balcony, FÜHRER VISITS DUCE, why?) in small, hastily constructed shacks, in their flimsy makeshift shops, selling untaxed and untariffed wares. "They leave us nothing," said the grocerwoman, "nothing, they want to ruin us." Amis lived in the grocerwoman's home. They had lived in the confiscated house for four years. They passed the place on to one another. They slept in the double bed of mottled birch, the bedroom set from her dowry. They sat in the baronial armchairs of her Old German suite, amid the splendor of the eighties, their feet on the table, and emptied their tin cans, their conveyorbelt food CHICAGO PACKS THOUSAND STEERS A MINUTE, a hoorah in their press. In the yard foreign children played, dressed in shoppingbag blue, eggyolk yellow, fire red, like clowns, girls seven years old with their lips made up like whores, the mothers in overalls, their pantlegs rolled up, itinerant folk, frivolous people. The coffee in the grocerwoman's shop molded, tariffed and overtaxed. Frau Behrend nodded. She never forgot the respect she owed the shopkeeper, the fear learned in the hard school of ration-coupon days CALLING UP SIXTY TWO AND ONE HALF GRAMS SOFT CHEESE. Now they had everything again. Here anyway. Who could buy it? FORTY MARKS PER CAPITA. Six percent of savings redeemed and ninety-four percent written on the wind. My own belly comes first. The world was tough. Soldiers' world. Soldiers were tough. Prove yourself. The scales were right again. For how long? Sugar was disappearing from the stores. England was short of meat. Where is the victor, I'll give him his laurels? They call Speck bacon. Ham is the same thing as Schinken. Fatty smoked meat lay in the display window at Schleck's butcher shop. "Lean meat, please." The butcher's knife separated the yellowed, whitishly wobbling fat from the reddish fiber of the center. Where is the victor, I'll give him his laurels? The Amis were rich. Their cars were like ships, Columbus's caravels returned. We discovered their land. We populated their continent. Solidarity of the white race. It was nice to belong among the rich people. Relatives sent packages. Frau Behrend opened the paperback she had started last night before going to sleep. A thrilling story, a true to life novel: FATE CLUTCHES AT HANNELORE. Frau Behrend wanted to know what happened next. The threecolor cover showed the picture of a young woman, good, sweet, and innocent, and in the background the scoundrels assembled, dug their pits, burrowing scavengers of fate. Life was dangerous, full of pitfalls the way of the respectable. Fate clutched not just at Hanne-lore. But in the last chapter the good triumph.

Philipp was having trouble with time. The moment was like a tableau vivant, the droll object of a kind of paralysis, existence cast in plaster, smoke that made you cough hung suspended around it like a mock arabesque, and Philipp was a little boy in a sailor suit, H.M.S. CRICKET across the band of his cap, and he was in a small town, sitting in a chair in German Hall, and on the stage, in a

sylvan setting, the ladies of the Queen Louise Circle were presenting scenes from the history of the fatherland, Germania and her
children, people used to love that, or pretended to love it, the
principal's daughter held the pan with the burning pitch that
evidently was supposed to give the scene something solemn, endur-
ing, timeless. The principal's daughter was long since dead. Eva, he
had tossed burrs in her hair. The boys were dead, all of them, who
had sat next to him on the chairs of German Hall. The town was a
dead town, like so many towns in the east, a town somewhere in
Masuria, yet you could no longer go to a train station and ask for a
ticket to that place. The town was extinguished. Curious: there was
no one in the streets. The classrooms of the Gymnasium were mute
and empty. Crows nested in the windows. He had dreamed just
that, during classes he had dreamed it: life in the town had died,
the houses were empty, the streets, the market square mute and
empty, and he, the only one left, had driven alone through the
dead town in one of the cars abandoned by the roadside. The
backdrop to that dream had been put into real life, but Philipp no
longer acted on that stage. Did he suffer when he thought of the
dead, of the dead places, his buried companions? No. The sensation grew rigid as it had before the tableaux of the Queen Louise
Circle, the whole idea was somehow pompous, sad, and revolting, a
triumphal avenue made of plaster of Paris and stamped tin laurel,
but above all it was boring. Meanwhile, though, this same time was
racing on, even though on the other hand it was standing still and
was the Now, this moment of sheer eternal duration, it hurtled
along, if one considered time as the sum of all days, the procession
of light and darkness that is given us here on earth was like the
wind, was something and nothing, measurable through cunning,
but no one could say what it was he was measuring, it coursed
around the skin, shaped one, and slipped away, impossible to grasp,
to hold: where from? where to? But in addition he, Philipp, stood
he, Philipp, stood in addition outside this procession of time, not

actually cast out of the stream, but rather originally called to man a post, an honorable post, perhaps, for he was to observe everything, but the dumb thing was, he got dizzy and couldn't observe anything at all, seeing finally only a ground swell in which a few dates flashed on like signals, no longer even natural signs, artificially, cunningly placed buoys in the ocean of time, swaying human marker on the unchecked waves, but now and then the sea solidified, and out of the water of infinity rose an image, frozen, meaningless, inviting ridicule, a tableau.

Into the Engel Picture Show you can flee, even in the morning, from the light of day. The Last Bandit is a box-office hit. The picture show owner telegraphs the attendance figures to the film distributor. House record, arithmetical acrobatics, like the news bulletins back then GROSS REGISTER TONNAGE SUNK. Wiggerl, Schorschi, Bene, Kare, and Sepp stood under the loudspeaker, stood under the cascade of words, victory and fanfares, little Hitler Youths, cub soldiers, brown shirt, short pants, bare legs. They shook the collection cans, rattled the pennies awake, clattered with their tin badges. "For Winter Assistance! For the front! For the Führer!" In the night the siren wailed. The flak was silent. Now the fighters flew out to fight. Diamonds to go with the Iron Cross. Mines. The light flickered. Duck! Water rushed through the cellar pipes. Next door they've drowned. All of them drowned in the cellar. Schorschi, Bene, Kare, and Sepp sit watching the last bandit. Their hard bottoms dig deep into the unstuffed, sagging cushions of the theater seats. They have no apprenticeship and no work. They have no money, yet they have the mark for the bandit; it flew their way, birdie in the cornfield. They skip classes at the trade school, since they have no trade, or rather a trade you don't learn in school, more likely on street corners, in the doorways of the dollar changers, the alleyways of the ladies, the side streets of the friendly boys in the shadow of the palace of justice, the trade of swift hands

13

that take and do not give, the craft of hard fists that beat and rob, and the gay route, the profession of the soft gaze, of swaying hips, swinging ass. Wiggerl is in the Legion, so far across the sea, with the Annamese in the bush, vipers and vines, crumbling temples, or with the French in the fort, girls and wine in Saigon, heavy odor of the quarters, the penal cell in the casemates, lizards in the sun. He doesn't care. Wiggerl fights. He sings: hold the colors high. He falls. A SOLDIER'S DEATH IS THE BEST OF DEATHS. So often heard, drilled into them during childhood, exemplified by their fathers and brothers, comfort for mother's tears, those words will never be forgotten. Schorschi, Bene, Kare, and Sepp are waiting for the drummer. They are waiting in the twilight of the movie theater. The Last Bandit. They are prepared; prepared to follow, prepared to fight, prepared to die. It doesn't need to be a god who calls them, a poster on every wall will do, a currently popular mask, a little trademark beard, no smiling augur, the robot face stamped out of tin, a face below average, no promise in the eyes, empty waters, polished mirrors that always show only you, Caliban, on whom the genii turned their backs, the synthetic Pied Piper, his call: PROVE YOURSELF, blood, pain, and death, I'll lead you to yourself, Caliban, you need not be ashamed of being a monster. The movie house is still standing; into the registers pours the cash. The city hall is still standing; amusement tax proceeds are recorded. The city is still growing.

The city is growing. MIGRATION BAN LIFTED. They come streaming back, a flood that ebbed away, trickled into the country, into peasants' rooms, while the cities burned, while in the alley daily traversed the asphalt melted, became Stygian water, caustic and burning, there where little shoes ran along to school, where bride and groom walked, the home of stone quaked, and then they perched there in the villages, their household things lost, lost the nest where their young came into the world, lost the things they'd

14

always kept, the what-you-were, the childhood banished to the
bottom dresser drawer, a baby picture, the class at school, the friend
who drowned, the faded writing of a letter, So-long-Fritz, Adieu-
Marie, a poem, did I write those lines? —

The small, delicately vigorous body of the doctor, well-con-
ditioned in brisk athletic exercises, lay on the table covered with an
oilcloth, and out of one vein in his arm flowed his blood, not visible
and not close by, to another person, no warm glance from the
recipient of new life gratified the donor, Dr. Behude was an abstract
Samaritan, his blood was transformed into a cipher, a chemical
formula, expressed in the language of mathematical symbols, it
flowed into a canning jar, received a label, raspberry juice, straw-
berry jam, the blood group was on the label, the juice was sterilized
and the preserves could be shipped, anywhere, through the air, far
across oceans, to wherever there happened to be a battlefield, and
there always was one, an originally harmless landscape, nature with
the changing seasons, a field with seed and harvest, to which men
now marched, rode, and flew in order to wound and kill each other.
There they lay, pale, on a field stretcher, the banner of the Red
Cross flapped in the alien wind and reminded them of the am-
bulances that rushed with a siren torrent through the streets of the
traffic-clogged cities, the cities they came from, the tetanus shot
stung and Dr. Behude's blood was pumped into their torn bodies.
Dr. Behude received ten marks for giving blood. The money was
paid in cash at the hospital cashier's desk. Young doctors who had
cut open, sawed open, rinsed off, and stitched back up the soldiers
of the Second World War, and now, working as unpaid volunteers
and aides, had to face the fact that they were superfluous, too many,
far too many war medics, crowded in to sell their blood, the only
thing they had to sell. Dr. Behude, too, needed the ten marks, but
it wasn't just the sum, money for blood, that prompted him to make
this transaction. Dr. Behude was chastising himself. It was an

ascetic castigation he subjected himself to, and the bloodgiving was an attempt, like the weightlifting, the morning running, the waist bends, the breathing exercises, to produce an equilibrium between the forces and the demands of body and soul. Dr. Behude analyzed himself while he lay on the cool oilcloth of the transfusion table. He was no philanthropist, no donor; the blood left him, became a medicine like any other, it could be transported, could be traded, used to save lives, it did not touch Dr. Behude; he was cleansing himself, he was preparing himself. Soon the rooms at his office will fill up, will fill up with people who want to tap strength and encouragement from him. The horde of halfcrazies loves and flocks to its Dr. Behude, the neurotics, the liars who don't know why they lie, the impotent, the queers, the paedophiles who go wild over children, follow little skirts around and bare legs, the literary sorts who don't fit in anywhere, the painters for whom life's colors run together into geometrical brushstrokes, actors who choke on dead words, Pan was dead, died a second time, they all came, those who needed their complexes like their daily bread, the timid and help-less, too helpless also to buy themselves health insurance or ever pay a bill. —

They had come away with their lives, a useless existence, they holed up, embittered, in tiny spots, in forest and field, in cabins and on farms, the smoke lifted, they listened for the steam shovels digging into the rubble, listened from afar, barred from Nineveh, from Babylon, Sodom, the beloved cities, the great, warming cauldrons, refugees, damned to summery freshness, tourists who couldn't pay up, eyed askance by the country folk, madly homesick for their stones. They returned home, the bar was raised, that despised ordinance, the migration ban, fell, their banishment was lifted, they streamed back, they flooded in, the high-water mark rose CITY FOCAL POINT OF HOUSING SHORTAGE. They were home again, joined the ranks, rubbed elbows again, got the jump on each other, haggled, created, built, founded, conceived, sat in the old pub, breathed the familiar stale air, kept an eye on their terrain, the lovers' lane, the new generation of asphalt alleys, laughter and quarreling and the neighbor's radio, they died in the municipal hospital, were driven out by the morgue, lay in the cemetery at the East-South-Crossing, surrounded by streetcar clanging, by hot gasoline haze, happy to be home. SUPERBOMBER STATIONED IN EUROPE.

Odysseus Cotton left the station. At the end of a long, loose arm, from a brown hand dangled a small case. Odysseus Cotton was not alone. A voice was with him. The voice came from the case, gentle, warm, soft, a deep voice, sensuous breathing, breath like velvet, hot skin under an old, torn army blanket in a corrugated tin shack, screams, bullfrog croaking, night on the Mississippi, Judge Lynch rides over the land, oh day of Gettysburg, Lincoln enters Richmond, forgotten the slave ship, the brand singed forever into the flesh, Africa, lost earth, the tangle of the forests, voice of a Negress. The voice sang Night-and-Day, its sound shielded the bearer of the case against the station square, entwined him like the limbs of a lover, warmed him in this foreign place, tented him in. Odysseus Cotton stopped, undecided. He looked past the taxi stands, looked across at the Rohn Department Store, saw children, women, men, the Germans, who were they? what did they think? how did they dream and love? Were they friends? enemies?

The heavy door of the telephone booth banged shut behind Philipp. The glass isolated him from the commotion on the station square, the noise was now just a murmuring, the traffic a play of shadows in the rippled surfaces of the walls. Philipp still didn't know how he was going to spend the day. The hour gaped before him. He felt like one of the empty wrappers the broom had swept into the dustpan, useless, bereft of his destiny. Of what destiny? Had he been destined for something, had he escaped it, and was it possible—assuming there was such a thing—to escape a destiny? THE ASTROLOGICAL CENTURY, HOROSCOPE FOR THE WEEK, TRUMAN'S AND STALIN'S STARS. He could have gone home. He could go home to the house on Fuchsstrasse. Spring had arrived. Weeds blossomed on the mansion's unkempt lawn. Home? A refuge full of leaks and spatterings: Emilia had probably calmed down toward morning. There would be scratches kicked into the doors, holes knocked in the walls, porcelain smashed. Emilia, exhausted by her rampage, wearied by her dreams, beaten by her fears, lay on the pink heir-loom bed, the deathbed of her grandmothers, who had lived a lovely life while that was still possible, Heringsdorf, Paris, Nice, the gold standard, and the luster of the wirklich geheimer Kommerzienrat title. The dogs, the cats, the parrot, jealous of each other, one another's enemies, yet united in a common front of hatred against Philipp, a phalanx of malevolent stares, just as everything in this house hated him, his wife's relatives, the other heirs, the crumbling walls, the dull parqueted floors, the trickling, whistling pipes of the broken-down heating system, the baths long in need of repair, the animals occupied the sofas and chairs like siege towers and watched over the sleep of their mistress through halfopened eyelids, the sleep of their prey, to whom they were chained and whom they guarded. Philipp phoned Dr. Behude. In vain! The psychiatrist hadn't yet returned to his office. Philipp didn't expect to gain anything from a session with Dr. Behude, no explanation, no insight, neither con-fidence nor courage, but he had got used to coming to see the nerve specialist, lying down in the darkened treatment room, and letting his thoughts run free, a rapid succession of images that swept over him on Dr. Behude's couch, a kaleidoscopic shifting of place and time, while the therapist of souls sought with gentle, soporific voice to free him from guilt and atonement. — Dr. Behude stood in the treatment room of the clinic and buttoned up his shirt. His face shimmered palely in the white-framed mirror on the wall. His eyes, which were supposed to be possessed of hypnotic power, were dull, tired, and a little inflamed. One hundred cubic centimeters of his blood stood in the hospital's refrigerator.

Night-and-Day. Odysseus Cotton laughed. He was happy. He swung his case. He showed his strong, gleaming teeth. He was confident. A day lay ahead of him. The day offered itself to one and all. Under the overhanging roof of the station waited Josef, the porter. The red porter's cap sat level, with military sternness, on his bald pate. What had bent Josef's back? Travelers' suitcases, the baggage of decades, half a century's daily bread earned by the sweat of his brow, Adam's curse, treks in army boots, the rifle over his shoulder, the belt, the sack with the hand grenades, the weight of the helmet, the weight of the killing, Verdun, the Argonne, Chemin des Dames, he had gotten out in one piece, and suitcases again, travelers without rifles, tourist traffic to the station for points south, tourist traffic to the hotel, the Olympic games, the youth of the world, and more flags, more marches, he carried officers' baggage, his sons left and did not return, the youth of the world, sirens, the old woman died, mother of the children devoured by war, the Americans came with colorful bags, duffel bags, light baggage, cigarettes as currency, the new mark, the savings gone with the wind, chaff, going on seventy, what was left? The seat in front of the station, the number badge on his cap. His body was wizened, his eyes still twinkled alertly behind the steelrimmed glasses, merry little wrinkles ran from his eyelids into the expanse of skin, rivulets flowing into the gray of old age, the outdoor brown, the beer ruddiness of his face. The fellow porters took the place of family. They left old Papa the easy commissions that came along between heavy loads of baggage, delivering a letter, fetching flowers, carrying a lady's handbag. Josef came by his tasks humbly, and craftily, too. He understood people. He knew how to win people over. Many a bag was handed him that people hadn't intended to give him. He trusted to what the day would bring. He saw Odysseus Cotton. His

19

eyes flirted with the little case that music came out of. He said: "Sie Mister, ich tragen." He wasn't deterred by the singing that had built a tent around Odysseus, he reached into the alien world, Night-and-Day-world, crowded the brown hand off the handle of the case, crowded in, small, modest, resolute, friendly, close to the dark giant, King Kong, who towered over him, unfathomable are the never felled, the forests primeval. Josef remained unhypnotized by the voice, voice of the broad, lazy, and warm current, engulfing voice, voice of the mysterious night. Like logs on a river they glided, one to the other; totems around the kraal, a taboo around the renegade of the tribe, Josef felt neither pleasure nor displeasure, nothing fascinated and nothing frightened him: no libidinal craving, Odysseus stood in no affectual relation to Josef, Josef was no mask of Oedipus for Odysseus, neither hate nor love moved them, Joseph sensed a liberal tipper, he drifted closer, gently and persistently, he saw a lunch, saw a beer Night-and-Day —

The parrot screeched, a love bird, Kama, the god of love, rides on a parrot, the narratives of the Parrot Book, fantastic and obscene, the adolescent girl had taken it from her father's cabinet, hidden it under her bed, the parrot in the old depictions of the Holy Family, symbol of the immaculate conception, it was a rosella parrot, rotund as an old, successful actress, red, yellow, agave green, steely blue its plumage, the gown that it shook in a fit of temper, its freedom was forgotten, was a forgotten dream, no longer even real, the bird screeched, screeching not for freedom, clamoring for light, to have the blinds raised, the heavy curtains shoved aside, the room's darkness rent, an end to the artificially prolonged night. The dogs and the cats grew restless as well. They sprang into the sleeping woman's bed, quarreled, yanked at the tattered silk of the bedcover, and down eddied through the room like snow, invisible in the darkness. Emilia still lay beneath the blanket of night which, outside, had ended hours before. Her consciousness was still

blanketed by night. Her limbs lay in the depths of night as in a
grave. The pink tongue of the black tomcat licked at the ear of the
youthful corpse. Emilia stirred, flailed about, tossed over onto her
back, groped along the crackling fur of the cat, took hold of one of
the dogs by its head, rasped: "what's happening, what do you want
now?" where had she come from? out of what dark abysses of sleep?
She heard the endless whistling in the house's pipes, the plaster
crumbling, the animals sniffing, purring, prowling, swishing bushy
tails. The animals were her friends, the animals were her companions, they were the companions of the happy childhood Emilia had
now been driven out of, they were comrades in the solitude in
which Emilia lived, they were play and joy, they were harmless,
devoted, spontaneous, they were the harmless and spontaneous
animal world, free of falseness and contriving, and they knew only
the good Emilia, an Emilia who was truly good to the animals. The
wicked Emilia turned against people. She sat up abruptly and
called: "Philipp!" She listened, her features wavering between crying and bitterness. Philipp had left her! She clicked on the bedside
lamp, jumped up, ran naked across the room, turned the switch for
the overhead light, silver candleshaped bulbs cradled in verdigrised
medlar boughs, wall brackets lit up, light that was repeated in
mirrors, multiplied, and colored by lampshades, yellow and reddish,
falling like yellow and reddish shadows on the woman's skin, on her
still almost childlike body, the long legs, the small breasts, the
slender hips, the smooth, elastic tummy. She ran into Philipp's
room, and in the natural light of the overcast day that came in here
through the curtainless window, her pretty figure suddenly paled.
Her eyes had an unhealthy sheen, sunk in shadows, the left lid hung
down as if robbed of all its resilience, the small, willful forehead was
wrinkled, particles of dirt stuck in her skin, black hair dangled in
her face in short, shaggy strands. She looked at the table with the
typewriter, the white, unused paper, the materials of the work she
abhorred and from which she expected miracles, fame, wealth,

21

security overnight, in a single inspired night in which Philipp would write an important work, in a single night, but not in many days, not in some kind of job, not with the constant clattering of the little typewriter. "He's a failure. I hate you," she whispered, "I hate you!" He was gone. He had run away from her. He would be back. Where else would he go? But he was gone; he had left her alone. Was she so unbearable? She stood naked in the workroom, naked in the daylight, a streetcar rolled past, Emilia's shoulders drooped, her collarbones stuck out, her flesh lost its freshness, and her skin, her youth, was as if doused with old, curdled milk for a second, pasty, sour, crumbly. She lay down on the rippled leather sofa that was firm and cold as a doctor's examining table, and therefore suspect to her, and she thought of Philipp, conjured him up in her thoughts, forced him back into the room, her comic, her failure, her unbusinessman, her companion, the man she loved and hated, defiler and defiled. She stuck a finger into her mouth, slid her tongue around it, moistened it, a little girl, reflective, abandoned, helpless, hold-me, she took her finger, played with herself, let it slip inside her, and fell into the deep trance of pleasure that permitted her, although she was at the mercy of the day and bathed in its hostile light, yet a bit of inward night, a span of intimacy and love, a delaying —

Night-and-Day. Odysseus looked down at the porter's red cap, at the much stained, threadbare cloth, he saw the visor placed squarely, in military fashion, over the eyes and glasses, he saw the brass number, he recognized the tired shoulders, the shabby wool of the coat, the frayed strings of the apron, and finally glimpsed a small, protruding belly hardly worth mentioning. Odysseus laughed. He laughed like a child who makes friends quickly, he perceived, childlike, in the old man an old child, a playmate of the streets. Odysseus was pleased, he was good-natured, he welcomed his companion, gave him a little of his own present abundance, gave him a little of the victor's role, let him have the case: the music, the voice now hung in the old porter's hand. Valiantly, a spindly little shadow, Josef strode beside the tall, broad form of the soldier across the open square in front of the station. Out of the case came blaring, rasping, shrieking: Limehouse Blues. Josef followed the black man, he followed the liberator, the conqueror, followed the protective and occupational force into the city.

A shrine, an altarpiece, a solemn shadow, mildewed remains of knowledge assumed and cast off again, a threat realized and not realized, fount of hope, deceptive wellspring for the thirsting: with its opened wings, the book cabinet was an unholy triptych of the written word behind the naked Emilia. For whom was she sacrificing herself, this priestess and doe in one, a debased Iphigenia, with no Artemis to protect her, no Tauris to be borne off to? The inherited books, the sumptuous editions of the 1880s, the untouched gilt-edged volumes, the German classics and the Pharos-on-the-Sea-of-Life for the lady's salon, the Struggle-for-Rome and the Bismarck's-Thoughts-and-Recollections for the gentlemen's drawing room, and the cupboard with the cognac and the cigars, the library of the forefathers who had made money and not read, stood beside Philipp's, the untiring reader's, collection of books carried home, all jumbled and disjointed, the heart laid bare, instinct dissected. And before these, the splendidly bound volumes and the dogeared ones consulted in vain, before them and, in a sense, at their feet, lay the unclothed woman, the heiress, one hand between her still childlike thighs, seeking to forget, to forget what they now called reality and hard facts and the struggle for survival and integration into society, and Behude spoke of unsuccessful adaptation to her surroundings, and it all really just meant that it was a bad life, a cursed world and the favored position lost, the being-well-off through a fortunate birth, the fall into the well prepared nest, what was there left now of the foolish torrent of flattery that inundated her childhood? 'You're rich, my lovely, you'll inherit, you pretty thing, inherit dear grandma's fortune, the Kommerzienrat factory millions, he thought of you, the geheimer Kommerzienrat with his restricted diet, the provident paterfamilias thought of his granddaughter, of the yet unborn child, he endowed her richly, richly providing for the future in his will, so that you might prosper, child, and the family might flourish and grow even richer, you needn't do a thing, he did so much, you needn't push yourself, he pushed himself and eight hundred workers, for you, little pigeon, you're floating at the top' (what floats at the top? what is there at the top of a pond? frog spawn, bird droppings, rotting wood, irridescent patches of color, shifting spectrums of grease, slime, and decay, the corpse of a young lover), 'you can celebrate, child, garden parties, you pretty thing, you'll always be queen of the ball, Emilia!' She wanted to forget, to forget the devalued mortgages, the lost privileges, the Reich treasury bonds in the depository, paper, waste paper, to forget the unprofitable, rundown houses she owned, the encumbrances on her property, the bricks she couldn't sell, her bondage to the authorities, the paperwork, the delays of payment granted and then rescinded, the lawyers, she wanted to forget, wanted to run away from what had deceived her, too late, to escape the material world, to devote herself now to the spirit, ignored until now, misunderstood, that was her new rescuer, its weightless powers, les fleurs du mal, flowers from the void, consolation in garret rooms, how-I-hate-poets, those-freeloaders, those-perennial-dinner-guests, spirit, consolation in rundown villas, yes-we-were-rich, une saison en enfer: il semblait que ce fut un sinistre lavoir, toujours accablé de la pluie et noir, Benn Gottfried Early Poems, La Morgue is—dark-sweet—onanie, les paradis artificiels going nowhere, Philipp going nowhere, helpless in the underbrush in Heidegger's mantraps, the scent of candies never tasted again after that outing with her girlfriends, the Lido of

Venice, the children of the wealthy à la recherche du temps perdu, Schrödinger What is Life? the essence of mutation, the behavior of atoms within an organism, the organism not a physics laboratory, a flow of order, you avoid disintegration in the anatomical chaos, the soul, yes, the soul, Deus-factus-sum, the Upanishads, order from order, order from disorder, the transmigration of souls, the multiplicity hypothesis, come-back-as-an-animal, I'm-friendly-to-animals, the calf-on-a-rope-that-screamed-so-in-front-of-the-Garmisch-slaughteryard, being whelped, Kierkegaard angst diarykeeping seducer not into Cordelia's bed, Sartre nausea I'm-not-nauseous, I'm practicing dark sweet onanie, the self, existence and the philosophy of existence, millionaire, was-once, once-upon-a-time, the grandmother's travels, Madame wirklich Geheime Kommerzienrätin, onanie dark sweet, Auer's glowing gaslight hums, if-they-had-invested-it-all-in-gold, the start of social security, I-ought-to-be-pasting-coupons-for-my-old-age, the young Kaiser, inflation in the trillions, had-it-been-in-gold, Immediate Aid Payment due, that was Nice, onanie, the Promenade des Anglais, the osprey hats, in Cairo Shepheard's Hotel, Mena House Hotel in front of the pyramids, the cure for the wirklich Geheimer Kommerzienrat's kidneys, drying out the clogged passages, desert climate, Photopostkarte, carte postale Wilhelm-and-Lieschen-riding-on-a-camel, the forebears, Luxor, the hundred gates of Thebes, the necropolis, field of the dead, city of the dead, I'll-die-young, Admet the young Gide in Biskra l'Immoraliste love without name, the wirklich Geheimer died pompes funèbres, millions, millions-not-in-gold, the devaluation mortgage, the temple to Ammon, Ramses something or other in the rubble, the Sphinx Cocteau: I-love, who-loves me?, the gene the nucleus of the fertilized ovum, don't-need-to-be-careful-twelve-times-regularly, the moon, no doctor, Behude-is-curious, all-doctors-lechers, my womb, body-belongs-to-me, no suffering, sweet-dark-depravity —

25

Exhaustion beaded on her forehead, each bead a microcosm of the underworld, a swarm of atoms, electrons, and quanta, Giordano Bruno sang at the stake the song of the infinity of the universe, Botticelli's Spring matured, became summer, became autumn, was it winter already, a new spring? an embryo of a spring? water collected in her hair, she felt moist to the touch, and before her glistening eyes, adrift in this moisture, Philipp's desk seemed to her once again a place of sorcery, a hated place to be sure, yet still the site of the possible miracle: wealth and fame, and she, too, famously wealthy and secure! She was reeling. The security that the time had taken from her, that the proclaimed, bestowed, and now worthless inheritance denied her, that the houses no longer provided her, the cracks in the walls, cracks everywhere in the material world, would this lost security that had turned up like a con man and let her down like one, be recovered for her by weak, penniless Philipp, plagued by heart problems and dizzy spells, who nevertheless, and this was new for her, was in touch with the invisible, with thought, with spirit, with art, who had nothing to call his own here, but might have some holdings there in the spiritual realm? For now, anyway, all security was gone. Philipp said there never had been any security. He lied! He didn't want to share what he had with her. How could he live without security? It wasn't Emilia's fault that the old security, in whose bosom two generations had made themselves at home, had collapsed. She wanted a reckoning! She demanded her inheritance from everyone older than herself. She had gone racing through the house in the night, a little, pitiful fury, followed by her animals, her darlings who couldn't speak and were therefore guiltless, last night, when Philipp had slipped out, unable to stand her screaming, her senseless railing upstairs and down to the custodian in the basement, feet and fists against the closed door: "You Nazis, why did you elect him, why did you elect misery, why the abyss, why destruction, why war, why the fortune shot into thin air, I used to have money, you Nazis" (and the custodian lay behind the

26

bolted door, held his breath, didn't stir, thought, 'wait and it will pass, a storm, it will blow over, she'll calm down') and the other Nazis behind other doors in the building, her father behind the secured latch of his springbolt lock, a fellow heir "you Nazi, you fool, squanderer, had to go march, had to march with the others, had to run with the pack, you pack hound, swastika on your chest, the money gone, couldn't you keep quiet? did you have to keep yapping?" (and her father sat behind the door, did not hear her shouts, did not face the accusations, justified or not, held the files up to his face, the bank bonds, the certificates of indebtedness, the letters of deposit, figured, 'and I've still got this left and this share and maybe the mortgage on the Berlin property, but in the eastern sector, who knows' USA AGAINST PREVENTIVE WAR). Why wasn't Philipp worried? Maybe because he too was living on what she had left, on the god of her grandparents, and his god was a false god? If only you could know all the answers! The pale face twitched. Her head was reeling, naked she reeled across to the desk, took a sheet from the stack of white, unused paper, from the little pile of purity of the inhibited conception, fed it into the little typewriter and typed carefully with one finger: 'Don't be mad. I do love you, Philipp. Stay here with me.'

He didn't love them. Why should he love them? He wasn't especially proud of his relatives. He was filled with indifference. Why should he be moved? No particular feeling tightened or swelled his chest. Richard thought no more about those who lived down there than about all the other old races: superficially. He was traveling on official business; no, on official business was what they down there would have said, the old parade grounds clan, the old princely servants, he was traveling for practical reasons, on behalf of his country and of his time, and he believed that now his country's time had come, the century of purged instincts, utilitarian order, planning, management, and efficiency, and for now it would be, along with the business, a kind of ironic-romantic look at the world and some castles. What they could expect of him was an open mind. That was a break for them. Augustus didn't set sail for Hellas to be a benefactor to the Greeks. History forced Augustus to do something about the confused state of Greek affairs. He wrought order. He subdued a mob of fanatics, zealous citizens, and provincial patriots; he supported reason, the moderates, capital, and the academies, and he accepted the insane, the sages, and the pederasts in the bargain. It was useful for him and a break for them. Richard felt free of enmity and prejudices, no hatred and loathing encumbered him. These negative feelings were poisons, diseases that civilization had overcome like the plague, cholera, and smallpox. Richard had been vaccinated, raised hygienically, the slag removed. Maybe he would be patronizing without meaning to be, for he was young, overrated his youth, and looked down, looked down on them quite literally, down on their countries, their kings, their borders, their feuds, their philosophers, their graves, their whole aesthetic, pedagogical, intellectual humus, their ceaseless wars and revolutions, he looked down on a single, ridiculous battlefield, the earth lay below him as if on a surgeon's table: badly cut up. Of course he didn't actually see it that way: he saw neither kings nor borders where right now there was only fog and night, nor did his mind's eye imagine it, it was his schooling that saw the continent that way. History was the past, the world of yesterday, dates in books, torture for schoolboys, but every passing day comprised history too, new history, history in the present tense, and that meant being there, becoming, growing, doing, and flying. You didn't always know where you were flying to. Not until tomorrow would everything get its historical name, and with the name its meaning, would it become real history, grow old in textbooks, and this day, this today, this morning would someday be for him 'my youth.' He was young, he was curious, he'd go have himself a look at it: the land of his fathers. It was a journey to the East. They were crusaders of order, knights of reason, of utility and proper middle-class freedom: they sought no holy grave. It was night when they reached the mainland. In the clear sky before them shone a frosty light: the morning star, Phosphor, Lucifer, the lightbearer of the ancient world. He became the prince of darkness. Night and fog lay over Belgium, over Bruges, Brussels, and Ghent. The cathedral at Cologne rose up out of the gray of daybreak. The red dawn pulled away from the earth like an eggshell: the new day was born. They flew upstream along the Rhine. Rest-calmly-fatherland-of-mine-firm-stands-and-true-the-watch-on-the-Rhine: song of his father when he was eighteen, song of Wilhelm Kirsch sung in classrooms, in barracks, on drill grounds, on marches, watch of his father, watch of his grandfather, watch of his great grandfather, watch on the Rhine, grave of ancestors, grave of blood relatives, watch on the Rhine, unfulfilled watch, misunderstood watch, they-shall-not-ever-have-it, who? the French, who did have it anyway? the people on the river, boatmen, fishermen, gardeners, wine growers, tradesmen, factory owners, lovers, the poet Heine, who should have it? whoever wants to, whoever is there, did he have it now, Richard Kirsch, soldier in the US Air Force, eighteen years old, looking at it from above, or might it even be that he was now taking up the watch, in good faith like the others, and perhaps again in the trap of a misunderstanding of the historical moment? He thought, 'if I were a bit older, maybe twenty-four instead of eighteen, then I too could have flown here at eighteen, destroyed here and died here, we would have brought bombs, we would have dropped bombs, we would have lit the place up like a Christmas tree, we would have laid down a carpet, we would have been their death, we would have plunged into the sky before their searchlights, where will that one day be? where will I practice what I'm learning? where will I drop bombs? whom will I bomb? here? them? farther ahead? others? father back? still others? Over Bavaria the land grew overcast. They flew over the clouds. When they landed, the earth smelled damp.

The airport smelled of grass, of gasoline, exhaust fumes, metal, and of something new, something foreign, it was a baking smell, a dough smell of fermentation, yeast, and alcohol, appetizing and animating, it was the odor of beer mash from the city's large breweries.

They walked through the streets, Odysseus first, a big king, a little conqueror, young, muscular, innocent, animal, and Josef behind, wizened, stooped, old, tired, and yet chipper nonetheless, and with his chipper little eyes he peered ahead through his cheap healthplan glasses at the black back, hopefully, trustingly, the light load, the good commission in his hand, the little musical case Bahama-Joe with his sound, Bahama-Joe with his musical chatter, voices a-patter Bahama-Joe with the muted trumpets, the drums, the cymbals, the screeching, howling, and the rhythm that radiated out and stirred the girls, girls who were thinking, 'the nigger, that fresh nigger, horrible nigger, no, I wouldn't do it' Bahama-Joe, and others thought, 'money they've got, so much money, a black soldier earns more than our chief inspectors, US Private, we girls have learned our English, League of German Girls, can you marry a Negro? no race laws in the USA, but ostracism, no hotel will let you in, the halfblack children, occupation babies, poor little ones, don't know where they belong, not their fault, no, I wouldn't do it!' Bahama-Joe, saxophone flourish. A woman stood in front of a shoe store, she saw the Negro walking by, mirrored in the window, she thought, 'the sandals with the spike heels, I'd like those, if you could just once, those boys do have some bodies, virile, saw a boxing match once, Papa was exhausted afterwards, but not him' — Bahama-Joe. They walked past the schnapps shacks, the stand-up drink counters, off limits for allied soldiers, and out from under the makeshift roofs they slunk, the pimps, the fences, the snatchers: "Hey, Joe, dollars? Joe, hast du gasoline? Joe, ein girl?" They were sitting right there, the wares, drinking soda, drinking Coca Cola,

30

bad coffee, stinking broth, the bed odor, the smell of yesterday's embraces not yet washed off, blotches and marks powdered over, doll's hair dead from bleaching and coloring like bundled straw, they were waiting, fowl ready to order fresh daily, looking through the glass to see what the pimps were up to, if they would wave, a black, they were good-natured, paid generously, it was only right, inferior fellows, tore you apart down there: 'lucky they can get a white woman at all, degrading for us, one pretty disgusting degradation.' "Hey, Joe, you got something to give?" — "Hey, Joe, you looking for something to buy?" — "Joe, I'll give!" — "Joe, I'll take!" They swarmed around them: maggots on pork belly, pasty faces, hungry faces, faces that God had forgotten, rats, sharks, hyenas, amphibians, scarcely masked by human skin, padded shoulders, checked jackets, filthy trenchcoats, loud socks, thick, bulging soles beneath their grease-stained suede shoes, caricatures of burlesque film fashions from across the Atlantic, poor slobs too, homeless, displaced, victims of the war. They turned to Josef, Bahama-Joe: "Does your nigger need German money?" — "We'll change money for your nigger." — "Does he want a fuck? Three marks for you. You get to watch, old man, make the music." Bahama-Joe, music with its silvery sound. Josef and Odysseus heard the whispering and they didn't hear it. Bahama-Joe: they left the whisperers standing there, the hissing vipers, Odysseus shoved them back, gently, mightily like a whale, pushed them aside, the paltry little crooks, the pimplefaces, the stinknoses, the run-down jerks. Josef followed the mighty Odysseus, waddled along in his wake. Bahama-Joe: they walked on, walked past the newly erected movie house UNDYING PASSION RELENTLESSLY GRIPPING STORY OF A DOCTOR'S FATE, past the newly erected hotels ROOF GARDENS OVERLOOKING THE RUINS COC-TAIL HOUR, were showered with lime dust, spattered with mortar, walked through the rows of shops erected on fields of rubble, right and left the single story huts, gleaming with their chrome trim, neon lighting, and plate glass windows: perfume from Paris, Dupont nylon, pineapple from California, Scotch whiskey, colorful news-stands: TEN MILLION TONS OF COAL MISSING. The traffic light was red and kept them from crossing. Streetcars, automobiles, cyclists, wobbling threewheelers, and heavy American army trucks streamed through the intersection.

The red light blocked the road in front of Emilia. She wanted to get to the pawn office, which closed at noon, then to Unverlacht, the used goods dealer in his damp, vaulted cellar, he would put his hand up her skirt, to the whining antique dealer, Frau de Voss, she wouldn't buy anything but she lived near Unverlacht, and finally, she sensed it, she knew it, the pearls would have to be sacrificed, the ornate, moonpale necklace, she would have to go to Schellack, the jeweler. She wore stylish shoes of genuine snakeskin, but the heels were worn down and crooked. Her stockings were of the very finest mesh, because Philipp loved sheer stockings and became amorous when she came home on biting cold winter days with nearly frostbitten calves, but, oh no, in this fabric advertised as runproof the strands came loose and fell like trickling brooks from knee to ankle. The skirt had a triangular tear at the seam: who was going to sew it up? Emilia's fur jacket, too warm for this time of year, was of the finest squirrel, tattered and torn, so what, it took the place of the spring coat Emilia didn't have. Her youthful mouth was made up, the paleness of her cheeks was remedied with a little rouge, her hair blew freely in the rainwet wind. The things she had brought along were wrapped in an English traveling plaid, the luggage of lords and ladies in the cartoons of Wilhelm Busch and Die Fliegenden Blätter. Emilia had a hard time carrying this delight of the old humorists. Any load she carried brought rheumatic pains in her shoulder. Any pain made her cranky and filled her with spite and bitterness. She stood ill-tempered beneath the red light and looked irritably into the stream of traffic.

In the consul's car, in the Cadillac gliding silently and shockfree, in the conveyance of the rich on the side of the rich, of statesmen, the successful, the shrewd managers, if you didn't let it fool you, in a spacious, gleaming black coffin, Mr. Edwin rode through the intersection. He felt tired. The journey, spent reclining but without sleep, had fatigued him. He looked despondently out at the overcast day, despondently at the unfamiliar street. It was the land of Goethe, the land of Platen, the land of Winckelmann, Stefan George had walked across this square. Mr. Edwin felt a chill. All at once he saw himself as a remnant, left alone, old, ages old, as old as he was. He pressed his thus old but even now still youthfully trim body down into the car's soft upholstery. It was a gesture of withdrawal. The brim of his black hat bumped against the cushions, and he lay the hat, a featherlight product of Bond Street, on his lap. His refined features, suggestive of asceticism, breeding, and contemplation, became angry. Beneath the carefully parted, silky soft, long, gray hair, his face took on the angular features of an old, greedy vulture. The consulate attaché and the literary impresario of the Amerika-Haus, who had been sent to meet Mr. Edwin's train, sat on the jump seats in front of him, leaned back toward him, and felt obliged to entertain the famous man, the award winner, the rare creature. They pointed out the city's supposed points of interest, talked about how they had made arrangements for his lecture, chatted—it sounded like charwomen tirelessly swishing wet mops back and forth across a dusty floor. Mr. Edwin found these gentlemen spoke in offhand slang. That was irksome. Mr. Edwin loved offhand slang, sometimes, in the company of beautiful people, but here, with these well-heeled gentlemen of his own social class, 'my social class? which class? with prejudice toward none, classless outsider, no community, none,' this slang, this American speech chewed like gum, was embarrassing, oppressive, and tiresome. Edwin slid even deeper into the corner of the car. What was he bringing to this country, Goethe, Winckelmann, Platen, what was

33

he bringing? They would be sensitive, perhaps receptive, this defeated people, they would be watchful, already awakened by the
catastrophe, they would be full of foreboding, nearer the abyss,
more familiar with death. Was he coming with a message, did he
bring comfort, could he explain the suffering? He was supposed to
speak about immortality, about the timelessness of the spirit, the
undying soul of the Occident, and now? now he had doubts. His
message was cold, his knowledge select. Select in both original
senses of the word: stemming from books, but also carefully chosen,
an extract of the spirit of the millennia, select, selected from all
tongues, the Holy Spirit poured out into the languages, select,
precious, the quintessence, sparkling, distilled, sweet, bitter, poi-
sonous, curative, itself almost the explanation, but the explanation
only of history, in the end this explanation, too, questionable, the
beautifully formed, clever stanzas, sensitive reactions, and yet: he
came with empty hands, without gifts, without comfort, no hope,
sorrow, tiredness, not inertia, an empty heart. Shouldn't he remain
silent? He had seen the war's destruction before, who in Europe was
not acquainted with it? he had seen it in London, in France, in
Italy, frightful, open wounds in the cities, yet what he saw here in
probably the hardest hit place on his itinerary, through the window
of the consulate's car, cradled in foam rubber, compressed air, and
an ingenious suspension, shielded from dust, was cleaned up, orderly, patched up, already restored, and for that very reason so
terrible, so invalid: it could never be made good again. He was
supposed to speak about Europe and for Europe, but did he perhaps
secretly wish the destruction, the smashing of the cloak in which
his beloved, in spirit so very beloved, continent showed itself, or
was it that he, Mr. Edwin, belatedly embarked on this journey to
accept the belated fame come to him through oh such misunderstandings, to be celebrated, that he knew the significance of the
offense, that he was a friend of the phoenix, who had to enter the
fire, into the ashes its bright plumage, those shops there, those

people, makeshift all of it, the glib slang in his car—foolish: what should he say to them? Perhaps he would die in this city. A news item. A note in the evening papers. A few memorial articles in London, in Paris, in New York. This black Cadillac was a coffin. Now they grazed a cyclist 'oh no, he's falling, he's caught himself' —

He caught himself and didn't fall. He balanced, pedaled hard, steered the bicycle into an opening, Dr. Behude, psychiatrist and neurologist, he worked the pedals, he rode on, tonight he will hear Mr. Edwin's lecture in the Amerika-Haus, the talk about the spirit of the Occident, the speech about the power of the spirit, the victory of the spirit over matter, spirit overcomes disease, diseases rooted in the psyche, ailments curable through the psyche. Dr. Behude was dizzy. The blood removal had weakened him this time. Maybe he was letting them tap his veins too often. The world needed blood. Dr. Behude needed money. Victory of matter over spirit. Should he turn here, get off the bicycle, go into a bar, drink something, be merry? He swam along in the flow of traffic. His head ached, a pain he ignored when he was with a patient. He kept pedaling down the road to see Schnakenbach, the tired vocational instructor, the gifted juggler of formulas, the nightschool Einstein, a shadow addicted to Pervitine and Benzedrine. Behude regretted having yesterday refused Schnakenbach the pills that kept the teacher awake. Now he was bringing him the prescription that would satisfy the addiction, preserve his pathetic life for a spell, while furthering its destruction. He would have liked to go see Emilia. He liked her: he felt she was in greater danger than Philipp, 'oh, he can survive anything, he'll even survive his marriage, a stout heart, neuroses, neuroses sure, a pseudo–angina pectoris, and what have you, but a stout heart, you wouldn't know it to look at him,' but Emilia didn't come to his office, and she hid whenever he visited Philipp at home. He didn't notice Emilia waiting for the green light at the intersection he was cycling past. He was bent over

35

the handlebars, his right hand on the brake, his left index finger on the bell: one mistaken ringing could kill, one slip leave him exposed, the mistaken ringing of the night bell, did he understand Kafka? —

Washington Price steered the horizonblue sedan through the intersection. Should he do it? Should he not do it? He knew that the tank trucks in his depot had secret taps. The risk was small. He would just have to go in fifty-fifty with the tank truck driver, drive up to the German gas station, every rig driver knew which one, and have them drain off a few gallons. It was good, safe money. He needed money. He didn't want to lose out. He wanted Carla, and he wanted Carla's child. There were no black marks on his record yet. He believed in respectability. To each citizen his chance. And to the black man his chance, too. Washington Price, sergeant in the army. Washington had to be rich. He had to be rich at least for a while; right here and now he had to be rich. Carla would trust wealth. She would sooner trust the money than his words. Carla didn't want to bring his child into the world. She was afraid. My God, why be afraid? Washington was the best, the strongest, the fastest crack player on the famous baseball team, the Red Stars. But he wasn't the youngest any more. This murderous racing around the bases! It wore him down. He couldn't catch his breath any more. But he'd be able to take it for another one, two years. He'd still be good in the arena. A rheumatic twinge shot through his arm; that was a warning. He wouldn't do the gas thing. He had to drive to the central exchange. He had to buy Carla a present. He had to make a phone call. He needed money. Right away —

Right off the number six and onto line eleven. She'd catch Dr. Frahm before he left. It was good if she got there a little after office hours. Frahm would have time then. She had to get rid of it. Right away. Washington was a good fellow. How frightened she had been!

36

The first day in the black soldiers' barracks. The lieutenant had said "I don't know whether you'll stay on." They crowded in at the window in the door, pressed their flat noses against the glass like putty, one face next to the other. Who was in the cage? who was representing their species in the zoo? the one on this side of the glass? the ones on the other side? Was it such a long way from the German Wehrmacht office, the commandant's secretary, to the black soldiers of the US transport unit? She typed, typed English quite well, bent her head over the machine so as not to see the foreign being, not the dark skin, not this suppleness in ebony, not the man, not to hear the guttural sound, just the text that he dictated, she had to work, she couldn't stay with her mother, not with Frau Behrend, she felt she was wrong in condemning the Musikmeister, she had to care for her boy, his father lay by the Volga, maybe drowned, maybe buried, missing on the steppes, no more greetings to Stalingrad, she had to come up with something, they were starving, the bad years, forty-five, forty-six, forty-seven, starving, she had to, why shouldn't she, weren't they people, too? At the end of the day, there he was. "I'll take you home." He led her through the barracks hall. Was she naked? The men were standing in the hall, dark in the shadowy dusk of the hall, their eyes like restless white bats and their gazes like suction cups on her body. He sat beside her at the wheel of the jeep. "Where do you live?" She told him. He said nothing while they drove. He stopped in front of her house. He opened the car door. He handed her chocolate, canned goods, cigarettes, quite a lot in those days. "Goodbye." Nothing more. Every evening. He picked her up at the office, led her through the hall with the waiting, staring, dark men, took her home, sat silently beside her in the car, gave her something, said: "Goodbye." Sometimes they sat in the car in front of her house for maybe an hour: in silence, neither one even stirring. Rubble from the bombed-out buildings still lay about in the streets in those days. The wind blew dust around. The ruins were like a field of the dead, outside all reality on those evenings, they were Pompeii, Herculaneum, Troy, sunken world. A damaged wall collapsed. New dust settled like a cloud over the jeep. By the sixth week, Carla couldn't take it any longer. She dreamt of Negroes. In her dreams she was raped. Black arms reached out for her: they came up out of the cellars under the ruins like snakes. She said: "I can't stand it." He came with her to her room. It was a kind of drowning. Was it the Volga? not icy a fiery stream. The next day, the neighbors came, her acquaintances came, her old boss at the Wehrmacht came, they all came, wanted cigarettes, canned goods, coffee, chocolate, "tell your friend, Carla" — "your friend can get it at the central exchange, in the American department store, Carla" — "if you could remind your friend, Carla, soap": Washington Price provided, picked up, brought by. The friends said their thanks casually. It was as if Carla were handing over a tribute. The friends forgot that the goods cost dollars and cents at the American base. Was it laughable? Was it nice? Was it something to be proud of? Carla as benefactress? Soon she wasn't sure anymore, and thinking about it was a strain. She gave up her job with the transport unit, moved into another building, where other girls associated with other men, lived with Washington, was faithful to him, although she now had many, in fact countless, opportunities to sleep with men, because every man, be he white or black, German or foreigner, believed, now that she was living with Washington, that she would go to bed with anybody, it turned them on, and Carla was unsure of her feelings and she asked herself, 'do I love him? do I really love him? foreign, foreign but I'll stay faithful to him, faithful that much I owe him, no other men,' and while doing nothing she grew accustomed to the picture world of countless magazines that showed her how ladies lived in America, the automatic kitchens, the washday wonders and dishwashing machines that cleaned everything while you watched television from your reclining armchair, Bing Crosby appeared in every home, the Vienna Boys' Choir made joyful noises in

38

front of the electric range, nestled into the luxurious cushions of the Pullman car you rode from east to west, in your streamlined automobile you enjoyed the spectacular lights and palms on the Gulf of San Francisco, you were offered security of every kind by pill manufacturers and insurance companies, no more troubled dreams will trouble you because you can sleep soundly tonight with Maybel's Milk of Magnesia, and woman was queen there and everything served her and lay at her feet, she was the gift that starls the home, and for the children there were dolls that cried real tears; they were the only tears cried in this paradise. Carla wanted to marry Washington. She was ready to follow him to the States. She had her former boss, the commandant, who was now a section chief in a district attorney's office, arrange for a death certificate for her husband missing on the Volga. And then came the child, a black being that stirred inside her, came too soon, made her nauseous, no, she didn't want it, Dr. Frahm had to help her out, had to take it out, right away —

"The downtown area you see here was entirely destroyed. Five years of rebuilding democratic administration and the good will of the Allies have made the city once again into a flourishing center of trade and industry." GERMANY ALSO TO GET MARSHALL PLAN AID, ERP FUNDS CUT BACK, SENATOR TAFT CRITICIZES EXPENDITURES. The bus with the tour group of teachers from Massachusetts rolled through the intersection. They were traveling, without knowing it, in disguise. No German who saw these women behind the panes of the bus would ever dream they were teachers. After all, those were ladies sitting there on red leather, well-dressed, nicely made up, youthful in appearance and indeed young, at least so people thought, rich, cultivated, idle women taking city tours to pass the time. 'If you hadn't sent the city up in flames, there'd be some different things to see, and you wouldn't be here at all, soldiers, fine, but now females too, adding to occupation costs, they're just a

39

bunch of drones.' An American teacher earns—what does she earn?—ah, infinitely more than her German counterpart in Starnberg, the poor, intimidated creature, 'don't dare risk offending anyone, a little powder on the face, the Herr Chaplain might notice and disapprove, the Herr Principal could mention it in the personnel files.' Education in Germany is a serious and gray affair, far removed from any joy of life, worldliness, humbug! and it remains forever inconceivable that a lady be seen behind the teacher's lectern in a German classroom, made up, perfumed, off to vacations in Paris, on study tours in New York and in Boston, Massachusetts, my God, it makes your hair stand on end, we're a poor country and that's our virtue. Kay was sitting beside Katharine Wescott. Kay was twenty-one, Katharine thirty-eight years old. "You're in love with Kay's green eyes," said Mildred Burnett. 'Green eyes cat's eyes lying eyes.' Mildred was forty-five and was sitting in front of them. They had one day for the city and two more for the American occupation zone in Germany. Katharine wrote down everything that the man from American Express standing next to the driver told them. She thought, 'I can use it in history class, it's an historic hour, America in Germany, the Stars and Stripes over Europe, I've gone and seen it, I've experienced it.' Kay had given up taking notes during the sightseeing tours. You got to see too little as it was. Only later, in the hotel, did Kay take down the most important information from Katharine's shorthand in her own travel log. Kay was disappointed. Romantic Germany? It was dreary. The land of poets and thinkers, of music and song? The people looked like people everywhere. At the intersection stood a Negro. A small portable radio was playing Bahama-Joe. That was like in Boston; like in a suburb of Boston. The other Germany had probably been invented by the professor of German literature at the college. His name was Kaiser and until 1933 he had lived in Berlin. He had been forced to leave. 'Maybe he's homesick,' thought Kay, 'it is his homeland after all, he sees it differently than I do, he doesn't like America, he thinks they're all poets here, they're not as good businessmen as people back home, but they forced him to leave, why? he's a nice man, in America we have poets too, Kaiser says those are writers, important writers, but he makes a distinction there, still: Hemingway, Faulkner, Wolfe, O'Neill, Wilder, Edwin lives in Europe, turned his back on us, Ezra Pound too, in Boston we had Santayana, the Germans have Thomas Mann, but he's in the States, funny, forced to leave too, they had, they had Goethe, Schiller, Kleist, Hölderlin, Hofmannsthal, Hölderlin and Hofmannsthal are Dr. Kaiser's favorite poets, Rilke's elegies, Rilke died in twenty-six, who do they have now? sit among the ruins of Carthage and weep, I ought to slip away from our tour group, maybe I'd meet someone, a poet, I'd like to talk with him, me, an American, I'd tell him he shouldn't be sad, but Katharine watches over me, bothersome, I'm an adult, she didn't want me to read Across the River a book they should never have allowed to be printed she says, why not actually? because of the little Contessa? wonder if I'd be that quick?' — 'The city is drab,' thought Mildred, 'and the women are badly dressed.' Katharine noted: Oppression of women still visible today, no positions equal to those of men. She would speak on that in Massachusetts at the women's club. Mildred thought, 'it's idiotic traveling with a bunch of females, we must stink, woman the weaker sex, all this riding wears you out, and what do you see? nothing, every year I get talked into it again, those dangerous Krauts, persecutors of the Jews, all Germans under steel helmets, I don't see anything, peaceable people, poor I suppose, a soldier people, BEWARE OF "COUNT US OUT" PROPAGANDA, Katharine doesn't like Hemingway, made a big fuss the silly goose when Kay started reading that book, an awful book, countess goes to bed with old major, Kay would go to bed with Hemingway too, there's no Hemingway here, but there is chocolate as a bedtime snack from Katharine, Kay-darling, her green eyes, she's quite taken with them, what do I see? of course a pissoir, I never see monuments, no, it's always things like that,

should I have my head examined? what for? too late, in Paris
corrugated metal around those places like little Hottentot skirts,
you'd think they'd be embarrassed —'

Green light. Messalina had spotted her. Alexander's sexfrantic
woman. Emilia wanted to slip away from her, wanted to hide, but
her line of retreat was ill-chosen: it was a pissoir right there on the
corner, and Emilia didn't notice it until she saw men walking
toward her buttoning up their trousers. Emilia gasped, stumbled,
and nearly fell, now also dazed by the harsh ammonia fumes and tar
smell, with her heavy plaid, the merry, comical plaid of the car-
icaturists, against the urinating backs, the backs above which heads
were now turning in her direction, pensive eyes gazing into space,
simple faces that slowly took on an astonished expression. Messalina had not let her prey out of her sights; she had discharged her
taxi, the car she had hired to go to the hairdresser to have her hair
bleached and fluffed up: now she stood waiting in front of the
retreat. Emilia came racing out of the male refuge with her face fiery
red, and Messalina called to her: "Emilychild, if it's gigolos you're
looking for, I can recommend Hänschen, he's Jack's friend, you do
know who Jack is, they get together at my place. Hi, how are you
dear, let's have a kiss, you have such fresh color in your cheeks, all
red. You're not getting enough, come to my house tonight, I'm
giving a party, maybe Edwin the poet will come, they say he's in
town, I don't know him, don't know what he's written, he's gotten
some prize or other. Jack might bring him along, he ought to get
acquainted with Hänschen, it really would be nice!" Emilia cringed
when Messalina called her Emilychild, she hated it when Messalina
mentioned Philipp, all Messalina's comments injured and embarrassed her, but since she saw in Alexander's wife, in this woman all
made up like a demon with the body of a wrestler, one enormous
piece of shit from whom there was no escape, a vast and violent

42

lady, the pompous, grotesque monument of a lady, Emilia was always intimidated by her and stood before her, the monument, almost as a little girl, curtsying and looking up to the monumental height, which in turn made Messalina all the more covetous of her, with dizzying admiration and exquisite courtesy. Messalina thought 'she is attractive, why does she live with Philipp? she loves him, that's the only possible explanation, funny, for a long time I couldn't figure it out, maybe he took her hymen, bonds like that do exist, the first man, I don't dare ask her, shabby, everything she has on is threadbare, a fine figure, a fine head, always looks good, that mangy fur, squirrel, ragamuffin princess, wonder if she's any good in bed? bet she is, Jack's hot on her, boyish body, if she would with Alexander, but she doesn't come to see me, or she comes with Philipp, he's ruining that girl, somebody ought to save her, he's using her, good for nothing, Alexander asked him for a film, what did he write? nothing, gave an embarrassed laugh, stayed away after that, can't figure him out, misunderstood genius coffeehouse poet in Berlin in the Romanisches Café, in Paris at the Dôme, but serious, a real scarecrow, too bad about the pretty little one, has a sensuous mouth.' And Emilia thought, 'what bad luck that I had to run into her, whenever I'm out carrying things I run into somebody, I'm ashamed, this stupid plaid, of course she notices that I have to sell something, that I'm on my way to the pawn office, to the used goods dealers, she can tell by looking at me, a blind man couldn't help seeing it, the pointed questions about Philipp, in a minute she'll ask about his book, the empty white pages lying there at home, I'm ashamed, I know he could write a book and he can't, ATTACK WOULD MEAN WORLD WAR, what does she understand? for her Edwin is a name out of the newspaper, she hasn't read a single line by him, she collects celebrities, miracle doctor Gröning visited her, wonder if it's true that she beats Alexander when he and other women, what does she understand? I have to hurry, the green light.' —

The green light. They walked on, Bahama-Joe. Josef squinted across the old tavern Zur Glocke; it had burned down to the foundations and now risen again as a plank shack. Josef tugged at his black master's sleeve: "Mister vielleicht Bier trinken wollen? Hier sehr gutes Bier." He looked at him hopefully. "Oh, beer," said Odysseus. He laughed, Bahama-Joe, the laughter raised and lowered his broad chest: waves on the Mississippi. He slapped Josef on the shoulder; his knees buckled. "Beer!" — "Bier!" They walked inside, walked into the famous old destroyed resurrected Glocke, arm in arm, Bahama-Joe, drank: the foam lay like snow on their lips.

In front of the typewriter shop, Philipp hesitated. He looked at the display window. That was a mistake. He didn't have the nerve to go inside. Spindly Countess Anne—she was an exceedingly enterprising, conscience-free, heartless lady everybody knew, from the family whose behind-the-scenes maneuvering helped Hitler into the chancellorship, for which Hitler, once in power, killed the family off except for the spindly Anne, a Nazi with a victim-of-Fascism identity card, the one by nature, the identity card was rightfully hers—spindly Countess Anne had come across Philipp, the author of a book banned during the Third Reich and forgotten after the Third Reich, looking sad in a sad café, and since she was always full of energy and in the mood to talk, she had struck up a conversation with Philipp. One-sided, very one-sided, 'my God, what does she want?' — "You can't let yourself drift about," she had declared, "Philipp, just look at you! A man with your talent. You can't let your wife support you. You've got to pull yourself together, Philipp. Why don't you write a film script? After all, you do know Alexander. You do have contacts. Messalina expects a lot of you!" But Philipp thought, 'what film should I write? what is she talking about? films for Alexander? films for Messalina? ARCHDUKE AMOURS IN THE ATELIER, I can't do that, she won't comprehend it, but I can't do that, I don't understand it, ARCHDUKE AMOURS, what is that to me? the false feelings, the genuine false feelings, no organ to feel them with, who wants to see that stuff? everyone, so they say, I don't believe it, I don't know, I don't want to!' — "But if you don't want to," said the countess, "then do something else, Philipp, deal in a product that's easily sold, I have a franchise for a patented glue, every business needs it, why not try peddling it? Today's packaging could not be done without it, it saves time and material, you need only to walk into the nearest quality store, and already you've earned two marks. Twenty, thirty packets you could sell in a day— add it up for yourself!" Such was the conversation with Anne the spindly, Anne the enterprising, suggestive patter, now he was sitting right in the stew, no, standing there with his paste—he opened the door. A warning device shrilled and alarmed him. He shrank back like a thief. His left hand was in his coat pocket, clutching the countess's patent glue. The typewriters sparkled in the fluorescent light, and Philipp had the sensation that their keyboards were grinning at him: the field of letters became a mocking cavernous mouth in which the alphabet bared its teeth and snapped at him. Was Philipp not a writer? Master of writing implements? A humiliated master! Were he to open his mouth, speak a magic word, they would start clattering away: willing servants. Philipp did not know the magic word. He had forgotten it. He had nothing to say. He had nothing to say to the people walking by out there. The people were condemned. He was condemned. He was condemned in a different way than the people walking by. But he too was condemned. Time had condemned this place. It had condemned it to noise and muteness. Who was speaking, what were they saying? HOW EMMY MET HERMANN GÖRING, the gaudy posters shrieked it from every wall. Noise for a century. What was Philipp doing here? He was superfluous. He was cowardly. He didn't have the courage to offer this businessman in the elegant suit, a much newer suit than Philipp's, the countess's patent glue, which now seemed to Philipp an utterly ridiculous and useless object. 'I have no sense for reality, I'm just not a serious man, this businessman here is a serious man, I simply cannot take what everybody runs around doing seriously, it strikes me as comical that I should sell this man something, at the same time I'm too cowardly to do it, let him glue his packages with whatever he wants, what's it to me? why does he glue packages? to ship his machines, why does he ship them? to earn money, to eat well, to dress well, because he wants to sleep well, Emilia should have married this man, and what do people do with the machines they have bought from him? they want to make money with them and live well, they hire secretaries, look at their legs, and dictate letters, 'Dear Sirs we acknowledge receipt of your recent enclosed please find our current,' I'd like to laugh in their faces, meanwhile they laugh at me, they're right, I'm the sucker, a crime against Emilia, I am a failure, cowardly, superfluous: a German writer. — "What may I show you, Sir?" The elegantly dressed businessman bowed a little to Philipp, he too was giving it all he had. Philipp's gaze swept over the display cases with the gleaming oiled machines, those malicious inventions, ready for all sorts of mischief, to which man entrusted his thoughts, his announcements, his messages, and declarations of war. Then he saw the dictating machine. It was a tape recording apparatus he recognized from two broadcast readings that he had spoken onto magnetic tape, and on the case stood the English word Reporter. 'Am I a reporter?' thought Philipp. 'I could make reports with this machine, report that I am too cowardly and too much a failure to sell a tube of glue, that I consider myself above writing a film script for Alexander to suit the tastes of the people walking by out there, and that I don't believe myself capable of changing people's tastes, that's what it is, I'm superfluous and comical, and I find myself superfluous and comical, but I see the others, like this businessman, who imagines he could sell me something, while I can't get up the nerve to palm this glue off on him, I find him no less superfluous and comical than myself!' The shopkeeper watched Philipp expectantly. "I'm interested in that dictaphone there," said Philipp. "It's the best system on the market,"

46

the elegant gentleman replied. He was most solicitous. "A first-rate piece of equipment. It pays for itself. You can dictate your letters anywhere, on trips, in your car, in bed. Here, try it for yourself—". He turned knobs on the box and handed Philipp a small microphone. The tape ran from one reel onto the other. Philipp spoke into the microphone: "Das Neue Blatt wants me to interview Edwin. I could take this machine here along, and it would record our conversation. I'll be self-conscious, approaching Edwin as a reporter. He is probably afraid of journalists. He'll feel obliged to say something general and civil. That will offend me. I'll be embarrassed. Of course he has never heard of me. On the other hand, I'm looking forward to seeing Edwin. I think highly of him. It may be a good first encounter. I could go walking with Edwin in the park. Or should I go ahead after all with the paste—" He gasped, fell silent. The businessman smiled civilly and said: "A journalist, are you, Sir? Many journalists have our Reporter—" He ran the tape back, and Philipp now heard his own voice recounting his thoughts about the interview with Edwin. The voice alienated him. What it said shamed him. It was exhibitionism, intellectual exhibitionism. He could just as well have taken off all his clothes. His own voice, the words it spoke, it alarmed Philipp and he fled from the store.

— like snow on their lips. They wiped them off and plunged once more into the earthenware steins, the bock rose up and into them, trickled sweet bitter sticky aromatic down their throats "Beer" — "Bier": Odysseus and Josef raised their steins to each other's health. The little radio stood on the chair next to Josef. Now it was playing Candy. Candy-I-call-my-sugar-candy. Somewhere miles away the record was playing, mute and invisible the sound passed through the air, and here on the tavern chair now a schmaltzy voice, the voice of a fat man who made a good living with his schmaltzy voice, sang the words Candy-I-call-my-sugar-candy. The Glocke was doing a good business. Country folk dressed in coarse wool, who were in the city to buy things, and businessmen who had shops nearby and wanted to sell the country folk things, were eating Weisswurst. Klett the barber peeled the skin off the white filling with his fingers and stuck the sausage plump and whole into his mouth. Candy-I-call-my-sugar-candy. Klett smacked his lips and grunted with pleasure. Just now his hands had been in Messalina's hair. 'Messalina, the actor's wife. Alexander's playing in ARCHDUKE AMOURS, sure to be a wonderful film.' "Hair's a bit on the dry side, perhaps Madame would like an oil treatment? Madame's husband in uniform, I can hardly wait, ARCHDUKE AMOURS, German films really are the best, they can't take that away from us." Now Messalina was sitting under the hair dryer. Five more minutes. Maybe one more Weisswurst? That tender meat, the juice on your fingers. Candy-I-call-my-sugar-candy. At one table, Greeks were throwing dice. Looked as if they were about to leap at each other's throats. Such theater! "Hey Joe, want a little action? Five times the ante?" — "Das sind schlechte Menschen, Mister, haben Messer." Josef lifted his face out of the beer stein and blinked loyally over at Odysseus the master. Odysseus's chest heaved with laughter, Mississippi waves, who could harm him? "Beer" — "Bier." The Glocke had atmosphere. Italian tradesmen were measuring out bales of material, cutting them with nimble scissors into lengths of cloth: spun rayon with English imprints. Two pious Jews transgressed against the laws of Moses. They were eating unkosher food, but they ate no pork, compromised, compromised as they traveled, compromised on their wanderings, always wandering, always on the way to Israel, always in dirt. BATTLES AT SEA OF GALILEE, ARAB LEAGUE CLAIMS JORDAN. One man was telling another about the landing at Narvik under Dietel: "We were at the Arctic Circle," and the other spoke of Cyrenaica, of the Libyan desert, "Rommel the Sun," they had gotten around in the world, advancing to victory, old buddies, it surged back up out of forgetfulness, one over there had been with

48

the SS: "in Ternopol man when the pack leader whistled I'll tell you they jumped." — "Shut up slug it down and shit." They laid their arms across each other's shoulders and sang: it-was-an-edelweiss. "Beer" — "Bier." Girls wandered through, chunky girls, coarse-faced girls Candy-I

call-the-States! In an upholstered telephone booth in the large post office of the central exchange stood Washington Price. He was sweating in the closed booth. He wiped the sweat from his fore-head, and his handkerchief fluttered beneath the booth's glazed electric light like an excited white bird in a cage. Washington was calling Baton Rouge, his home town in the state of Louisiana. In Baton Rouge it was four o'clock in the morning, the sun had not risen yet. The ringing of the telephone had awakened and alarmed them, so early, that was nothing good, bad news, they stood anx-iously in the hall of the small, tidy house, the trees along the road rustled, the wind rustled through the tops of the elms, trains made their way to the grain silos, wheat-filled barges glided up to the docks, a tug shrieked, Washington saw them, the two old folks, him in striped pajamas, she had quickly put on a housecoat, in his mind's eye he saw them hesitate, saw how they were afraid, his hand extended to pick up the receiver, hers to hold his back, news in the morning, foreboding in the house they had toiled to preserve and protect, Uncle Tom's cabin, a stone house, home of an upstanding colored citizen, a respected man, but the telephone with its voice from far away, call from the white world, the hostile world, alarming voice and yet so yearned for, they knew even before the rustling came in the receiver and it was there, his voice, the voice of their son, why did he stay? prodigal son, no calf was to be slaughtered, he himself slaughtered, stayed beyond the end of the war, beyond the call of duty, stayed in the army, what business was it of his? Germany, Europe, how remote their squabbles seemed, the Rus-sians, why not the Russians? our son a sergeant, his picture in

49

uniform on the buffet beside the nickel silver pitcher, beside the radio, RED OFFENSIVE, KIDS LOVE LUDENS COUGH DROPS, what does he want? ah, they've guessed it, and he knows that they've guessed: entanglement. The old man lifts up the receiver and speaks, his father, superintendent at the grain silo, Washington played in the grain, nearly suffocated, a boy in red and white striped overalls, a little black imp amid the abundance, in a sea of yellow grain: bread. "Hello!" Now he has to say it: Carla, the white woman, the child, he's not coming home, he is going to marry the white woman, he needs money, money to get married, money to save the child, he can't tell them that, Carla threatening to go to a doctor, Washington wants money from the old folks' savings, he tells them of wedding plans, and the child, what do they know? They know. Entanglement, their son in need. Nothing good: sin. Or not sin before God but before men. They see this foreign daughter in the Negro quarter of Baton Rouge, see the woman with different skin, the woman from over there, woman from the other side of the ditch, they see the compartment for colored, the street of apartheid, how will he live with her? how be happy when she cries? the house too cramped, the house in the ghetto, Uncle Tom's tidy cabin and the rustling of the trees along the road, the lazy flow of the river broad and deep and in the depths peace, music from the neighbors' house, the murmuring of voices, dark voices in the evening, too much for her, too much of the voices and yet only one voice too cramped too closed too near too dark, blackness and night and the air and the bodies and the voices are like a heavy curtain of velvet that falls with a thousand folds over the day. When evening comes—will he take her dancing at Napoleon's Inn? Washington knows, knows as well as they know, the old folks, the good old folks in the hall of the house under the rustling trees by the murmuring river in the velvet folds of the night, in front of Napoleon's taproom there will be a sign the night before the dance for the enemy woman the enemy girlfriend the enemy lover who was not captured, who was earned the way Jacob got Rachel's hand, no one will see the sign and all will read it, it will be there to read in every eye WHITES UNWELCOME. Washington telephones, speaks across the ocean, his voice speeds ahead of the rosy dawn, and his father's voice joylessly emerges from the night, and the sign that once hung on the phone booth door that Washington has closed behind him read NO JEWS ALLOWED. President Roosevelt had heard of this sign, the diplomats and the journalists reported it to him, and he spoke of the afflicted Star of David by his fireside, and the fireside chat beamed through the airwaves and beamed out from the sound box next to the nickel silver pitcher in Uncle Tom's cabin and unfolded in their hearts. Washington became a soldier and went to war, ONWARD CHRISTIAN SOLDIERS, and in Germany the infamous commandments disappeared, town down, burned, and hidden were the tablets of the antilaw that shamed every human being. Washington was decorated, but in his fatherland, which had recognized him with the ribbons and the medals for bravery, in his fatherland the arrogant signs remained, the subhuman code, whether posted or not, remained intact NO BLACKS ALLOWED. Entanglement, Washington is entangled. While he talks with his parents about his love (ah, lovable! is she lovable? is it arrogance? arrogance on his part? Washington versus everyone? Washington a knight fighting prejudice and proscription), he dreams, and in his dream he owns a little hotel, a nice, comfortable bar, and NOBODY IS UNWELCOME stands written inside a wreath of constantly lit colored lights by the door— that would be Washington's Inn. How can he make them grasp it? him far away in Germany, them far away on the Mississippi, and the world is wide and the world is free and the world is evil and there is hatred in the world and the world is full of violence, why? because all are afraid. Washington dries his sweaty face. The white handkerchief bird flutters, trapped in the cage. They will send the money, the good old folks, money for the wedding, money for the child's bed: it is toil, it is sweat, it is full, heavy shovelfuls, shovels

51

full of grain, it is bread, and new entanglement, and ill fortune is
our companion —

But as the child stirred within her, she too feared signs visible
and invisible, Nebuchadnezzar dreams, Belshazzar handwriting that
could drive her out of the paradise of the automatic kitchens and
pharmaceutical security, WHITES UNWELCOME, BLACKS UNWELCOME,
both applied to them, and it had been for JEWS UNWELCOME that the
father of her son, without knowing it or particularly wanting it so,
had gone to war. This new child was unwelcome to her, dark,
mottled, unaware in its hollow that it was to be unwanted fruit, cast
aside by the gardener, laden with guilt and reproach before it was
able to draw guilt and reproach to itself, and she stood in the
examination room, what was there for him to examine? she was sure
after all, there was no need to sit on the chair, she wanted the
operation, the scraping, he should get rid of it, didn't he owe her
something? what had he gotten? coffee, cigarettes, that expensive
whiskey at a time when there was neither coffee, nor cigarettes, nor
hard liquor, not even the cheapest rotgut, what had he taken it for?
for rinses, squeezes, tablets, 'he put his hands on my breasts, now he
should do something for me.' And he, Dr. Frahm, gynecologist and
surgeon, knew what he was supposed to do, knew it without her
putting it into words, knew what the protruding abdomen meant,
and he thought, 'Hippocratic oath, thou shalt take no life, and how
they go on about this oath, wonder whose idea it was to use it,
hangover after the euthanasia trials, murder of the mentally ill,
murder of the unborn, I have the thing hanging in gothic script in
the hall outside my office, it's a little dark in the hall and the text
looks very good there, what is life? quanta and life, now the
physicists are struggling with biology, I can't read their books, too
much mathematics formula scribbling abstract knowledge mental
acrobatics, a body isn't a body any more, dissolution of objective
reality in the works of the new painters, that says nothing to me,

I'm a doctor, too uncultured maybe, don't have the time anyway, barely enough for the journals, always something new, I'm tired at night, my wife wants to go to the movies, an Alexander film, I think he's a twerp, but women? human life even in the sperm? the ovum? then protect against gonococci too, the priests say the soul, of course, they ought to take a look at one all cut open, Hippocrates, did he work under socialized medicine? did he have a metropolitan practice? the Spartans threw their freaks into the gorges of the Taygetus, military dictatorship, totalitarian state, despicable to be sure, Athens better, philosophy and pederasty, but Hippocrates? he should come to my office some time and listen for himself, "I'll kill myself" — "if you don't do it, Herr Doktor" — "I want it out," and to know where they'll go then, the botched abortions, die by the thousands, shop girls, secretaries, can hardly support themselves, and what does something like that grow up into? charity soup lines institutional care foster homes unemployment prison war, I was a medic, what landed all red on my table, like newborns again, limbs torn away, born to die, eighteen-year-olds, better never to have been born, what awaits this Negro child? they ought to outlaw intercourse for them, hopeless, they'll never stop, wouldn't mind some depopulation, Malthus, when you see what comes in here during office hours, ought to find myself another profession, mule of socialized medicine, for the insurance companies palatial offices and for us the pennies, good old uncle doctor, my father drove a horse and buggy through the countryside, the horse wore a straw hat in the summer, and what did my father give them? rapped and tapped on their stomachs and ordered lime blossom tea, today everyone prescribes a chemical formula that nobody can read or pronounce, secret signs of the medicine men in the bush, opposition to it, the psychotherapists another odd bunch, wife's amenorrhea because her husband has the hots for the messenger boy at the office and doesn't dare try anything, the old spells for banishing warts, patients always want the newest things, today ultrasonics, tomorrow something with nuclear fission, comes from those magazines, keep that stuff in my waiting room, all the equipment, it gleams and sparkles, patients treated on a conveyor belt, who pays for it? uncle doctor does, tribute paid to industry, the car payments, she'll have fun with her Negro, in Paris they're supposed to be crazy about them, NEGROIZATION, war propaganda in the Völkischer Beobachter, RACE BETRAYAL, where did their racial purity laws get them? a race of bunker dwellers, social grounds would cause difficulties, eugenic grounds not allowed, black and white make for pretty children too, what would my wife say if I wanted to take one in? medical grounds' — "let's have a look" — 'healthy, we need a name, INFRINGEMENT UPON DOCTOR/PATIENT CONFIDENTIALITY' — "constant vomiting?" — 'hardly by injection any more, over to Schulte's clinic in comfort, real nurses, like to work with them, we'll have to talk about fees, only-scoundrels-are-modest, as Goethe would say.' — "Frau Carla, it's best if we do it right away in the clinic." —

'The best for Carla.' Washington was on the large sales floor of the central exchange. He went over to the ladies wear section. What did he want? 'The best for Carla.' The German salesgirls were friendly. Two women were picking out nightgowns. They were the wives of officers, and the nightgowns were long robes of pink and pale green crepe de Chine. The women would lie in bed like opulent Greek goddesses. The salesgirl left the women alone with the gowns. She turned toward Washington and smiled. What did he want? There was a buzzing in the air. He felt as if he still had the telephone receiver up to his ear and was hearing words spoken across the ocean. Through technological magic he was at home in Baton Rouge. Through what magic was he standing here in the central exchange of a German city? What did he want? It was good and it was disgraceful: he wanted to get married. Was he harming anyone, making anyone unhappy? Was every step dangerous? Even

54

here? In Baton Rouge they would have killed him. The salesgirl thought, 'he's shy, these giants are always shy, they come looking for underthings for their girlfriends and don't dare say what it is they want.' She laid out what she thought appropriate in this case, panties and chemises, light delicate veils, regular hookers' underwear, 'just right for the Fräuleins,' ultra sheer, more to entice than to conceal. The salesgirl wore the same underwear. 'I could show it to him,' she thought. Washington didn't want the underwear. He said: "Baby clothes." The salesgirl thought, 'oh no, he's already got her pregnant.' — 'They're supposed to be good fathers,' she thought, 'but I don't want a child by one of them.' He thought, 'it's time to start thinking about baby things, need to get everything together ahead of time, but Carla would have to pick it out, she'll be furious if I pick it out and take it to her.' — "No. No baby clothes after all," he said. What did he want? He gestured uncertainly toward the sheer fabrics of erotic seduction. The officers' wives had found their nightgowns and were glaring at Washington. They called the salesgirl over. 'He's going to leave her with the baby,' the salesgirl thought, 'he's already got another lover, he's giving her the lingerie, that's how they are, black the same as white.' She left Washington standing at the counter and wrote out the purchase slip for the officers' wives. Washington laid his big brown hand on a piece of yellow silk. The silk disappeared like a trapped butterfly beneath his hand.

The black hand of the Negro and the yellowish, filthy hands of the Greeks took the dice, tossed them onto the cloth, sent them hopping, skipping, and rolling. Odysseus had won. Josef tugged at his jacket: "Mister, wir gehen, schlechte Menschen." The Greeks crowded him away. Josef held the music case tight in his hand. He was afraid someone could steal the little case. The music was still for a while. A man's voice was reading the news. Josef didn't understand what the man was saying, but some words he did

understand, the words Truman Stalin Tito Korea. The voice in
Josef's hand spoke of war, spoke of discord, talked about fear. Again
the dice fell. Odysseus lost. He looked in surprise at the hands of
the Greeks, magician hands, tucking his money away. The brass
band in the Glocke began its noonday shift. They played one of the
popular booming marches. 'Nobody makes them like we do.' The
people hummed along with the band. A few pounded their beer
steins to the beat. The people had forgotten the sirens, had forgotten the bunkers, the collapsing houses, the men no longer thought
of the sergeant's shouts as he drove them into the mud of the drill
grounds, not of the trenches, the field first-aid posts, the drumfire
barrages, being surrounded, retreating, they thought of triumphant
marches and flags. 'Paris if only the war had been over when we got
there, it was unfair that it wasn't over right there.' They had been
cheated out of their victory. Odysseus lost a second time. The dice
fell against him. The magician hands conjured. It was a trick.
Odysseus wanted to figure the trick out. He didn't let himself be
fooled. NO NEW MILITARISM BUT DEFENSIVE READINESS. Amid the
noise of the brass band Josef raised Odysseus's music box to his ear.
Did the voice in the box have a message for Josef the porter? The
voice was very insistent now, an insistent rushing. Josef understood
a word only here and there, names of cities, distant names foreign
names, names pronounced in a foreign tongue Moscow, Berlin,
Tokyo, Paris —

In Paris the sun was shining. Paris was undestroyed. If you wanted
to trust your eyes, you might think World War II had not taken
place. Christopher Gallagher was connected with Paris. He stood
in the booth from which Washington Price had telephoned Baton
Rouge. Christopher too held a handkerchief in his hand. With the
cloth he wiped his nose. The nose was large-pored and a bit
reddish. His complexion was rough. His hair red. He looked like a

56

sailor; but he was a tax lawyer. He was talking with Henriette. Henriette was his wife. They lived in Santa Ana in California. Their house stood on the Pacific Ocean. You could imagine you were looking out the windows of the house across to China. Now Henriette was in Paris. Christopher was in Germany. Christopher missed Henriette. He hadn't thought beforehand that he would miss her. But he did. He would have liked to have her there with him. He particularly would have liked to have her with him in Germany. He thought, 'we're so formal with each other, I wonder why that is? after all, I do love her.' Henriette was sitting in a room in a hotel on the Quai Voltaire. In front of the hotel flowed the Seine. Over on the opposite bank lay the Tuileries, an often painted, even more often photographed, always enchanting view. Christopher had a loud voice. Through the receiver his voice sounded like shouting. He shouted the same sentences over and over: "I understand you; but believe me, you'd like it. I'm sure you'd like it. You'd like it a lot. I like it a lot, too." And she said the same words over and over: "No. I can't. You know that. I can't." He knew it, but he didn't understand it. Or he did understand, but the same way someone understands a recounted dream and then says: "Forget it!" She looked out at the Seine while she was speaking with Christopher, she saw the Tuileries in the sun, she saw the lovely Parisian spring day, the landscape before her window resembled a Renoir, but it seemed to her as if another image were pushing up through the primer coat, a darker painting. The Seine was transformed into the Spree, and Henriette was standing at the window of a house on Kupfergraben and over there lay the museum island, lay the Prussian-Hellenic temples that were forever under construction, and she saw her father walking to work in the morning, he strode like a figure in a Menzel painting, erect, proper, spotless, top hat set squarely over his gold pince-nez, across the bridge into his museum. He was not an art historian, he had nothing directly to do with the

pictures, though of course he knew every one of them, he was an
Oberregierungsrat on the central governing board, an administrator
in charge of maintaining order on the premises, but for him it was
his museum, which he didn't let out of his sight even on holidays,
and whose resident art historian at any given time he regarded as
something less than adult, as an entertainer hired to amuse visitors,
whose doings and blusterings need hardly be taken seriously. He
refused to move to the new residential districts in the west, out of
sight of the museum, he stayed in the apartment on Kupfergraben,
where things were spare and Prussian (stayed there even after his
dismissal, and until the day they came for him, him and the timid
woman, Henriette's mother, who had wasted away, devoid of will
and wholly dependent, in the shadow of so much Prussiandom).
Henriette played as a child on the steps of the Kaiser Friedrich
Museum beneath the monument and its bellicose equestrian statue
of the three-month emperor with the dirty, loud, and glorious brats
from Oranienburgstrasse, the hellions from Monbijouplatz, and
later, after the lyceum, when she was a pupil of Reinhardt's at the
Deutsches Theater and walked across the bridge to Karlstrasse, the
teenagers, her former playmates, who now met beneath the hooves
of the Kaiser's horse to kiss in the dark, called to her fondly
"Henri," and she, delighted, waved back and called "Fritz" and
"Paule," and the proper spotless Oberregierungsrat said "Henriette,
that won't do." What would do and what wouldn't do? It would do
that, in Berlin, she receive the Reinhardt Prize as the best pupil in
her class; but it wouldn't do that, in southern Germany, where she
was under contract, she play the romantic lead in Eichendorff's Die
Freier. It would do that she be abused, it would not do that she
remain with the company. It would do that she lead a vagrant life
and play cabarets and clubs with an émigré troupe in Zurich,
Prague, Amsterdam, and New York. It wouldn't do that she receive
an unlimited residence permit anywhere, working papers, or a
permanent visa for any country at all. It would do that she, along

58

with other members of the cabaret troupe, be stripped of her citizenship in the German Empire. It wouldn't do that the proper Oberregierungsrat continue to work in the museum. It would do that he be forbidden to use the telephone or a park bench. It would do that she wash dishes in a diner in Los Angeles. It wouldn't do that the daughter be sent money from Berlin so that she could wait for a film role in Hollywood. It would do that she, fired from her dishdrying job, stand on the street, a very foreign street, and that she, hungry, accept the invitation of a stranger who happened to be a Christian. He married her, Christopher Gallagher. It would not do that her father retain his name, Friedrich Wilhelm Cohen; it would do that he be named Israel Cohen. Did Christopher regret having married? He did not. It would not do that the figures Menzel might have drawn, the Prussian civil servant and his timid wife, remain any longer in their native city, Berlin. It would do that they be among the first Jews to be taken away: for the last time they stepped out of the house on Kupfergraben, in the dusk, they climbed into a police car, and Israel Friedrich Wilhelm, proper, spotless, calm, with classic Prussian bearing, helped her up, Sarah Gretchen, who was crying, and then the door of the police car closed and nothing more was heard from them until, after the war, all was heard, nothing of them personally, just in general, the anonymity of their fate, the widespread death—it was enough. Christopher's loud voice shouted: "So you're staying in Paris?" And she said: "Please understand me." And he yelled: "Sure, I understand. But you'd like it. You'd really like it. Everything has changed. I really like it." And she said: "Go to the Bräuhaus some time. Across from it there is a café. Café Schön. I used to study my lines there." And he bellowed: "Sure. Of course I'll go there. But you would like it." He was furious because she was staying in Paris. He missed her. Did she love Paris? Now she saw the Renoir again, saw the Seine, the Tuileries, the clear light. Surely, she loved that view, undestroyed as it was, but in Europe what was destroyed

59

crowded in on what had been spared, came to the fore, was a noonday specter: the Hellenic-Prussian temples on the museum island in Berlin lay plundered and in ruins. She had loved them more than the Tuileries. She felt no satisfaction. She no longer hated. She was only afraid. She was afraid to travel to Germany, even for three days. She longed to be away from Europe. She longed to be back in Santa Ana. By the Pacific Ocean there was peace, there was forgetting, peace and forgetting for her. The waves were the symbol of eternal recurrence. In the wind was the breath of Asia. She had never been in Asia, ASIA GLOBAL PROBLEM NUMBER ONE, but the pacific sea gave her some of the calm and security of a being that surrenders itself to the moment, her sorrow became a melancholy undulating across the open spaces, her ambition to be admired as an actress died, it was not contentment, it was acceptance of her lot that filled her, something like sleep, acceptance of the house, of the terrace, of the beach, of this single point in infinity arrived at by good fortune, coincidence, or destiny. "Tell Ezra hello," she said. "He's just great," he shouted. "He gets along fine with your German. He translates everything for me. You'd enjoy it. You'd really like it here." — "I know," she said, "I understand you. I'll be waiting for the two of you. I'll be waiting for the two of you in Paris. Then we'll go home. It will be glorious. It will be glorious at home. Tell Ezra that, too! Tell him that I'm waiting for you both. Tell him he should take a good look at everything. Tell Ezra—"

Ezra was sitting in Christopher's spacious car with its wood paneling the color of mahogany. The car looked like an older model of a sports plane that had been relegated to ground duty. Ezra circled above the square. He let them have it with all his guns. He fired merrily into the street. Panic spread through the crowd, the swarm of pedestrians and murderers, this mob of hunters and victims, they fell to their knees, they prayed and whimpered for mercy.

his mind

the target is not delivered

They rolled on the ground. They held up their arms to protect their heads. They fled like frightened deer into the houses. The display windows of the big stores shattered. The bullets flew with luminous trails into the stores. Ezra made a strafing run at the monument in the center of the American central exchange parking lot. On the steps of the monument sat boys and girls, Ezra's age. They chatted, yelled, and played heads or tails; they haggled, traded, and fought over small amounts of American goods; they teased a scraggly young dog; they fought and made up. Ezra poured a sheaf of his luminous ammunition over the children. The children lay dead or wounded on the steps of the monument. The young dog limped into a ditch. One boy shouted: "That was Ezra!" Ezra flew over the roof of the central exchange and climbed steeply. When he was high above the city, he dropped a bomb. SCIENTISTS WARN AGAINST USE.

A little girl wiped the dust off the horizonblue paint of a sedan. The little girl was hard at work; one might think she was cleaning the celestial vehicle of an angel. Heinz was hiding. He had climbed onto the base of the monument and crouched under the prince elector's horse. The historians called the prince elector The Pious. In the religious wars he had gone into battle to defend the true faith. His enemies fought to defend the true faith as well. In the matter of faith, then, there was no victor. Maybe faith in general was defeated by people fighting over it. But by means of the war the pious prince elector had become a powerful man. He had become so powerful that his subjects had nothing to laugh about. Heinz didn't care about the religious strife and the prince's power. He was looking around the square.

A nation of car drivers was making itself at home here. The cars were parked in long rows. If their gas supply ran out, they would be helpless crates, huts for shepherds, if people herded sheep after the next war, hideaways for lovers if people still wanted to hide away and make love after they were dead. Now the cars were shiny and sleek, a proud automobile exhibition, a triumph of the technological

61

century, a saga of the lordship of man over the forces of nature, a symbol of his apparently outwitting inertia and resistance in space and time. Maybe the cars would be left behind someday. They would be left standing on the lot like sheetmetal corpses. People wouldn't be able to drive them. They would take out what they could use, a cushion to sit on. The rest would rust. Women, women dressed in fashion and like tomboys, women proudly ladylike and boyish, women in olive-green uniforms, female lieutenants and female majors, smartly made-up teen-age girls, a whole lot of women, and then civilian employees, officers and soldiers, Negroes and Negresses, they were all part of the occupation force, they populated the square, they called out, laughed, waved, they steered the lovely automobiles that hummed the song of wealth skillfully among the already parked vehicles. The Germans admired and despised all this display on wheels. Some thought, 'ours used to march.' In their minds, it was more respectable to march in a foreign land than to drive; marching was more suitable to their idea of soldiering; it conformed better to the rules of the game as they had learned it to be watched over by foot soldiers than by casual motorists. The casual motorists were surely friendlier, the foot soldiers would probably have been rougher on them; that was beside the point; it was a matter of rules, of the traditional practices to be adhered to in war, victory, and defeat. German officers, scraping by as traveling salesmen and waiting with their bags of samples for the streetcar, were annoyed when they saw ordinary American soldiers, looking like rich tourists on comfortable cushions, drive past their superiors without saluting. That was democracy and disorder. The luxurious automobiles gave the occupation force a tinge of cockiness, wickedness, and extravagance.

Washington approached his horizonblue sedan. He was the angel for whom the little girl had shined up the celestial transport. The little one curtsied. She curtsied and ran her cloth along the car door. Washington gave her chocolate and bananas. He had bought

62

the chocolate and bananas for the little girl. He was a regular customer of the little girl. Heinz, beneath the pious prince elector's horse, smirked. He waited until Washington had driven off, then he climbed down from the pedestal. He spat on the tablet with the list cast in bronze of the prince elector's victories. He said: "That was my mother's nigger."

The children looked at Heinz with respect. He impressed them, the way he stood there, spat, and said: "That was my mother's nigger." The industrious little girl had come over to the monument and munched reflectively on a banana given her by his-mother's-nigger. The young dog sniffed at the discarded banana peel. The little girl paid no attention to the dog. The dog was not wearing a collar. A string had been tied around his neck. He seemed to be captive but homeless. Heinz was bragging: he had steered the Ami-car once, he could do it every day if he wanted to: "My mother is going with a Negro." The dark friend, the black breadwinner of the family, the generous and yet alien and disturbing figure in the apartment constantly occupied his thoughts. Some days, he lied the Negro out of his life. "What's your Negro up to?" the boys would ask. "Don't know. There's no nigger," he would say then. Another time he would build a kind of cult around Washington, describing his tremendous physical strength, his wealth, his importance as an athlete, so that finally he could hurl his last trump at the others, that placed all the accomplishments of this important, black man in their proper, personal light, the trump that Washington was living with his mother. The other children knew the often-related story, they themselves passed it on at home, yet they waited again and again in suspense like at the movies for the climax, this unbeatable trump: He is going with my mother, he eats at our table, he sleeps in our bed, they want me to say Dad to him. That came from the depths of joy and of pain. Heinz could not remember the father who was missing in action on the Volga. A photograph that showed his father in gray uniform meant nothing to him. Washington could be

63

a good father. He was friendly, he was generous, he didn't punish,
he was a well-known athlete, he wore a uniform, he was one of the
victors, to Heinz he was rich and drove a big, horizonblue car. But
Washington's black skin spoke against him, the obvious sign of
being different. Heinz didn't want to be different than others. He
wanted to be exactly like the other boys, and they had white-
skinned, native-born fathers accepted everywhere. Washington was
not accepted everywhere. People spoke of him with contempt.
Some made fun of him. Sometimes Heinz wanted to defend Washington, but then he didn't dare have a different opinion than the
many, the adults, the local folks, the smart ones, and he said: "That
nigger!" People said ugly things about Carla's relationship with
Washington; they did not hesitate to use vulgar terms in the presence of the boy; but what Heinz hated most was when they patted
him on the head with false sympathy and blubbered: "poor boy,
after all, you are a German boy." So Washington, without suspect-
ing it (or maybe he did suspect it, knew it even, and stayed away
from Heinz, withdrawn, gazing off into space), was a problem for
Heinz, irritation, suffering, and a continual conflict, and Heinz
came to avoid Washington, only reluctantly accepted his gifts any
more, and rode seldom and without pleasure in the admired and
splendid car. He hung around here and there, talked himself into
believing he despised the blacks and the Amis, the whole lot of
them, and to torment himself for the sake of an attitude he basically
considered cowardly, and to prove that he himself could say the
words that others thought they could use to put him down, he
crowed tirelessly his "she's going with a nigger." When he noticed
Ezra watching him from the car that looked so much like an
airplane, he shouted in fairly fluent English (which he had learned
from Washington for the sole purpose of listening in on the conversations between his mother and the Negro in order to hear what
they were planning, which, after all, was his affair, too, the trip to
America, the move both away and home, which he, Heinz, didn't

64

know whether he would go on or not, maybe he would insist on being taken along, maybe he'd go and hide once everything was packed): "Yes, she goes with a nigger."

Heinz held the dog on its string. The boy and the dog looked like they were tied together. They looked like a couple of poor condemned wretches tied together. The dog tugged at the string. Ezra watched Heinz and the dog. It was as if he were dreaming it all. The boy who called out: "Yes, she goes with a nigger," the dog tied on the string, the equestrian monument of dark green bronze were unreal, they were not a real boy, not a real dog, not a real monument; they were ideas; they had the light, dizzying transparency of dream figures; they were shades and at the same time they were him himself, the dreamer; there was an intimate and evil bond between them and him, and the best thing would be to scream and wake up. Ezra had foxred, shortcropped hair. His little forehead wrinkled beneath the foxred cap. He had the feeling he was lying in his bed at home in Santa Ana. The waves of the Pacific Ocean beat monotonously against the shore. Ezra was ill. In Europe there was war. Europe was a distant continent. It was the continent of the gruesome sagas. There was an evil land there, and in the evil land there was an evil giant HITLER AGGRESSOR. America, too, was in the war. America fought against the evil giant. America had a big heart. It fought for the rights of man. What kind of rights were they? Did Ezra possess them? Did he have the right not to eat his soup, to kill his enemies, those kids from the north beach, to talk back to his father? His mother sat by his bed. Henriette spoke German with him. He didn't understand the language, and yet he did understand it. This German was his mother tongue, that was to be taken literally, it was the language of his mother, older, more mysterious, than the only language used around the house, the familiar, everyday American, and his mother wept, in the child's room she wept, she wept over strange people who had disappeared, been robbed, kidnapped, slaughtered, the Jewish-Prussian Ober-

65

regierungsrat and his silent, gentle Sarah Gretchen, taken away IN
THE COURSE OF THE LIQUIDATION, became, at the bedside of a sick
child in Santa Ana, California, figures from Grimm's Fairy Tales,
just as real, just as kindly, just as sad as King Drosselbart, as Tom
Thumb and grandmother and the wolf, and it was just as eerie as
the story of the Juniper Tree. Henriette taught her boy her mother
tongue by reading him German fairy tales, but when she thought he
was asleep she would go on by herself, watching over his feverish
sleep, worrying about him, would tell the fairy tale about his
grandparents and, like the droning of the latest language instruction phonographs that teach you the foreign sounds in your sleep,
the German vocabulary of suffering, the murmured and sobbed
words, sank deep into Ezra's mind. Now he was in the thicket, in
the eerie, enchanted forest of dream and of fairy tale—the parking
lot was the forest, the city was the thicket: the aerial attack had
done no good, Ezra would have to win this battle on the ground.
Heinz had long, blond hair, an unruly mane. He looked disap-
provingly at the short, now popular American hair style, Ezra's
modified barracks cut. He thought, 'this guy is stuck up, I'll show
him.' Ezra asked in German: "Do you want to sell the dog?" Because
of his uncertainty with the language, he thought it appropriate to
use the formal *Sie* instead of *du*. Heinz took the *Sie* to be further
proof of the arrogance of this foreign boy who sat rightfully in the
interesting car (unlike Heinz's dubious position in Washington's
car), it was a rejection, a keeping-at-a-distance (perhaps, perhaps
the *Sie* was indeed intended as a check, a protective barrier for Ezra,
and not linguistic confusion), and he, Heinz, used it now as well,
this *Sie,* and the two eleven-year-olds, the two children begotten in
the fear of war, stood conversing stiffly like old-fashioned adults.
"Do you want to buy the dog?" said Heinz. He had no intention of
selling the dog. It wasn't even his dog. The dog belonged to the
gang of children. But maybe he could sell it after all. He'd have to
keep the conversation going. Heinz had a feeling that something

would come of all this. He didn't know what, but something would come of it. Ezra wasn't at all interested in buying the dog. For a while he had felt that he ought to rescue the dog. But then rescuing the dog was forgotten, was not the main thing, the main thing was the conversation and something that would turn up. You couldn't see it yet. The dream wasn't far enough along yet. The dream was just beginning. Ezra said: "I am a Jew." He was a Catholic. He had been baptized a Catholic like Christopher and went to a Catholic school. But it went with the tone of the fairy tale that he was a Jew. He looked at Heinz expectantly. Heinz didn't know what to make of Ezra's confession. It perplexed him, this obscure move by the other boy. It would also have perplexed him if Ezra had told him he was an Indian. Was he trying to make himself interesting? Jews? They were merchants, shady businessmen, they didn't like the Germans. What was it? What was Ezra trading? There was no merchandise in the airplane car. Maybe he wanted to buy the dog cheaply and sell it later at a higher price. He'd wreck that plan! Just in case, Heinz repeated his own confession: "My mother, you should know, lives with a Negro." Was Heinz threatening him with a Negro? Ezra had had no contact with Negroes. But he knew of white and black gangs of children who fought each other. Heinz belonged to a black gang, that was surprising. Ezra had to be careful. "What do you want for your dog?" he said. Heinz answered: "Ten dollars." That could be done. For ten dollars it could be done. If that stupid kid paid ten dollars, then he was the sucker. The dog wasn't even worth ten marks. Ezra said: "Fine." He didn't know yet how he'd do it. But he'd do it. It would work all right. He'd have to make up a lie to tell Christopher. Christopher wouldn't understand that this was just part of a dream, and not real. He said: "I have to get the ten dollars first." Heinz thought, 'you wish you could, you son of a bitch.' He said: "You don't get the dog until you give me the money." The dog, indifferent to their haggling, tugged at its string. The little girl had thrown him a piece of chocolate from Heinz's-mother's-Negro. The

67

chocolate lay in a puddle and slowly dissolved. The dog couldn't reach the puddle. Ezra said: "I have to ask my father. He will give me the money." — "Now?" Heinz asked. Ezra thought a moment. Again his little forehead furrowed beneath the foxred cap of close-shorn hair. He thought, 'can't do it here.' He said: "No, tonight. Come to the Bräuhaus. My father and I will be in the Bräuhaus tonight." Heinz nodded. He shouted: "Okay!" He knew the area around the Bräuhaus well. On the Bräuhaus square was the Negro soldiers' club. Heinz often stood in front of the place and watched his mother and Washington climb out of the horizonblue sedan and walk past the black MP into the club. He knew all the hookers who prowled around the square. Sometimes the hookers gave him choc-olate that they had gotten from the Negroes. Heinz didn't need the chocolate. But it satisfied him to take the chocolate from the hookers. Then he could say to Washington: "I don't like choco-late." He thought: 'You'll get your dog, I've already given you the slip.'

Odysseus gave them the slip. He gave the Greeks the slip, slipped free of the quick hands whisking across the bar-room table like quick yellow lizards. The dice fell their way. They snatched up the dice, passed them to Odysseus; Odysseus lost; they grabbed them up again, hurled them down, luck on their side; they were playing for marks and dollars, for manly marks and hussy dollars, playing for what they called life, playing for a bellyful of food, for drunkenness, for pleasure, for the day's money, because what they derived from each day cost money, the chow, the booze, the sex, it all cost money, marks or dollars, here they were laid on the line: what were the Greeks, what was King Odysseus without money? He had deerslayer eyes. The Glocke band played I'll-shoot-the-stag-in-the-forest-green. Everyone in the Glocke was hunting the white stag of their wishes and illusions. The beer had set them upon imaginary horses; they were proud hunters on horseback. Their drives were off

68

on the chase, on pleasure hunts after the white stag of self-deception. The mountain gunner sang along with the band's song, the Africa veteran, the man from the Eastern Front joined in. Josef, crowded by the machinations of the Greeks away from his black master of the day, heard a lecture from Odysseus's music case about the situation in Persia PARATROOPERS SENT TO MALTA, and again it was only a rushing in the air to Josef again only a breaking wave of history, a breaker washed down from the air to him, unintelligible firsthand seething history, a sourdough rising. Names were kneaded into it, names and more names, names often heard, the names of the historical hour, the names of the major players, the names of the managers, the names of the settings, scenes of conferences, scenes of battles, scenes of murder, how will the sourdough rise? what kind of bread will we eat tomorrow? "We were the first ones on Crete," shouted the Rommel soldier, "first they sent us to Crete. We just jumped right in." There was the stag! Now he'd seen through it, deerslayer eyes! The black hand was quicker than the magic trick of the yellow lizards. Odysseus made his move. He had the dice. This time they were the right ones, the loaded ones, the tricky ones that brought luck, the ones so often, so cunningly switched. He rapped them down onto the wood: a winner! He threw them again and threw lucky again. He made room with his elbows. The Greeks staggered back. Odysseus's back covered the table. The table was the battlefront. He fired salvos into the wood, a bombardment of luck: Chief Odysseus King Odysseus General Odysseus Chairman of the Board Mister Odysseus Cotton Esquire. "We mopped up in the White Mountains. When we went down into the valley, we needed cluster charges, and in the underbrush, our knives, tommy guns, and pellet spitters. We got the Crete medal." — "Big shit!" — "Did you say—" — "I said big shit. There was a war in Russia. Everything else is little boys' stories. Dime novels with bright pictures on the cover. Fairy tales, man! Bright pictures! Here a naked whore, there a paratrooper with the look of death in his eye. The same thing,

69

man! I'll tan my boy's butt if he brings that stuff home." The voice
in the music case said: "Cyprus." Cyprus was strategically important. The voice said: "Teheran." The voice did not say Shiraz. The
voice did not mention the roses of Shiraz. The voice did not say
Hafiz. The voice did not know of Hafiz the poet. For this voice,
there had never been a Hafiz. The voice said: "Oil." And again
there was a rushing, a rushing of sound a dull pattering of syllables,
the river of history rushed past, Josef sat on the bank of the river,
old man, tired man, battleworn man, man still peering after happiness in his twilight years, unintelligible the river, unintelligible
the pattering, the rushing syllables lulling him to sleep. The Greeks
didn't dare go for their knives. The white stag had slipped away
from them. Black Odysseus had escaped them: cunning, great
Odysseus. He gave Josef money to pay for the beer. "Zu viel,
Mister," said Josef. "Nix zu viel money," said Odysseus. The waitress
tucked the big bill away: mighty and magnanimous Odysseus.
"Come on," called Odysseus. "Appeal to the Hague," said the
voice. The voice was being carried by Josef, WILHELM II KAISER OF
PEACE MAKES DONATION FOR THE HAGUE, being shaken by Josef,
with his old man's gait he shook the trickle of great words. The river
of history flowed. From time to time the river overflowed its banks.
It flooded the land with history. It left behind the drowned, it left
behind the muck, the manure, the stinking mother field, a slime of
fertility: where is the gardener? when will the fruit be ripe? Josef
followed, small and peering, he too in the muck, still in the muck,
back again in the muck, followed the black overlord, the master he
had chosen for this day. When was the blossoming? When would
the golden age come, the time of milk and honey—

He was a honeymooner. The horizonblue sedan stopped in front
of the apartment house where Carla lived. Washington had brought
flowers, longstemmed and yellow. As he got out of the car, the sun
broke through the overcast sky. The light reflected off the car body,

70

giving the flowers a sulfurous yellow gleam. Washington felt them watching him through the windows of the apartment house. The little people who lived in many units here, three, four people to every space, every room a cage, the accommodations were roomier at the zoo, the little people crowded against the often mended and repeatedly starched curtains and poked one another. "Flowers he brings her. See the flowers? He ought to be—." Due to some complex or other, it infuriated them that Washington was bringing flowers into the building. Washington himself drew relatively little attention; he was a person, even if he was a Negro. The flowers drew attention, the packages he carried were counted, the car drew embittered stares. In Germany, the car cost more than a small house. It cost more than the little house on the edge of town that people yearned for all their lives in vain. Max said so. Max ought to know. Max worked in a garage. The horizonblue sedan at the front door was a provocation.

A couple of old women had complained about the goings on in the apartment on the fourth floor. Old lady Welz must have had connections with the police. The police did not intervene, CAN-CEROUS EFFECTS OF DEMOCRACY. In reality, the police simply saw no reason to intervene. They couldn't always intervene where something was rotten in the city. Besides, the old women would have regretted it, had the police intervened. The police would have deprived them of the only entertainment they could afford.

Washington climbed the steps: jungles surrounded him. Behind every door they stood and listened. They were domesticated predators; they still sniffed out their prey, but the time was not yet favorable, the time did not allow the herd to pounce on the foreign creature that had violated the herd's domain. Old lady Welz opened the door. The woman was stringy-haired, fat, droopy-assed, filthy. For her, on the other hand, Washington was a tame pet: not a cow exactly, but maybe a goat, 'I'll milk that black billy goat' — "Not home," she said. She started to take his packages. He said: "Oh,

71

that's all right." He said it with the friendly, impersonal voice blacks use when they're talking to whites, but the voice had a strained and impatient undertone. He wanted to be rid of the woman. He loathed her. He walked down the dimly lit corridor to Carla's rooms. From several doorways, the girls who met with soldiers at Frau Welz's were watching him. Washington suffered because of this apartment. But he could do nothing about it. Carla couldn't find any other rooms. She said: "With you there, I can't find any others." Carla suffered because of the apartment as well, but she suffered less from it than did Washington, whom she never tired of assuring how terribly she was suffering, how degrading all this was for her, and that meant by implication how much she was giving herself away, how far she was lowering herself, down low to him, and that he would have to bring her ever new love, new presents, new sacrifices, to make up for it a little bit, just a very little bit. Carla despised and reviled Frau Welz and the girls, but when she was alone, when she was bored, when Washington was at work at the base, she would make up to the girls, invite them over, talk with them, girl talk, whores' gossip, or she would sit by the stove in Frau Welz's kitchen, drinking Mischkaffee from the pot kept constantly bubbling over the fire, and tell Frau Welz (who then passed it along to the neighbors) whatever she wanted to know. The girls in the hall showed Washington what they had; they opened their house dresses, adjusted their garters, shook out clouds of scent from their dyed hair. There was a competition among the girls to see if one could get Washington into bed. Since they knew Negroes only in heat, their little brains concluded that all Negroes were lechers. They didn't understand Washington. They did not comprehend that he was no frequenter of brothels. Washington was born to lead a happy family life; but, sadly, unfortunate coincidences had led him off course and into this apartment, into muck and jungles.

In the living room Washington hoped to find a message Carla might have left him. He thought Carla would be back soon. Maybe she had gone to the hairdresser's. He looked on the dresser for a note that would tell him where she had gone. On the dresser stood bottles of nail polish, face lotion, creme jars, and powder boxes. There were photographs stuck inside the frame of the mirror. One picture showed Carla's missing husband, who was now about to receive his death certificate, his official death, from whom the fetter was being removed that bound him and Carla in this world until-death-do-ye-part. He was in a battlegray uniform. On his chest was the swastika, against which Washington had gone into battle. Washington looked at the man with equanimity. With equanimity he looked at the swastika on the man's chest. The hooked cross had become meaningless. Maybe the racist cross had never meant anything to the man. Maybe Washington had never fought against this cross. Maybe they had both been deceived. He didn't hate the man. The man didn't trouble him. He was not jealous of his predecessor. At times he envied him the fact that he had it all behind him. That was such a dark feeling; Washington always suppressed it. Next to her husband in the frame of the mirror hung Carla in her wedding dress and with a white veil. She was eighteen years old when she married. That was twelve years ago. In those years, the world in which Carla and her husband had expected to live long and secure lives had collapsed. Of course, their world had no longer been the world of their parents. Carla was pregnant when she went to the magistrate's office, and the white veil in the photograph was a lie, and yet it wasn't a lie, because no one was deceived, nor could they have been, for the white veil had long since stopped serving any but a decorative purpose, and it became an embarrassing masquerade, the object of ridicule, if one took it to be the sign of undefiled virginity, and it was not at all disrespectful for people to think this, for the time was rather inclined to consider it disrespectful and shameless to think of the bridegroom, after the bride is publicly handed over to him and the ceremony completed, pouncing upon her, upon the white lamb whose hymen was then sacrificed, and yet

73

the marriage was necessary, propriety and official sanction of their joining together, the blessing of the community, all this was necessary because of the children, the children who were to be born into the community and were lured into this life even with advertising, VISIT BEAUTIFUL GERMANY, and Carla and her husband, freshly married, believed then in an empire upon which you could bestow your children, trusting, dutiful, responsible, CHILDREN THE NATION'S WEALTH, GOVERNMENT LOANS FOR YOUNG MARRIED COUPLES. Carla's parents also hung in the mirror frame. Frau Behrend had chosen to be photographed with an armful of flowers, the Musikmeister was in uniform, but instead of a baton, his left hand held the neck of a violin, which he propped against his legs as he sat. Thus were Herr and Frau Behrend joined, a pair of devotees of poetry and of the muses, in harmonious union. Heinz was photographed as an infant. He stood upright in his baby carriage and waved. He no longer knew whom he had waved to, some adult probably; the adult had been his father, who had stood behind the camera taking the picture, and soon thereafter, father had gone off to war. One picture that was larger than the others showed him himself, Washington Price: he was in his baseball uniform with the white visored cap, the fielder's gloves, and the bat. The expression on his face was dignified and serious. That was Carla's family. Washington belonged to Carla's family. For a while, Washington stared dully at the pictures. Where might Carla be? What was he doing here? He saw himself with his flowers and packages in the mirror. It was funny how he was standing in this room in front of the family pictures, the toilet things, and the mirror. For a moment, Washington had the feeling his life was meaningless. His reflection in the mirror made him dizzy. From one of the girls' rooms came radio music. The American station was playing the mournfully dignified tune Negro Heaven by Duke Ellington. Washington could have cried. While he listened to the tune, a song from home coming from a whore's room in an alien place (and what places were

74

not alien?), he felt the whole ugliness of existence. The earth was not a heaven. The earth was certainly not a Negro heaven. But quickly his optimism came hurrying after a mirage, he clung to the thought that soon another picture would be stuck in the mirror, the picture of a little brown child, the child that he and Carla were going to bestow upon the world.

He stepped into Frau Welz's kitchen, stood by the stove, by the bubbling pots, and she let him know, a witch amidst clouds of smoke, steam, and odors, that she did know where Carla was, he should keep calm, things weren't quite right with Carla, there had been a little something, he would know, sometimes you aren't careful, when you love somebody you aren't careful, she knew about these things, maybe you couldn't tell anymore by looking at her, but she knew how it was, and the girls here, they all knew how it was, and, well, Carla's little thing wasn't so bad (he didn't understand, he, Washington, didn't understand, didn't understand the German witch's ABC, an evil woman, what did she want? what was that about Carla? why didn't she say she was at the hairdresser's, had gone to the movies? why all the mumbling? so much wicked talk), so it wasn't bad at all, she did have such a good doctor and she had always provided for the doctor through the bad time, "I used to say to Carla, it's too much, Carla, but Carla wanted to take him the best things, and now we know what good it did, Carla's taking him the best things like that," there was no cause for worry at all, "Washington, Doctor Frahm will do it all right." This he understood. He understood the name Dr. Frahm. What was going on? Was Carla sick? Then it struck Washington. Or had she gone to the doctor because of the child? But that couldn't be, that couldn't be. She couldn't do that, of all things, she couldn't do that —

It was a joke. Somebody had pulled the practical joke of tying Emilia to too many possessions. But maybe it wasn't even a joke, maybe Emilia was so completely insignificant to any powers that be, to any kind of planning, to any premeditation, to any good or wicked fairy, to the spirit of chance, that it wasn't even a joke, and she had been thrown, along with what she owned, into the trash, without anyone in particular wanting to throw her there, it had happened by chance, by chance to be sure, but it was a completely mindless, dumb, utterly meaningless coincidence that had tied her to goods that had constantly been described to her by others, and then by her own wishes as well, as the means to a glorious life, while her inheritance actually made possible only a bohemian existence, with disarray, uncertainty, begging forays, and days of going hungry, a bohemian existence that was grotesquely coupled with capital management and tax deadlines. Time had made no designs on Emilia, had had neither good nor bad intentions in regard to her, it was only Emilia's inheritance that had fallen prey to the spirit of the times and its planning, capital was being dissolved, in some countries it had already been dissolved, in others it was going to be, and in Germany each hour loosened like nitric acid the bonds of possession, ate away with corrosion what wealth had been accumulated, and it was foolish of Emilia to take the spatters of corrosive, insofar as the caustic solution struck her, personally, to take them for the vengeful stabs of fate intended personally for her. Nothing had been done with her in mind. This life, which Emilia did not master, was a time of change, a fateful time, but only in general, individual people could go on being happy or unhappy, and Emilia had the bad luck to be clinging, stubbornly and fearfully, to what she was losing, while it lay in the throes of a distorted, disordered, disreputable, and a bit ludicrous final agony; yet the birth of the world's new age was no less fringed with the grotesque, disordered, disreputable, and ludicrous. People could live on the one side and on the other, and they could die on this side and on that side of the trench of time. "Great religious wars are coming," said Philipp. Emilia got all this mixed up, she saw herself lowered by financial difficulties to the level of the bohemians, saw herself in the company of people who, in her parents' house, had enjoyed free meals and fool's license but never respect, and her grandparents, who had so fruitfully multiplied the family fortune, wouldn't have let these fly-by-nights through the front door in the first place. Emilia hated and scorned the bohemians, the penniless intellectuals, the idle windbags incapable of doing a day's work, wearers of threadbare trousers, and their cheap girlfriends dressed in secondhand things based on long since passé Parisian Taboo Cellar fashions, with whom she now lay in the same dust heap, while Philipp simply avoided this group that Emilia so despised, because he did not accept them as bohemians, the Bohème was long since dead, and the crowd that acted as if the young intellectuals still existed, radicals spawning revolutions and aesthetic theories in coffeehouses, they were people in costume for the evening, out for a night's conventional entertainment, and by day they worked, not nearly as idle as Emilia thought, as commercial artists, wrote advertising copy, earned their income in film and radio studios, and the Taboo girls sat primly at typewriters, the Bohème was dead, it had already died when the Romanisches Café in Berlin was hit by bombs and burned, it was already dead when the first SA man set foot in the café, it had, strictly speaking, already been strangled by politics even before Hitler. When he left for Russia, the Zurich bohemian Lenin had closed behind him the doors of the literary café for centuries to come. What remained in the café after Lenin was basically conservative, was conservative adolescence, conservative love for Mimi, was conservative effort to alarm the bourgeoisie (although it must be remembered that both Mimi, who was to be loved, and the bourgeois, who was to be alarmed, had also died by then and become fairytale characters), until the Bohème finally found its tomb in certain nightspots, changing from a thing conservative to a thing preserved, a museum piece, a tourist attraction. And incongruously, it was these establishments, the boîtes, the mausoleums of the Scènes-de-la-vie-de-bohème, that Emilia liked to frequent, she who had to go through the bohemian routine that she loathed in order to raise the money to go there, while for Philipp these places, with their dancer types and the businessman's glass-of-wine-patronage-of-the-arts, were one unmitigated horror. "We never go anywhere," Emilia would shout then, "you forget that I'm young." And he thought, 'is your youth so withered that it requires such a watering, a watering of intoxication, alcohol, and syncopation, do your feelings need the air of nonfeelings, your hair the wind of will-you-sleep-with-me-tonight "but hurry, I have to get up early"?' Emilia stood, threatened on all sides, in no man's land. She was rich and was barred from enjoying the benefits of being rich, she was no longer accepted by Pluto, she did not belong, was not his child, but neither did she belong nor find acceptance in the working world, and she viewed this having-to-get-up-early with blind, cold, but completely innocent contempt.

Now she had made headway, she had walked on, she had part of her Scottish plaid route behind her. Emilia had been to the pawn-broker. She had stood among the poor in the hall of the municipal pawn office. The hall was lined with marble and looked like a swimming pool with the water let out. The poor were not swimming. They had gone under. They were not at the top. They were at the bottom. The top, up above, life, ah, that gleam, ah, that plenty, life lay beyond the marble walls, lay above the glass roof that covered the hall, above the milky panes, this foggy sky above the pond of people gone under. They were at life's bottom and led a ghostly existence. They stood at the counters and held their former belongings in their arms, the possessions of another life, one that no longer had anything to do with their present life, a life that they had led before they had drowned, and the goods that they brought to the counter seemed to them like someone else's belongings, like stolen goods they were trying to hock, and they were skittish, like thieves caught in the act. Was it all over for them? The end was near, but it wasn't all over yet. These possessions still connected them with life, just as ghosts cling to buried treasures; they belonged to the halfworld of the Styx, for the moment there was a reprieve, the counter would lend out six marks for the overcoat, three for the shoes, eight for the eiderdown quilt, the drowned gasped for air, once more they were released back into life, for hours, for days, fortunate ones for weeks, VOID AFTER FOUR MONTHS. Emilia had handed across the counter a set of fish knives and forks. The Renaissance pattern on the silverware was not inspected, the artistry of the silversmith ignored, one glance at the silver stamp and then the silverware was thrown onto the scales. The fish course of the sumptuous Kommerzienrat dinner service lay upon the scales of the pawn office. "Your Excellency, the salmon!" The Kaiser's general was served a second helping. FULL STEAM AHEAD, KAISER'S MESSAGE FOR THE NEW CENTURY. The silverware did not weigh much. The silver handles were hollow. Kommerzienrat hands, hands of bankers and government ministers had held the handles, had helped themselves to salmon, sturgeon, and trout: fat hands, bejeweled hands, fateful hands. "His Majesty mentioned Africa in his address. I say colonial bonds—" — 'Fools! They should have put it in gold and buried it, fools, in gold all would have been saved, I wouldn't be standing here!' The pawn office lends three pfennig per gram of silverware. Eighteen marks and the receipt were handed across the counter to Emilia. The drowned in the stygian pool envied her. For now, Emilia still belonged to the elite among the shades; for now, she was still the princess in the tattered fur coat.

And she had walked farther, path of Calvary, made headway in her tattered princess fur and with her bundle of goods in the comical Scottish traveling plaid: she stood before the vaulted cellar of Herr Unverlacht, this, too, an entrance to the underworld, slippery steps led downward, and behind dirty windowpanes Emilia saw, by the light of alabaster lamps, ponderous, pearshaped, opalescent luminous domes that he had bought once from the estate of a

79

suicide and hadn't been able to get rid of to this day, Unverlacht's broad, bald pate gleaming. He was stocky and broadshouldered; he looked like a furniture mover who had one day discovered that it was easier and more profitable to trade in old household goods than to carry them, also like the stubby, fat man who plays the bad guy in a troupe of performing wrestlers, but surely he had been neither a mover nor a wrestler, maybe a frog, a devious, fat frog perched in its vault, waiting for flies. Emilia descended the steps, opened the door, and immediately she shuddered. Her skin drew up taut. That was no frog prince watching the door with cold, watery eyes, Unverlacht was as he was, unenchanted, and no breaking of a spell was to be expected, no prince would ever hop forth from that frog costume. A musical mechanism, set in motion by Emilia's entrance, played A-Mighty-Fortress-Is-Our-God. That was meaningless, no confession of faith. Unverlacht had acquired the mechanism, like the lamps, cheaply, and now he was waiting to find a buyer for these treasures. As for the lamps, it was dumb of him to try and sell them: with their alabaster glow, they lent his vault a gloom truly worthy of Hades. "Well, Sissy, what have you brought?" he said, and already the frogflipper hand (really, his fingers seemed joined by horny scaled webbing) had hold of Emilia by the chin, her little chin slid into the hollow of the frog hand as if into an open maw, while Unverlacht's other hand felt along her young and firm behind. For some unclear reason, Unverlacht called Emilia Sissy; perhaps she reminded him of someone who really had this name, and Emilia and this unknown, perhaps long since buried, Sissy had merged in this vault into a single entity which its proprietor greeted with lecherous affection. Emilia pushed away from him. "I want to talk business," she said. All at once she felt nauseated. The musty vault air took her breath away. She let her plaid fall to the floor and threw herself into a chair. The chair was a rocker, and the force with which she had dropped into it sent it rocking violently. Emilia felt like she was in a boat crossing the ocean; the boat was rocking on the high seas; a monster reared its head up out of the waves; shipwreck was imminent; Emilia was afraid she was going to be seasick. "Cut it out, Sissy," called Unverlacht. "I don't have any money. What do you expect? Business is bad." He watched Emilia lurching back and forth, he saw her stretched out before him, below him in the rocking chair, her skirt had ridden up, he looked above the stockings at the bare thighs; 'a child's legs' he thought; he had a fat and jealous wife. He was in a bad mood. Emilia excited him, the child's legs excited him, the tired, spoiled face of a tired and spoiled girl could have beguiled him, had he been capable of following any impulse other than that of his greed. For Unverlacht, Emilia was something fine, 'this good family,' he thought, he desired her, but he desired her no more really than a picture in a magazine one might use to get excited, and he wanted no more than to fondle her, but even the fondling could get in the way of business: he did want to buy from Emilia, he just acted as if he had no money, that was part of doing business, they were good things that Emilia offered him 'from such a fine family from such a wealthy house,' and she let him have them cheap, had no idea what they were worth, 'what little panties she has on, it's as if she doesn't have any on at all,' but at any second Frau Unverlacht, a grease-encrusted, loathsome toad, might enter the vault. "Quit that rocking! What have you brought, Sissy?" He used the familiar *du* with Emilia; it gave him pleasure to say *du* to her like some whore of a street urchin, and again he thought, 'the fine family, such a fine family.' Emilia pulled herself together. She opened the plaid. A little prayer rug appeared; it was torn, but it could be mended. Emilia unrolled it. Philipp loved this rug, loved its fine pattern, the swinging blue lamp on a red background, and Emilia had purposely taken this one, she had taken it because Philipp loved it and because she wanted to punish Philipp, because he had no money and because she had to go to the pawn office and to Unverlacht's, and because it seemed to make no difference to him that he was always penniless and that she was

81

allowed to sell her things off for a pittance like some beggar, sometimes Emilia saw Philipp as an ogre, then again other times as a rescuer sent to her from whom she could expect anything, surprise, pain, but fortune as well, fame and wealth, and she was sorry that she tormented him, she felt like kneeling down on the prayer rug and praying, asking God and Philipp for forgiveness for being bad (she used that childhood expression), but where was God and which direction was Mecca, where was she supposed to turn with her prayer? Unverlacht, bothered by no remorse, tormented by no religious scruples, pounced eagerly upon the tears in the rug. They inspired him to triumphant shouts: "Such a rag! Nothing but holes! These tears! Worthless, Sissy, rotted, crumbling, worthless!" He crumpled the wool in his hand, held it up to his bald skull, lay his ear against the rug, shouted: "It sings!" — "It does what?" asked Emilia, momentarily flustered. "It sings," said Unverlacht, it crackles, it's crumbling, I'll give you five marks, Sissy, because it's you and you've lugged it over here." — "You're insane," said Emilia. She did her best to make her face show cold indifference. Unverlacht thought, 'it's worth a hundred,' if worst came to worst, he'd pay twenty. He said: "Ten, on commission; I'm doing you a favor, Sissy." Emilia thought, 'I know he'll sell it for a hundred.' She said: "Thirty, in cash." Her voice sounded firm and decisive, but her heart was tired. From Unverlacht she had learned the tricks of the business. Sometimes she thought, if she could manage to sell a house (but she would never manage it, it would never happen: who buys houses? crumbling walls? who takes on burdens? who lets the bureaucrats run his life, gets involved with tax authorities and building inspectors? who asks for headaches? exposes himself to court summonses? who wants to contend with tenants constantly clamoring for expensive repairs, tenants whose rent has to go straight to the tax office, instead of being like the old landlords in that fairytale time, contented, comfortable, hands in their laps, living from the rent?), if it could be managed!—it was one of her

82

greatest dreams, to someday finally get rid of one of her houses, but the purchasers would hardly accept such a bad investment, so vulnerable to every action of the state, even if you gave it to them— maybe then Emilia, too, would open a used goods shop, and, like Unverlacht, live on the riches of the past and the estates of the dead. Was that the transformation, the way to break the spell? Not Unverlacht leaping, a prince, out of his frog costume, but she, the darling Emilia, the beautiful young heiress to the Kommerzienrat fortune, the ragamuffin princess, wanted to journey into the underworld of the basest haggling, to descend into the cellar of petty greed, out of simple fear of the future to wear the mask of the frog, of the coldblooded creature that sits waiting for poor flies. Was that her true nature, life in a stagnant pool, the lurking mouth that snaps shut? But her used goods shop was still a long way off, there was no housebuyer in sight, and by then Philipp would have written his book and the world would have changed.

Philipp had already feared them beforehand, and his fear had perhaps attracted the misunderstandings the way carrion draws flies, or as they say in the country, you're asking for a storm if you keep watching the clouds. He had been caught in a whirlpool of ludicrous misunderstandings, meant for him alone, set like traps in his path alone, as he went on assignment for the Neues Blatt (gladly and yet inhibited by shyness, the latter precisely because of the newspaper's assignment, which would have given others courage) to visit Edwin. The Abendecho, which mentioned the names of poets only when they became public figures by virtue of some award, could no longer be overlooked, and had died besides, a note that then came under the heading Other-news-of-the-day, in the column of light patter ARGENTINIAN CONSUL'S TOMCAT MISSING, ANDRE GIDE PASSED AWAY YESTERDAY, this paper that took such an avid interest in literature had sent a staff trainee to Mr. Edwin's hotel to interview the famous author, to ask him on behalf of the readers of the

Abendecho whether he believed in a World War III before the end of the summer, what he thought of the new bathing attire for women, and whether in his opinion the atom bomb would turn mankind back into monkeys. By means of some miscalculation, maybe because Philipp looked concerned and because they had told the young eager writer, the news-huntress-in-training, that the prize-winning creature she was to bag was a serious man, she took Philipp, who was not famous and still quite a bit younger, for Edwin and pounced on him with her schoolgirl English, mixed with bar room slang learned from an American she had met during Fasching, while two brash and arrogant young men, in the company of the reporter and, like her, members of the press, toted pieces of heavy, dangerous-looking equipment and illuminated Philipp with flashes of light.

As a result of this commotioncausing, flashlit, embarrassing scene, which had shamed Philipp in several ways (ways that bystanders did not notice, it was a shame that pained Philipp inwardly), other guests in the hotel lobby, having grown curious, learned that there had been some confusion, a mixup that had something to do with the famous Mr. Edwin, a misunderstanding that still hadn't been cleared up, and people now seemed inclined to think Philipp was Edwin's secretary and, filled with sudden interest in the poet's life, they stormed him with questions as to when the master could be spoken to, interviewed, seen, and photographed. A man in a trenchcoat with many belts, who seemed to have just flown around the globe on an important mission, though he had experienced nothing on the flight and spent the whole time solving a crossword puzzle, this man, well fortified against possible inclement weather and second thoughts, inquired of Philipp whether the renowned Mr. Edwin might be willing to state, and have his statement appear with his photograph in all the illustrated magazines, that, were he not able to enjoy a certain brand of cigarettes, which the trenchbelted man represented, he would not be able to live or

84

write. While Philipp succeeded here in escaping by remaining silent and rapidly walking on, he soon found himself encircled and called to account by the group of teachers from Massachusetts. Miss Wescott fixed Philipp on the spot, looking at him through her thick, hornrimmed glasses like a friendly owl, and inquired whether he couldn't ask Edwin to hold a small reading, a quite private session, for the touring group of teachers and, one might well say, admirers of Edwin's, to give them an introduction to his work, which was after all so very difficult, so very obscure, and in need of interpretation. At this point, before Philipp could even begin to explain that they were talking to the wrong man, Miss Burnett interrupted Miss Wescott. Never mind all that about private sessions and admiration, Miss Burnett said, Edwin would have other things to do, better, more entertaining things, than to spend his time with a bunch of traveling schoolmarms, but Kay, the youngest among them, the Benjamin of the group, so to speak, young and pretty, Miss Burnett nearly blurted out "the one with the green eyes," truly revered poets in an honest, adoring way not spoiled by too much sophistication, and Edwin of course in particular, and perhaps, Philipp the secretary must agree, it would refresh the celebrated man, refresh him amid his travels and in this foreign land, to be revered by so much youthful charm, in short, Philipp should go ahead and risk taking Kay to see Edwin so that he might write a dedication, to remember the day they met in Germany, in her copy of his poems, a volume she had with her now in the flexible, thinpaper edition. Miss Burnett pushed Kay into the light, and Philipp was touched as he looked at her. He thought, 'my feelings would be just what this energetic lady says Edwin will feel when his young devotee appears.' Kay seemed so unaffected, so fresh, there was a youthfulness about her that one seldom sees here any more, she was untroubled, that must have been it, she came from different air, from bracing, pure air, it seemed to Philipp, from another land with open spaces, freshness, and youth, and she admired poets. Of course, Edwin had fled from the land Kay came from: had he fled from the open spaces or from the youth of the country, but no, he surely hadn't left, never to return, to escape from Kay, maybe from Miss Wescott, the friendly owl with the glasses, but surely she wasn't that frightful either, it was hard to judge why Edwin had fled when one didn't know the country, for him, Philipp, the New World, represented for the moment by Kay, was likable. He envied Edwin. But that made it all the more embarrassing that he could do nothing for the charming admirer of poetry come here from open and young America, and that it would be all too ridiculous and all too difficult to speak now of himself and to explain all the confusions and misunderstandings involved in this malicious farce. He tried to reveal to the older ladies that he was by no means Edwin's secretary and had himself come only to talk with Edwin, but this gave birth to yet another error, for they all took Philipp's words to mean that he was Edwin's friend, a trusted comrade, Edwin's German friend, his German colleague, as famous in Germany as Edwin was in the world, and the teachers apologized right away, they were polite and had good manners (they were much politer and had much better manners than German teachers), that they didn't know who Philipp was, they asked his name, and Burnett pushed Kay even closer to Philipp and said: "he's a poet, too, a German poet." Kay extended her hand and expressed her regret at not having a book of Philipp's along as well, so she could ask him to sign it. Kay smelled of mignonette. Philipp was no lover of flowery scents, he liked perfumes made of artificial, indeterminate ingredients, but the mignonette smell suited Kay, it was an attribute of her youthfulness, an aura of her green eyes, and it reminded Philipp of something. Mignonette had grown in the garden of the rectory, sweetsmelling mignonette, and the sweet smell had been part of those summer days when Philipp, a child, and Eva, the rector's daughter, had lain in the grass. Mignonette was light green. And there was a light green about Kay. She was a light green spring. Kay thought, 'he's looking at me, he likes me, he's not young any more, but I'm sure he's very famous, I've only been here a few hours and already I've met a German poet, the Germans have such frightfully expressive faces, they have heads full of character like the bad actors back home have, that must be because they are an old people and have been through so much, maybe this poet was buried in a bomb cellar, they say it was horrible, my brother says it was horrible, he was with the fliers, he dropped bombs here, I couldn't stand being bombed, or could I? maybe you only think beforehand that you won't be able to stand it, the poets in Dr. Kaiser's history of German literature all look so terribly romantic, like people out of the rogue's gallery, though they all have beards there, he probably works all night, that's why he's so pale, or is he sad because of his fatherland's misfortune? maybe he drinks, too, lots of poets drink, he'd drink Rhine wine, I'd like to drink Rhine wine, too, Katharine won't let me, why do I go on trips anyway? he goes walking in an oak forest and composes poetry, actually, poets are funny people, I think Hemingway is less funny, Hemingway goes fishing, it's less funny to go fishing than to go walking in the forest, but I'd go walking with the German poet in his oak forest if he asked me to, I'd go walking with him just so I could tell Dr. Kaiser about it, Dr. Kaiser will be pleased when I tell him that I've gone walking with a German poet in an oak forest, but the poet won't ask me at all, I'm too young, maybe he'll ask Katharine, or Mildred, but I'm the one he would love, if he trusted himself to love an American woman, he'd love me much more than he'd love Katharine or Mildred.' Katharine Wescott said: "You must know Mr. Edwin quite well." — "His books," replied Philipp. But apparently they didn't understand his English. Mildred Burnett said: "It would be nice if we were to see each other later on. Maybe we'll see each other while you're with Mr. Edwin. We may end up imposing on Mr. Edwin after all." They still believed Philipp was going as a trusted and expected friend to visit Edwin. Philipp said:

"I don't know whether I'll go to see Edwin; it's not at all certain that you will find me at Mr. Edwin's." But again the teachers seemed not to understand him. They all gave him a friendly nod and chirped in chorus: "at Edwin's, at Edwin's." Kay mentioned that she was studying German under Dr. Kaiser, history of German literature. "Maybe I've read something of yours," she said. "Isn't it funny that I've read something of yours and now I'm meeting you?" Philipp bowed. He was embarrassed and felt insulted. He was being insulted by foreigners who didn't intend to insult him. It was as if the foreigners had been prompted to say the insulting sentences, and they repeated them trustingly, with the best of intentions, as flattering expressions of respect, and only Philipp and the malicious prompter, who remained invisible, understood the offense. Philipp was furious. But he was also attracted. He was attracted to the young girl, to her fresh, honest, and unaffected respect for values that Philipp also respected, qualities that he had had and lost. There was a bitter fascination amid all this misunderstanding with Kay. Kay reminded him somewhat of Emilia, too, only Kay was an unaffected, untroubled Emilia, and she, it did him good, didn't know him or anything about him. Nevertheless, it still pained him to be shown respect in such a mean, deceptively mocking way, that here was respect for a Philipp who didn't exist, but who easily could have existed, a Philipp whom he had wanted to become, a distinguished author whose works were read even in Massachusetts. And right away it was clear to him that this 'even in Massachusetts' was a dumb thought, for Massachusetts was just as far away and just as near as Germany, from the author's point of view, of course, the author stood in the center and the world around him was everywhere equally far and near, or the author was outside and the world was the center, the task around which he circled, something never to be attained, never to be mastered, and there was no such thing as far away and near; maybe there was another dumb writer sitting in Massachusetts, wishing he would be read 'even in Germany,' to dumb people geographical distances always meant the wilderness, nonculture, the end of the world, the place where coyotes howl at the moon, and light was only there where they themselves groped about in the dark. But unfortunately, Philipp had not become a distinguished author, he was after all just someone who called himself an author because he was listed as an author in the city register: he was weak, he had remained in the fields of the dead, where the heinous politics and the vilest war, madness, and crime had raged, and Philipp's small appeal, the first attempt, his first book, had gone under amid the shouts of loudspeakers and the noise of gunfire, had been drowned out by the screams of the murderers and the murdered, and it was as if Philipp were crippled and his voice were suffocated, already, as he watched in horror, how the cursed scene, which he could not leave, maybe didn't want to leave either, was being fitted out for a new, bloody drama.

After the misunderstandings in the hotel lobby, after the con-versation with the traveling teachers, it was impossible for Philipp to really go see Edwin now. He had to give up his assignment from the Neues Blatt to visit Edwin. It was another failure. Philipp wanted to run out of the hotel. He was ashamed, though, after causing a commotion, to go out, to slink off in front of all those people like a beaten dog. Most of all, he would be ashamed before Kay's green eyes. He walked up the stairs that led to the hotel rooms, but he hoped to find a back stairway somewhere that he could take back down and get to an emergency exit. But on the main stairs he met Messalina. "I've been watching you for a long time," the massive woman called out and placed herself squarely in Philipp's way. "You're visiting Edwin?" she asked. "Who's the little one with the green eyes? She's sweet!" — "I am not visiting anyone," said Philipp. "Then what are you doing here?" — "Walking up the stairs." — "You can't fool me." Messalina made an attempt to tap him coquettishly on the shoulder. "Now listen, we're giving a party tonight, and I'd like to have Edwin there. It'll be very chic. It'll be nice for Edwin, too. Jack's coming, so is Hänschen. You know what I mean, all authors are that way." Her freshly waved hair quivered like raspberry gelatin. "I don't know Mr. Edwin," said Philipp angrily. "You're all crazy. All of you associate me with Edwin. What do you think you're doing? I just happen to be in the hotel. I have things to do here." — "Just now you said you were Edwin's friend. Are you trying to seduce the greeneyed girl? She looks like Emilia. Emilia and the girl would make a pretty couple." Messalina looked down into the lobby. "It's all a misunderstanding," said Philipp. "I don't know the girl either. I'll never see her again." He thought, 'it's a shame, I would like to see you again, but would you like me?' Messalina remained stubborn: "So what are you really doing here, Philipp?" — "I'm looking for Emilia," he said in desperation. "Aha! She's coming here? You two have a room here?" She moved closer to him. 'It was wrong, it was wrong to tell her that,' thought Philipp. "No," he said, "I'm just looking for Emilia. But she certainly won't come here." He tried to get past the monument, but the raspberry gelatin was quivering all too pre-cariously, any moment it could begin to slide, become a cloud, a red cloud dissolving into red fog, smoke, in which Philipp would die. "Let me go," he cried out in desperation. But now she was whisper-ing, her alcohol-ravaged face pressed against his ear, as if she had something confidential to impart: "How's the film doing? The film for Alexander. He's always asking when you might bring the film by. He's really looking forward to it. We could all meet at Edwin's lecture. You bring Emilia and the little green girl along. Before the party, we'll go to Edwin's lecture, and afterwards I hope—" — "Don't hope anything," Philipp interrupted her sharply. "There's nothing to hope for. There's no hope left at all. And especially not for you." — He hurried up the stairs, reached the landing, regretted his frankness, started to go back, then was afraid to, and opened a door that led past linen closets to a descending corridor and finally into the famous hotel kitchen, distinguished with stars in the traveler's handbook.

Had Edwin lost his taste for culinary delights? The food didn't taste good to him. Not indifferently, no, with distaste he spurned the creations of the renowned oven, the tasty, palatepleasing specialties of the house, carried into his room in silver pots and porcelain bowls. He drank a little wine, Franconian wine, he had read and heard about it and had been curious to try it, but then the brightly sparkling beverage from the potbellied bottle struck him as all too tart for this midday hour on an overcast day. It was a sunny wine, and Edwin saw no sun, the wine tasted of graves, it tasted the way old cemeteries smell in wet weather, it was an accommodating wine, it made the cheerful laugh and the unhappy cry. Decidedly, Edwin was having a bad day. He had no idea that, down in the lobby, another was serving as unwilling surrogate for him, receiving and tolerating the trivial annoyances and little homages that came with the fame of having one's picture in the press, approaches and blandishments that were just as repugnant to him as they were acutely embarrassing for Philipp, who had to endure them and for whom they were not intended. Philipp's misfortune would have contributed further to Edwin's ill mood; Edwin would not have seen himself as having been relieved of anything by Philipp, he simply would have found all that was questionable and comic about his own existence enlarged by Philipp's scene, as if by a shadow, sharply outlined, and betrayed. But Edwin heard nothing about Philipp. Clad in black and red leather house shoes, wrapped in a Buddhist monk's cloak, his working clothes, he stepped around the ornate table upon which the spurned delicacies steamed and simmered. The untouched meal annoyed him, he was afraid of offending the chef, a master whose artistry he would normally have appreciated. With a guilty conscience he left the dining table and stepped along the edge of the carpet, into whose pattern were set gods and

91

princes, flowers, and fabled animals, so that the woolen painting resembled an illustration to a story within a story about the Thousand-and-One-Nights. The floor covering was so splendidly fairytale oriental, so flowerfully laden with myth, that the poet didn't care to walk directly across the field of knots and, though wearing house shoes and dressed like a sage of India, he stayed respectfully on the edge. The genuine carpets, along with the good cuisine, were the pride of the old hotel, which had, essentially, been spared the manifold destruction of the war. Edwin loved old-fashioned accommodations, the caravanserais of cultured Europe, beds in which Goethe or Laurence Sterne had lain, nice, rather wobbly writing desks that maybe Platen, Humboldt, Hermann Bang, or Hofmannsthal had used. He preferred by far the hostelries of better standing since time immemorial to the newly constructed palaces, the housing machines of a Corbusier-architecture, the gleaming steel tubes and revealing walls of glass, and so it happened on his travels that he had to suffer because of an occasional heater that didn't heat, or too cold bathwater, discomforts that he preferred to overlook, but to which his large, exceedingly sensitive nose generally reacted by catching cold. Mr. Edwin's nose would have preferred warmth and technologically assured comfort to the smell of woodworm dust in the antique secretaries, the odor of mites, human sweat, fornication, and tears that wafted up from the fabric of the old tapestries. But Edwin did not live for his nose, nor for creature comforts (although he loved comfort but never could surrender himself to it completely), he lived in discipline, in the stern discipline of the spirit, and in the harness of active, humane tradition, a most sublime tradition, to be sure, of which the old lodgings, too, were part and parcel, the Elephant, the Unicorn, and the Seasons, on the fringes of course, yet otherwise he was consumed with agitation, for this poet born in the New World considered himself (and he indisputably was) part of the European elite, of the late and, as one had more and more reason to fear, final one on this, his beloved Occidental continent, and nothing outraged and injured Edwin more than that barbarian shout, that prediction unfortunately not lacking genius and greatness, and thus all the more alarming, the cry of that Russian, of that holy madman, of that man possessed, of that great unwise man, unwise in the sense of the enlightened Greeks, as Edwin asserted, yet who was also a visionary and an elemental poet, as Edwin had to admit (a poet he admired and avoided, for he felt an attachment not to the demons, but rather to Hellenic-Christian reason, from which things transcendental, within certain bounds, were not excluded; but already the banished ghosts of the inhuman and the absurd seemed to be turning up again), his words about the small peninsula that lay before Asia, which after three millennia of independence, of precocity, of impertinence, of orderly disorder, of megalomania, would turn back or fall back to Mother Asia. Had they come that far? Was the time again fulfilled? Weary from traveling, Edwin had wanted to lie down, but he found neither rest nor sleep, and the meal, spurned and viewed with distaste, had not been able to refresh him. The city alarmed him, the city did not suit him, it had been through too much, it had experienced the horror, seen the severed head of the Medusa, wanton enormity, a parade of barbarians that emerged from its own underground, the city had been punished with fire and with the smashing of its walls, it was a city smitten, it had had a brush with chaos, the collapse into unhistory, now it hung once more on the slope of history, hung slantwise and prospered, was it sham prosperity? what held it on the slope? the strength of its own roots? (how eerie the gourmet meal on the ornate table in this place) or was it held in place by the thin fetters that linked it with all sorts of interests, with the transitory and conflicting interests of the victors, the loose bond with the daily agenda of strategy and of money, the belief, superstitious belief, asinine belief in the spheres of influence of diplomacy and in the positions of power? not history but economics, not befuddled Clio but Mercury with his full sack

93

ruled the scene. Edwin saw in the city a spectacle and an example, it hung, hung at the edge of the abyss, was suspended, maintained its perilous, wearying balance, it could swing into the old and, after all, proven ways, it could swing into new and unfamiliar ones, could remain true to traditional culture, yet also sink into perhaps only temporary culturelessness, perhaps disappear as a city altogether, perhaps become a mass prison, fulfill in steel, concrete, and super-technology the vision of a fantastic prison by Piranesi, the remarkable engraver whose Roman ruins Edwin so loved. The stage was set for tragedy, but what was taking place in the foreground, on the apron of the hour's stage, the personal contacts with the world, remained for the moment farcical. In the hotel, people were waiting for Edwin. He had been told they were there, journalists, photographers, one woman interrogator had sent her urgent queries ahead to him, senseless questions, a moronic conversation—. Edwin did not always avoid the public and its representatives, they were taxing for him, true, it did require an effort to speak to strangers, but on occasion, indeed often, he had done it, had brought it off, with a jest he had satisfied their foolishness and won the sympathies of the makers of public opinion, but here in this city he feared the journalists, he feared them because here, where earth and time had quaked once already and could break off suddenly into the void or into the new, into the other, into the unfamiliar future about which nothing was known, here he wouldn't be able to jest, not easily find the good, wittily tripping phrase that was expected of him. And what if he were to tell the truth? And did he know the truth? Oh, oldest of questions: what was truth? He could only have spoken of apprehensions, senseless fears perhaps, let the melancholy that had come over him here take its course, but fear and grief, it seemed to him, had been banished to the cellars here, to the cellars above which the buildings had collapsed, and they were being left there for a while. The smell of these rubblefilled cellars lay over the city. No one seemed to notice it. Perhaps they had forgotten these tombs entirely. Should Edwin remind them?

The city attracted him. In spite of everything, it attracted him. He removed his silk monk's robe and dressed, adapting to worldly ways, in the style of the time. Maybe it was a disguise. Maybe he wasn't human. He hurried down the stairs, the lightweight black hat from London's Bond Street tilted slightly over his brow. He looked exceedingly elegant and a little like an old pimp. On the landing above the lobby he noticed Messalina. She reminded him of an odious person, a ghost who worked in America as a society columnist, a professional gossip, and Edwin ran back up the stairs, searched for the door to a back entrance, went past linen closets, past giggling girls, they were swinging bedsheets, linen sheets, winding sheets, wraps for corpses and wraps for caresses, for em-braces, procreation, and final breaths, he hurried through a women's world, through marginal areas of the maternal realm and, thirsting for a change of air, he opened a door and found himself in the spacious and famous kitchen of the hotel. Awkward! Awkward! The untouched meal in his room oppressed him anew. How gladly would Edwin otherwise have chatted with the chef about the physiologie-du-goût and watched the pretty kitchen boys scrape the scales from placid fish that gleamed like gold. As it was, he charged through meat-broth steam and bitter clouds smelling of greens to yet another door that he hoped would lead out into the open—but it didn't really lead into the open either. Edwin now stood in the courtyard of the hotel before an iron rack that held the bicycles of the employees, the cooks, waiters, pages, and bellboys, and behind the rack stood a gentleman whom Edwin took in the confusion of the moment to be himself, his mirror image, his double, a welcome-unwelcome figure, but then he saw that it was of course an illusion, an absurd thought, it was not his likeness standing there, but rather a younger gentleman who didn't even remotely resemble him, but

95

who nevertheless remained familiarly welcome-unwelcome and was more or less comparable to a brother one didn't like. Edwin understood: the gentleman was an author. What was he doing here among the bicycles? Was he lying in wait for him? Philipp recognized Edwin and, after the first moment of surprise, he thought, 'this is my opportunity to speak with him.' — 'We could have our conversation,' he thought. 'Edwin and I, we'll talk, we'll get along well; maybe he will tell me what I am.' But already Philipp's hope had deserted him, his confusion triumphed, his amazement at seeing Edwin here in the hotel courtyard, and he thought, 'it's ludicrous, I mustn't speak to him now,' and instead of stepping up to him, he took a step backward, and Edwin, too, stepped back, and thought as he did so, 'if this man were young, he could be a young poet, an admirer of my work,' and he was not conscious of how ludicrous the thought and its formulation were, put to paper, Edwin would never have let the sentence stand, he would have blushed, yet here in the invisible lilt of the just now enticing thought, victory went not to reflection but rather to the wish, yes, he would have welcomed it, encountering in this city a young poet, striving, eager to follow, he would gladly have found a disciple, a poet from the land of Goethe and Platen, but this was no youth here, no radiant believer, the other man's own doubt, his own sorrow, his own concerns were written in his face, and both thought in the hotel courtyard, having fled from the company of others, 'I must avoid him.' Philipp had been in the courtyard for a while already. He couldn't get out. He hesitated before the hotel employees' exit, he was afraid to walk past a time clock and the porter. The doorkeeper would think he was a thief. How was he to explain his desire to slip out of the building unnoticed? And Edwin? He, too, seemed uncertain. But, standing in the foreground of the courtyard, Edwin was more conspicuous than Philipp, and the porter stepped out of his cubicle and called: "What can I do for you gentlemen?" Both poets now strode, gingerly maintaining the distance separating them, to

96

the gate, they walked past the time clock, the mechanical slave driver, an hour meter and work counter, to which neither of them had ever subjected himself, and the porter took them for men who had to use the employees' exit because of some woman, and thought 'riffraff' and 'idlers.'

Idle gossiping dreaming, dreaming little shallow agreeable dreams in an eternal halfslumber, a slumber of happiness, STYLISH LADY LATE FORTIES SEEKS GENTLEMAN WITH SECURE POSITION, sat the women who lived on state pensions, successful life insurance claims, divorce settlements, and separation payments, in the Domcafé. Frau Behrend, too, loved the place, the preferred gathering spot for ladies of like heart, where over coffee and cream one could surrender contentedly to the recollection of marital joys, contentedly to the bitterness of disappointment. Carla had not yet come by a pension settlement, and Frau Behrend watched in fear and discomfort as her daughter emerged from the shadow of the cathedral tower and stepped into the tinted light of the candycane pink lamps, into this unhurried port of life, into the quietly lapping bay, into the retreat of those amicably provided for: a lost soul. Carla was lost, she was the victim, a victim of the war, she had been thrown to a Moloch, people avoided the victims, to her mother she was lost, lost to her mother's thoroughly respectable circles, lost to all culture and breeding, wrenched from the family hearth and home. But what difference did it make? There was no more family home. By the time the house was destroyed by a bomb, the family had broken up. The bonds had dissolved. Maybe the bomb had only shown that they had been loose bonds, strands of coincidence, error, misjudgment, and foolhardiness wound into the rope of habit. Carla was living with a Negro, Frau Behrend in an attic with the yellowing scores of the open air concerts, and the Musikmeister, thrown away on some trollop, played dance tunes for tarts. Once she had seen Carla, Frau Behrend gave a worried look around the room to see if there were friends, enemies, friendly enemies, acquaintances sitting nearby. She disliked being seen with Carla in public (who knows? maybe her Negro would show up, too, and the ladies in the café would see the shameful thing), but Frau Behrend had an even greater fear of conversations with Carla in the solitude of the attic. Mother and daughter had nothing more to say to each other. And Carla, who had sought out Frau Behrend in the café, which she knew to be her mother's afternoon headquarters, with the feeling that she had to see her before going to the clinic to have aborted this unwelcome fruit of love, ach, was it love? was it not just twosomeness, the desperation of people cast into the world, the warmth of two bodies lying together? and the near but foreign being in her body, was it not just the fruit of habit, of growing accustomed to the man, his embrace, his penetration, fruit of being a kept woman, fruit of fear, of not being able to survive alone, which had in turn begotten new fear, would give birth again to fear? Carla saw her mother, fishfaced, flounderheaded, cold, fishlike, distant, her hand stirred coffee and cream with the little spoon and was like the fin of a fish, the slightly trembling fin of a pitiable fish in a living room aquarium, that was how Carla saw it, were her eyes distorting things? was it her mother's true face? surely a different one had bent over Carla's crib, and only later, much later, when there was nothing more in the household to care for and to do, had the fish emerged through the skin, the flounder head, and the feeling that had driven Carla here, to see her mother, to try talking to each other, died as she reached Frau Behrend's chair in the café. Frau Behrend had for a moment the sensation that not her daughter, but rather the cathedral tower loomed before her.

Odysseus and Josef had mounted the tower. Josef was out of breath and took deep gulps of the thinner air when, after surmounting crumbling masonry steps and steep ladders, they had finally reached the uppermost platform of the tower. The little music case

was silent. There was a broadcast intermission. The only sounds
were the gasping breath, maybe the tiredly pounding heart of the
old porter. They looked out over the city, over the old roofs, over
Romanesque, Gothic, Baroque churches, over the ruins of the
churches, over the newly constructed roof frames, over the wounds
of the city, the vacant lots of the demolished buildings. Josef
thought how old he had grown, always he had lived in this city,
never had he traveled, except for the trip to the Argonne Forest and
to Chemin des Dames, he had always just carried the bags of the
people who traveled, yet in the Argonne Forest he had carried a
rifle and at Chemin des Dames, hand grenades, and maybe, he had
had this thought back then in the shelter during an hour of death,
during the drumfire, maybe he was shooting at travelers and throwing explosives at travelers, people who, back home, as traveling
foreigners, would have given him a good tip, so why didn't the
police prohibit him from shooting and throwing murderous mis-
siles? it would have been so simple, he would have obeyed: war
prohibited by order of the police; but they were just crazy, all of
them were crazy, even the police had gone crazy, they let the
murdering go on, ach, you shouldn't think, Josef stuck to that, the
drumfire passed, they had grown tired of the killing, and life,
travelers' bags, lunch hour, and beer once again resumed their
rightful places, until they all went crazy a second time, it must be a
disease that always recurred, the plague had got his son, it had
taken away his son and, for today, it had given him a Negro, a
Negro with a speaking and musicmaking case, and now the Negro
had dragged him up the cathedral tower, never before had Josef been
up the tower; only a Negro could come up with the idea of climbing
the tower. 'He really is a very foreign gentleman,' though Josef as he
squinted into the distance. He was even a little bit afraid of
Odysseus, and he wondered, 'what do I do if the black devil
suddenly decides to throw me down there?' He was dizzy from so
much thinking and so much open space. Odysseus gazed con-

tentedly over the city. He was standing at the top. It lay below him. He knew nothing about the old history of the city, he knew nothing about Europe, but he knew that this was a capital city of the white people, a city they had come from and then founded places like New York. The black boys had come from the forest. Had there never been forest here, always just houses? Of course, there had been forest here, too, dense primeval forest, green underbrush, Odysseus saw mighty jungles growing below him, underbrush, ferns, vines overran the houses; what had been once could always come again. Odysseus clapped Josef on the shoulder. The old porter staggered beneath the blow. Odysseus laughed, laughed his broad King Odysseus laugh. Wind stirred in the heights. Odysseus patted the leering face of a protruding Gothic demon, a stone figure from the Middle Ages, which banished their devils to the towers, and Odysseus took a red pencil from his jacket and proudly wrote across the demon's body his signature: Odysseus Cotton from Memphis, Tennessee, USA.

What did the Americans get you? It was shameful that Carla had gotten involved with a Negro; it was dreadful that she was pregnant by a Negro; it was a crime that she wanted to kill the child inside her. Frau Behrend refused to think about it any longer. Horrible things could not be spoken about. When something that shouldn't happen did happen, one had to keep silent. Here there was no love, here there were abysses. That wasn't the love song the way Frau Behrend heard it on the radio, that wasn't the movie she liked to watch, this wasn't a matter of the passions of a count or a chief engineer, like in the paperback novels that were so uplifting to read. Here were only yawning abysses, lostness, and disgrace. 'If only she were already in America,' thought Frau Behrend, 'let America figure out how to deal with this disgrace, we don't have Negroes here, but Carla will never go to America, she'll stay here with the black bastard, she'll come with the black child in her arms into this

100

café.' — 'I don't want to,' thought Carla, 'how did she find out? does the fishhead have visionary eyes? I wanted to tell her, but I didn't tell her, I can't tell her anything.' — 'I know everything,' thought Frau Behrend, 'I know what you want to tell me, you got yourself stuck, you want to do something bad, you want advice where I can't advise you, go ahead and do the bad thing, run to the doctor, you've got no choice left but to do the bad thing, I don't want you here with that Negro child' —

He wanted the child. He saw the child of his love in danger. Carla was not happy. He had not made Carla happy. He had failed. They were in danger. How should Washington say it? How could he say what it was he feared? Dr. Frahm had stepped reluctantly into the corridor. The examination room was being cleaned. The door stood open. A woman was wiping the linoleum floor with a damp cloth. The damp cloth ran along the white legs of the large examining chair. Dr. Frahm had been busy eating. He had gotten up from the table. He held a white napkin in his hand. On the napkin was a fresh, red spot: wine. An odor of carbolic acid came from the examination room, the woman who was wiping down the room was spraying a mist of the old wound cleanser into the air. How should Washington tell the doctor? Carla had been here? Dr. Frahm said so. He said everything was all right. What was wrong with Carla then? Why had she been here if everything was all right? "A small disturbance," said Dr. Frahm. Was there trouble brewing here? So that was him, the black father. A handsome man, once you got used to the skin. "We're expecting a child," said Washington. "A child?" asked Frahm. He gave Washington an astonished look. He thought, 'I'll play dumb,' Dr. Frahm had the disconcerting impression that the Negro in the dark corridor, he stood directly beneath the framed inscription, that so-called Hippocratic Oath, turned pale. "Didn't she tell you?" Washington asked. "No," said Dr. Frahm. What was wrong with this Negro? Frahm folded up his napkin. The red spot disappeared in the white folds. It was as if a wound were closing. The thing could not be done. Carla would bring her child into the world. The little Negro would live. Here was the threat of disgrace.

Frau Behrend sat in silence, obstinate, offended, and flounderheaded silence, and Carla continued to guess what she was thinking. They were thoughts that Carla could guess and understand, her own thinking moved in areas not far from these mother thoughts, maybe it was a disgrace, was a crime, what she was doing and wanted to do, Carla thought nothing of her life, she would gladly have disavowed her life, she endured it, she didn't lead it, she believed she had to excuse herself, and she thought she could use the excuse of the time, the excuse of the time gone chaotic, bringing crime and disgrace and making its children criminal and disgraceful. Carla was no rebel. She was a believer. In God? In convention. Where was God? God might have approved of the black bridegroom. A God for all seasons. But even for her mother, God had been only a holiday God. Carla had not been led to God. They had brought her, at Communion, only as far as His table.

She wanted to lead her to God. Emmi, the nursemaid, wanted to lead the child that had been put in her care to God; she looked upon it as her God-given duty to bring up Hillegonda, the actor's child, the child of sin, the child that got no attention from its parents, in the fear of God. Emmi scorned Alexander and Messalina; she was employed by them and paid by them, paid very well, but she scorned them. Emmi thought she loved the child. But one could not show Hillegonda love, one could show her only sternness, to snatch her back from the hell into which her birth had already delivered her. Emmi spoke to Hillegonda about death in order to prove to her the vanity of life, and she led her into the tall, dark churches in order to direct her thoughts to eternity, but little

Hillegonda shuddered in horror at death and shivered with cold in the churches. They were standing in the side chapel of the cathedral before the confessional. In the pillar that Hillegonda was looking at, a tear gouged by a bomb had been hastily smeared over with bad mortar and extended like a barely scarred wound up to the pillar's capital of stone leaves. 'Lead the child to God,' the child had to be led to God. Emmi saw how small, how helpless the child looked standing beside the mighty, mortar-smeared pillar. God would help Hillegonda. God would stand by her. He would look after the little and helpless girl, the guiltlessly guilty child laden with sin. Hillegonda should confess. Even before she was of age for confession, she should confess in order to be absolved of her sins. What should she confess? Hillegonda didn't know. She was just afraid. She was afraid of the silence, she was afraid of the cold, of the size and grandeur of the nave, she was afraid of Emmi and of God. "Emmi hold hand." The sins of her parents? What kind of sins were those? Hillegonda didn't know. She only knew that her parents were sinners, outcasts before God. 'Actor child, comedian child, film child,' thought Emmi. — "Is God angry?" asked the child.

"Splendid! Terrific! Magnificent!" The Archduke was being undressed, the golden fleece laid aside. "Splendid! Terrific! Magnificent!" The producer had seen the proofs: the day's takes were splendid, terrific, and magnificent. The producer praised Alexander. He praised himself. A SUPERFILM. The producer felt he was the creator of a work of art. He was Michelangelo, telephoning the press ARCHDUKE'S AMOURS UNDERWAY, HUGE CAST AT WORK. Alexander had heartburn. The greasepaint had been wiped off his face. He looked once again like curdled milk. Where might Messalina be? He would have liked to call her. He would have liked to tell her: "I'm tired. Tonight there'll be no party, no social evening. I'm tired. I want to sleep. I must sleep. I will sleep. Dammit, I will sleep!" On the telephone he would have said it. He would have told Messalina how tired, empty, and miserable he felt. That evening he wouldn't say it.

She was sitting in the hotel bar and drinking a Pernod. Pernod, that was so wicked, it picked you right up: 'Pernod Paris, Paris the city of love, PUBLIC HOUSES CLOSED, HARMFUL TO FRANCE'S REPUTA- TION.' Messalina turned the pages in her notebook. She was looking for addresses. She needed women for the evening, girls, pretty girls for her social evening. It was unlikely that Emilia would come. Philipp wouldn't let her come. And the little green girl he wouldn't bring over either, the charming little American with the green eyes. But there had to be girls at the party. Who would take off their clothes? Just the ephebes? But there were heterosexuals, too. Should she ask Susanne again? Always Susanne? She was boring. She had no spark. There were no girls any more. Susanne was just a dumb tart.

'There are so many tarts,' thought Frau Behrend, 'and of all of them he has to pounce on Carla, and she has to say yes, has to fall for him, you'd think it would give her the creeps, it would give me the creeps, why did she go to the base, why did she go to the Negroes? because she didn't want to stay with me, because she couldn't stand listening to me complain about her father, back then I still used to complain about his crime, she had to defend him, had to defend him with his trollop, she got that from him, the musician blood, they're gypsies, only the Wehrmacht kept them in line, her and him, what a man he was when he strode at the head of his regiment, the war turned him bad.'

It wasn't so awful. The newspapers had exaggerated. Here, at least, the war seemed not to have raged so awfully, and yet about this city in particular the reporters had written that the furies of war had struck it harder than others. Richard, riding the airport bus into the city, found the vistas of destruction that met his eye disappointing. He thought, 'here I've flown so far, yesterday I was still in America, today I'm in Europe, in the heart of Europe, as good old Wilhelm would say, and what do I see? I don't see any heart, a faded light, I'm lucky I don't have to stay here.' Richard had expected to see awesome devastation, streets buried under rubble, pictures like those that had appeared in the press right after the German capitulation, photos that he had looked at, curious, as a boy, and that his father had wept over. The hemp rag his father had used to wipe his eyes had been soaked with cleaning oil, and his smudged eyelids looked like someone had punched him. Richard Kirsch was riding through a city that was not all that different from Columbus, Ohio, yet in Columbus, Ohio, Wilhelm, his father, had mourned the fall of this very city. What had fallen here? A couple of old buildings had collapsed. They had long since been ready to come down. The gaps in the row of buildings would close up. Richard was thinking he'd like to be a builder here; for a while anyway, and an American builder of course. What skyscrapers he would set on their rubble heaps! The whole place would take on a more progressive look. He left the bus and ambled through the streets. He was looking for the street where Frau Behrend lived. He looked into the store windows, he saw the well-stocked displays, COST OF LIVING INDEX RISES, a wealth of goods that surprised him, a little short on advertising here and there, but otherwise the stores looked exactly like stores back home, in fact they were often more spacious and grand than his father's gun shop in Columbus. This avenue of businesses was now the border, the border land, that Richard was to protect. From high up, from the airplane, everything looked simpler, flatter, you thought in terms of vast spaces, thought geographically, geopolitically, inhumanly, drew fronts across continents like a pencil line across a map, but down there on the street, among these people who all had something silly and alarming about them, as it seemed to Richard, they were living in an unhealthy disproportion between languor and frantic hurrying, collectively they looked poor, but then individually they looked rich. Richard had the feeling that there were several things amiss here, amiss in the whole scene, and that these people were an enigma to him. Did he want to protect them? Let them figure out for themselves how to sort out their European confusion. He wanted to defend America. If need be, he would defend America in Europe as well. The old Reichswehr soldier Wilhelm Kirsch had left Germany after ten years in the service. He had been able to retreat across the ocean with his military pay while there was still time. Afterwards came Hitler and with Hitler came the war. Wilhelm Kirsch would have become a dead hero or a general. Maybe as a general he would have been hanged by Hitler, or by the Allies after the war as a war criminal. Wilhelm had escaped all the historical possibilities, the honor as well as the hanging, by emigrating to America in time. But he hadn't eluded the dishonor completely. Richard who, ever since his first baby steps sent him tumbling into the shop, had always seen his father handling weapons, the firm grips, the cool, deadly barrels of handguns, Richard was stunned, as if a bullet from one of the guns had struck him, that his father, unlike his classmates' fathers, didn't go off with the army into battle, but instead, as an experienced armorer, settled into a factory post that carried a draft exemption with it. Richard was mistaken: his father was no coward, it hadn't been a matter of sparing himself the demands, sufferings, and dangers of war, nor did indifference toward the new fatherland he had chosen cause him to stay in the States, but rather, if anything, a reluctance and hesitancy to attack the old fatherland he had abandoned, but the real reason that Wilhelm Kirsch refused to offer himself to the war was his training in the Reichswehr, was the keen edge, the instruction according to Seeckt, teaching the smooth, quick way to kill the enemy, that had convinced Wilhelm Kirsch that all use of force was loathsome, and

every conflict was better solved by discussion, negotiation, a will-
ingness to compromise, and reconciliation, than with gunpowder.
For the emigrated Reichswehr soldier Wilhelm Kirsch, America had
been the promised land, the new empire of the peacemakers, the
seat of tolerance and of the renunciation of force, Wilhelm Kirsch
had journeyed with the faith of the Pilgrim Fathers to the New
World, and the war America was fighting, righteous though it
might have been, was a blow to the faith he had found in a German
barracks, faith in reason, understanding, and a peaceful frame of
mind, and in the end, Wilhelm Kirsch doubted the truth of America's old ideals. The old German Reichswehr soldier was, an anom-
aly that life produced, a pacifist who traded in handguns, but
Richard, his son born in America, had yet other ideas about
soldiering and war, and it almost seemed to the father as if his son
resembled the young officers of the Reichswehr of the twenties, in
any case Richard enlisted, as soon as his age allowed it, in the
American Air Force. Wilhelm Kirsch had not fought in the war.
Richard Kirsch was prepared to fight for America.

Schnakenbach didn't want to fight. He rejected war as a form of
human conflict and he despised the military, which he regarded as a
remnant of barbaric times, as an unworthy atavism in advanced
civilization. On his own, he had quietly both won and lost World
War II. He had won his war, the righteous, perilous, and tricky war
against the draft board, but he had returned from the fray an
invalid. Schnakenbach had had an idea, a scientific idea, since for
him everything was based on scientific principles, and he might also
have been prepared to wage war scientifically, a war without soldiers, a global battle of minds, whose solitary participants would
hatch deadly formulas, sit behind switchboards and, by pressing
some button or other, wipe out all life on some distant continent.
In World War II, Schnakenbach had not been tempted to press a
death button, and this war hadn't been his war anyway, but he had

107

taken pills. They were stayawake pills that he took, pills that, when taken in sufficient quantities, allowed him to spend days, weeks, months with almost no sleep, so that finally the constant depriva- tion of sleep had reduced him to such a state of physical collapse that even a military doctor had to send him home from his induc- tion physical as unfit. Schnakenbach did not fall victim to the service, not to this atavism of human degradation, but he remained, even after the war had ended, a victim of the drugs. His hypophysis, the adrenal gland, gave the wrong directions, in the face of the chemical competition his organs went on strike, and they stayed on strike unrelentingly after the draft board was dissolved and there was no danger of being made a soldier in Germany for a while. Schnakenbach had become a narcoleptic, sleep was taking its revenge on him, a deep sleep had come over him, he slept wherever he walked or stood, and he needed unusually large doses of Per- vitine and Benzedrine to achieve, for a few hours a day, a half- waking state. The stimulants were prescription drugs and, since Schnakenbach no longer could get enough of them, he hounded Behude for prescriptions, or he tried, talented chemist that he was, to produce the powders himself. Dismissed from his job because of the narcolepsy, spending his little money on scientific experiments, the impoverished Schnakenbach was living in the cellar beneath the house of a baroness, a patient of Behude, who, ever since she had received a summons to the employment office years ago, suf- fered from the belief that she had been drafted into service on the city's streetcars, and who now left her lovely home early every morning and uselessly rode around the city on a certain streetcar line for eight hours, which cost her three marks a day, and worse, "enervated" her, as she said to Dr. Behude, whom she approached for medical leave from work, but which he couldn't give her, since she was not employed to begin with. Behude tried using an analysis of her early childhood to talk her out of her streetcar riding. He had spotted in the eight-year-old girl an incestuous inclination toward her father, a commanding general, and transferred onto a streetcar conductor. But Behude's disclosure of her buried past had first resulted in the Baroness missing days at her imagined job, because of which, as she told Behude, she had had great difficulties. Behude didn't find Schnakenbach in his cellar. He found an unmade bed grimy with coaldust, he found the trade school instructor's torn coats and pants lying on the floor, on a lawn table he saw the tubes, retorts, and burners of the poison kitchen, and scattered everywhere, on bed, floor, and table, he found slips of paper with chemical formulas, drawings of molecular structures that looked like greatly enlarged microphotographs of cancer tumors, they were somehow proliferating, dangerously diseased, and always consuming more and more, out of dots and circles branched off more dots and circles, carbon, hydrogen, and nitrogen divided, united, and multiplied in these pictures made of ink lines and splotches, and together with phosphorus and sulfuric acid, they were supposed to banish Schnakenbach's sleep and yield the desired stimulant. As he looked at the formula drawings, Behude thought, 'this is how Schnakenbach sees the world, the universe, this is how he sees himself, in his mind everything is abstract and grows from the smallest particles into gigantic calculations. Behude laid a package of Pervitine on the lawn table. He had a guilty conscience. He sneaked out of the cellar like a thief.

The waitress cleared the table. Frau Behrend's regular seat in the Domcafé was free for today. Mother and daughter had left. Outside the café door, in the shadow of the cathedral tower, they had parted company. What they might have wanted to say to each other had remained unsaid. Each had felt the fleeting urge to embrace the other, but their hands had only brushed, coldly, for a second. Frau Behrend thought, 'you wanted it like this, you have to go your own way, leave me in peace,' and that meant, 'don't come bothering my Domcafé, my quiet, my settled state, my belief,' and her belief was that respectable women like herself had to be preserved somehow, that the world could never come so badly unstrung that she wouldn't be left her afternoon chat with the ladies of her kind as a consolation prize. And Carla thought, 'she doesn't know that her world doesn't exist anymore.' But what world was there? A dirty world. An utterly godforsaken world. The cathedral clock struck an hour. Carla had to hurry. Before Washington came home from the baseball game, she wanted to pack her things and go to the clinic. The child had to go. Washington was insane to want to convince her to bring his child into the world. The other world, the beautiful, colorful world of the magazines, the mechanical kitchens, the TV sets and the Hollywood-style apartment didn't belong with this child. But hadn't it already stopped mattering? Hadn't even this child, its birth or its death, stopped mattering? Carla doubted now whether she would ever get to the beautiful dreamworld of the American magazines. It had been a mistake to move in with Washington. Carla had gotten on the wrong train. Washington was a good fellow, but unfortunately he was on the wrong train. Carla couldn't do anything about it, she couldn't change the fact that he was on the wrong train. All Negroes were on the wrong train. Even the leaders of the jazz bands were on the wrong train; they were in the luxury compartment of the wrong train. How stupid Carla had been. She should have waited for a white American. 'I could have had a white man instead, a white man, too, would have been satisfied, do these breasts sag? they do not, they're firm and round, what did the guy call them? milkapples, they're still milkapples, my body is white, a little too fat, but they love full thighs, the cuddly type, I'm cuddly, in bed I'm always cuddly, it's fun, wasn't I supposed to have any fun? what does it get you? a bellyache, but I could have had a white man instead.' Carla could have gotten on the right train. It could never be put right again. Only the train of the white Americans led into the dreamworld of the magazine pictures, the world of affluence, of security, and of comfort. Washington's Amer-

110

ica was dark and shabby. It was a world as dark, as shabby, as abandoned by God as this world here. 'Maybe I'll die' thought Carla. Maybe it would be best to die. Carla turned around, she looked back across the square, looked back once more for her mother, but Frau Behrend had already left the cathedral square, fleeing with quick, cowardly steps before this calamity, and without looking back for her daughter. From the church, from its not yet replaced windows, came the rumbling of the organ beneath the hands of the rehearsing organist, swelled the Stabat Mater.

Stormy-weather: the music of the theater organ wafted, welled, quaked, and wheezed. It wafted, welled, quaked, and wheezed from all the loudspeakers. Synchronous with the loudspeakers came sound wafting, welling, quaking, and wheezing from the music case, which Josef had set beside him on the bench. He was chewing part of a sandwich. He had a hard time chewing the thick, multi-layered bread. He had to wrench his mouth open as far as it would go to be able to bite off part of the thick sandwich. It tasted bland. On the ham they had spread a sweetish paste. The ham tasted spoiled. The sweetish flavor bothered Josef. It was as if the ham had spoiled, and then they had perfumed it. The lettuce leaves they had put between the ham and the bread weren't to Josef's taste either. The sandwich was like the grave of a ham roll, with ivy growing on it. Josef reluctantly choked down the bread. He thought about his own death. He ate the unfamiliar, foreign-tasting food only out of ingrained obedience. He mustn't offend Odysseus, his master. Odysseus was drinking Coca Cola. He put the bottle to his mouth and drank it empty. He spat the last mouthful under the seats of the next row. It hit square against the bottom slat of the seats. Josef had been able to get out of that. He had been able to get out of drinking Coca Cola. He didn't like that newfangled stuff.

Washington ran. He heard the ball be hit, heard it come down with a thud. He heard the wafting, welling, quaking, and wheezing

111

of the theater organ. He heard voices, the voices of the crowd, voices of the sports community, shouts, whistles, laughter. He ran around the playing field. He panted. He was bathed in sweat. The stadium with its bleachers looked like a giant, ribbed clamshell. It seemed as if the shell were trying to shut, trying to take the sky away from him forever, trying to press together and squash him. Washington fought for air. The theater organ fell silent. The announcer at his microphone praised Washington. The loud-speakers said the reporter's words along with him. The reporter spoke from Odysseus's case. Washington's name filled the stadium. He had won that run. The winner's name braced itself against the clamshell and kept it from snapping shut. For a while, Washington had defeated the clamshell. It wouldn't snap shut, it wouldn't squash him, wouldn't, in this instant, eat him alive. Washington had to keep winning again and again.

'He's not in shape,' thought Heinz. He could tell by looking that Washington wasn't in shape. He thought, 'the next run he'll lose, if he loses the next run, they'll eat him alive.' It angered Heinz that they would whistle derisively after Washington, laugh at him, and taunt him. Anybody could have an off day. Were they in better shape? 'Snotnoses.' He was ashamed. He didn't quite know why he was ashamed. He said: "Next time he's not going to make it." — "Who's not going to make it?" the boys asked him. They had gotten the tickets to the stadium from the American-German youth club. They had brought the little stray dog on his string into the bleachers with them. "Who do you think? My mother's nigger," said Heinz, "the nigger's not going to make it."

Richard had found his way to Frau Behrend's house. He spoke with the janitor's daughter. The janitor's daughter was talking down to him, talking down literally, because she stood two steps above Richard on the stairs, but talking down in the idiomatic sense as well. Richard was not the radiant figure, the consummate success, the hero that the ugly girl was waiting for. Richard had come on foot; the beloved of the gods came by car. Richard, she saw that, was a simple soldier, even if he was a flier. Of course, the fliers were something better than ordinary soldiers, the fame of Icarus elevated them, but the janitor's daughter knew nothing of Icarus. If Richard had landed his airplane on the stairs and had leapt out with flowers in his arms, then he might have been the bridegroom this unattractive creature was expecting; but no, he couldn't have been the bridegroom: even then he would be lacking an Iron Cross. The girl lived in a world of horrifying class prejudices. She had thought up a hierarchy of the classes, the code of morals and mores in her head was stricter and more rigid than in the days of the Kaiser, unbridgeable was the gulf that separated one class from the other. The notion of a social ladder with a top and bottom made the janitor's daughter's lowly position in the house, lowly in her opinion, bearable, for it made that which was to be her fate all the more alluring, the climb up the social ladder that the horoscope of the Abendecho prophesied: she of all people would succeed at what hardly anyone succeeded at, she was at the bottom, to be sure, but a prince would come, or an executive, and lead her to the rung of status and respect that was intended for her. The prince or the executive was staying, temporarily, by a quirk of fate, and maybe in disguise, in the lower realm of society, but surely the prince or the executive would conduct her into the splendor of the upper realm. Fortunately, the janitor's daughter knew she would recognize anyone in disguise right away; so there could be no mistake. Richard was no high ranking officer in disguise, she saw that, he was one of the lowly masses and had to be treated as such. All Americans belonged among the lesser people. They only acted at times as if they belonged to the better class. But even if they were rich, the janitor's daughter saw through them: they were people at the bottom. The Americans weren't real princes, weren't real officers, weren't real executives. They didn't believe in hierarchy: DEMOCRATIC PRINCIPLE FIRMLY ROOTED IN

GERMANY. The girl sent Richard off with an impatient wave of her hand to the grocer's. Maybe Frau Behrend was at the grocer's. Richard thought, 'what's with her? she's so funny, doesn't she like us?' The girl watched him go with fixed eyes. She had the fixed eyes and the mechanical movements of a doll. She had opened her mouth and her teeth protruded some. She was like a shabby, ugly doll that someone had left on the stairs.

This time Washington wasn't fast enough. He lost the run. He panted. His chest rose and fell like a blacksmith's bellows being pressed up and down. He had lost the run. The man at the microphone was no longer Washington's friend. From every loud-speaker the reporter criticized. He criticized excitedly from the little case between Josef and Odysseus. Odysseus hurled a Coca Cola bottle onto the playing field. Josef looked around, peering anxiously, for policemen. He didn't want Odysseus to be taken away. In all the bleachers they were hooting and whistling. 'Now they've got him, now they'll do him in,' thought Heinz. He didn't like it that they were hooting at Washington and doing him in. But he, too, hooted and whistled. He howled with the wolves: "The nigger's had it. My mother's nigger has had it." The children laughed. Even the little stray dog howled. A fat boy said: "That's right, give it to him!" Heinz thought, 'I'll give it to you, you snotnose, stinky.' He howled, hooted, and whistled. It was the Red Stars against the visiting team. The crowd was rooting for the visitors.

Ezra wasn't rooting for the one team or the other. The game on the baseball field bored him. One of the sides would win. It was always that way. One side always won. But after the game they shook hands and walked together into the dressing rooms. That was boring. You ought to fight with your real enemies. He knotted his little forehead. Even the crown of his closecropped red hair wrinkled. He had seen the boy with the dog again, the boy and the dog from the parking lot in front of the central exchange. That problem occupied his thoughts. That was no game, it was war. But he still didn't know how he should do it. Christopher asked: "What's the matter with you? You're not even watching!" — "I don't like baseball," said Ezra. Christopher was annoyed. He liked going to ball games. He had been glad that they'd had a chance to see a game even in Germany. When they had walked into the stadium, he had thought he was doing Ezra a favor. He was disgruntled. He said: "If you don't like it, we might as well leave." Ezra nodded. He thought, 'that's how I'll have to do it.' He said: "Can you give me ten dollars?" It surprised Christopher that Ezra wanted to have ten dollars. "Ten dollars is a lot of money," he said, "do you want to buy something?" — "I don't want to spend the money," said Ezra. He glanced over at the section of the bleachers where the children sat with the dog. Christopher didn't understand Ezra. He said: "If you don't want to spend the money, why should I give it to you?" Ezra was tormented by a headache behind that little, wrinkled forehead. Christopher was always so dense! You couldn't explain it to him! He said: "I need the ten dollars because I might get lost. I mean we could get separated." Christopher laughed. He said: "You worry too much. You worry just as much as your mother does." But then he decided Ezra's idea was quite reasonable. He said: "Fine. I'll give you the ten dollars." They stood up and edged down the row. Ezra made one last quick ascent with an airplane and dropped a bomb onto the playing field. There were casualties on both teams. Ezra looked over at Heinz and the dog again and thought, 'wonder if he'll come tonight? it'd be sickening if he didn't come.'

"Frau Behrend would be happy," said the grocery shopkeeper. "If Frau Behrend came in now, would she be happy!" She crowded Richard into the corner of the shop where, hidden beneath a stack of paper wrappers, she kept the sack containing sugar, which was once again in short supply. All at once, Richard felt hungry and thirsty. Between himself and the shopkeeper, he saw a ham lying on a platter, and by his feet stood a crate of beer. The air in Germany, or the air in this shop with its smells of old food, seemed to make you thirsty and hungry. Richard would have liked to ask the shopkeeper to sell him a bottle of beer and a slice of ham. But the woman was pressing him too hard. He felt like a prisoner in the corner of the shop. It seemed to him as if he were to be held, like the sugar, in safekeeping and parceled out at her discretion. It annoyed him that he had followed his father's sentimental idea and looked up Frau Behrend, a distant relative to whom they had sent packages shortly after the war. The shopkeeper was talking just now about the packages. She was describing the hardship of those months at the war's end, leaning as she did so over the ham, at which Richard was staring with steadily growing appetite. "They had taken everything, there was just plain nothing left," said the shopkeeper, "and Negroes they've sent us, you're from a German family, you'll understand what I mean, we had to put up with Negroes to keep from starving. And that is Frau Behrend's sad plight!" She looked at Richard expectantly. Richard's command of German was less than complete. What was this about Negroes? They had Negroes in the Air Force. The Negroes flew in the same planes as the other fliers. Richard had nothing against Negroes. He was indifferent towards them. "Her daughter," said the shopkeeper. She lowered her voice and leaned even farther over toward Richard. The edge of her apron touched the fatty rim of the ham. Richard didn't know Frau Behrend had a daughter. Frau Behrend had not mentioned the daughter in her letters to Wilhelm Kirsch. Richard considered whether Frau Behrend might have had a daughter by a Negro she had given herself to to keep from starving. But she was too old to have been able to sell herself for bread. Did Richard still have his appetite for that ham? He thought of Frau Behrend's daughter and said: "I would have brought playthings." — "Playthings?" The shopkeeper didn't understand Richard. Was this

116

young man, born in America but the son of a German father, so americanized that he had lost all sense of decency? Was he trying to make fun of the Germans' hardship and confusion? She asked sternly: "Playthings for whom? We don't associate with the daughter any more." She assumed that Richard would not associate with Frau Behrend's daughter either. Richard thought, 'what do I care? what do I care about Frau Behrend's daughter? it's as if I were sinking into something, it's my roots, my father's old native land, the family that's at home here, the narrowness, they're swamps.' He tore his eyes away from the ham and freed himself from the entanglements of this shop that was a curious mixture of hardship and fatty foods, of ill will, shortages, and illusions. His foot bumped against the beer. He said he would be in the Bräuhaus that evening, his father had advised him to go there, Frau Behrend could come look for him there if she wanted to. He had no interest at all in seeing Frau Behrend—Frau Behrend and her Negro daughter.

"No bed has been reserved. No bed has been reserved for you," said the nurse. The nurse had the monotone voice of a telephone service recording, which, when its number is dialed, always repeats one and the same statement. "Nothing has been reserved. There is nothing in our records," said the voice. "But Dr. Frahm said—" Carla was dumbfounded. "It must be a mistake, nurse. Dr. Frahm told me he would call ahead." — "There is nothing in our records. Dr. Frahm has not called." The nurse had the face of a stone statue. She looked like one of the stonecarved figures at a municipal fountain. Carla stood holding a small suitcase in the admissions room of the Schulte Clinic. In the suitcase she had underclothes, she had a rubber bag with cosmetics in it, she had the latest American magazines; the colorful picture magazines that described the domestic happiness of the Hollywood actors. Armed with this happiness from Hollywood, Carla was ready to have her child taken from her, to have the child of her black boyfriend, of her friend/

117

enemy from the dark America, killed. "A bed must have been reserved for me. Dr. Frahm promised. I'm supposed to have an operation. It's urgent," she said. "No reservation has been made. No bed has been reserved." It would take at least an earthquake to shake that stone statue, and only on a doctor's instructions would she clear the way to the abortion bed. "I'll wait for Dr. Frahm," said Carla. "I told you, nurse, it's a mistake." She could have cried. She felt like telling the nurse about the many presents she had brought Dr. Frahm at a time when there was nothing, no coffee, no schnapps, no cigarettes. She sat down on a hard bench. The bench was hard as a poor sinner bench. The nurse answered the telephone and spoke exactly like a postal service recording: "Sorry, nothing is free. Sorry, there are no beds free." In an indifferent, mechanical monotone, the nurse dispatched the invisible supplicants. The beds in this clinic seemed to be very much in demand.

Josef was asleep. He had fallen asleep sitting up. He had fallen asleep while sitting in the bleachers of the stadium, but it seemed to him as if he were sleeping in a bed. He was used to hard beds, but this was an infirmary bed he was sleeping in, a bed in a poorhouse infirmary, an especially hard bed, his deathbed. It was the end of his life's journey. Fallen asleep in the stadium and in service, in a servant's service, in service to a foreign master come here from a foreign, faraway land, Josef, surrounded by the loudspeaker torrent of a senseless lawn game, senselessly addressed by the same noise and torrent, which emerged, quieter and directed with a senseless message at him personally, once more from the small case that he was to carry and to guard today, the sleeping Josef knew that this had been his last job, transporting this little case, carrying the little music case, an easy job, pleasant actually, in the service of a large and openhanded, albeit black, master. Josef knew that he would die. He knew that he would die on this infirmary bed. And how could it have been otherwise than that, at the end of his life's course, he should die in a poorhouse? Was he prepared to go, equipped to set out upon the great journey? He thought, 'God will pardon me, he will forgive me the little tricks of the tourist business, after all, foreigners come here to be cheated a little, to be led a little farther than they intend to be led.' There were strange nurses in this infirmary. They walked around in baseball uniforms and held bats in their hands. Was God angry with Josef after all? Was Josef to be beaten? At the gate of the infirmary stood Odysseus. But it was not the friendly, openhanded Odysseus of the city streets. It was the Odysseus of the cathedral tower, a dangerous and fearsome devil. He had become one with the leering devil protruding from the tower, the leering devil on which he had written his name and where he was from; Odysseus was a black devil, really, an evil, black devil; he was nothing but a plain old frightful devil. What did the devil want with Josef? Hadn't Josef always been good, except for the little tricks of the tourist business that were part of his trade? Hadn't he carried any man's bags? Hadn't he gone to war? Or had that very going-to-war been a sin? Had doing his duty been a sin? Duty a sin? the duty they all talked, wrote, and screamed about, and praised to the sky? Had his duty now been chalked up against him, was it chalked up there on God's blackboard the same way a bartender marks up unpaid beers? It was true! It had always tormented Josef. Secretly, it had always tormented him. He hadn't liked to think about it: he had killed, he had killed people, he had killed travelers; he had killed them at Chemin des Dames and in the Argonne Forest. Those were the only trips he had taken in his life, Chemin des Dames, Argonne Forest, not beautiful areas, and they had made the trip there in order to kill and be killed. 'Lord, what should I have done? what could I have done, Lord?' Was it fair that for this debt, chalked up and never crossed out, for this involuntary killing, he was now being handed over to the devil, the black devil Odysseus? 'Hey! Hey! Hooray!' Already he was being beaten. Already the devil was beating him. Josef screamed. His scream was lost amid

119

other screams. He was hit on the shoulder. It startled him. It startled him back to life. Odysseus the Devil, Odysseus the Friendly, King Odysseus the Friendly Devil hit Josef on the shoulder. Then Odysseus leapt up onto his seat. He held a Coca Cola bottle like a hand grenade ready to be thrown. The loudspeakers roared. The stadium hooted, whistled, pounded feet, screamed. The reporter's voice came hoarse from the little radio case. The Red Stars had won.

He had won. Washington had won. He had won the most runs. He had drawn victory for the Red Stars from his own lungs. The shell did not snap shut. The shell had not snapped shut yet. Maybe the two halves of the shell would never snap together over Washington, never take the sky away from him. The stadium didn't eat him alive. Washington was the hero of the bleachers. They shouted his name. The radio announcer had made up with Washington. Washington was once again the announcer's friend. They all cheered Washington. He panted. He was free. He was a free citizen of the United States. There was no discrimination. How he was sweating! He would always go on running. He would run farther and farther and faster and faster around the playing field. The run made him free, the run led into life. The run made room in the world for Washington. It made room for Carla. It made room for a child. If Washington would just keep running well, keep running faster, there would be room in the world for all of them.

"He was in shape after all." — "Of course he was in shape." — "He was in shape after all, that nigger." — "Don't say nigger." — "I'm saying he was in shape." — "He was in great shape." — "You said he wasn't." — "I said he was. Washington's always in shape." — "You said your mother's nigger wasn't." — "Shut up, jerk." — "Want to bet? You said so." — "I said shut up, creep, lousy." They began scuffling at the exit to the stadium. Heinz was fighting for Washington. He had never said that Washington was out of shape. Washington was in great shape. He was great, period. Schorschi,

Bene, Kare, and Sepp stood in a circle around the fighting boys.
They watched the boys punch each other in the face. "Give it to
him!" shouted Bene. Heinz stopped punching. "Not for you, fag-
got." He spat blood. He spat it at Bene's feet. Bene raised his hand.
"Let him alone," said Schorschi. "Don't get all excited! Let him
alone, the jerk." — "You're the jerk," screamed Heinz. But he did
move back a little. "The game was a drag," said Sepp. He yawned.
The boys had gotten their tickets from the American-German
youth club. The tickets hadn't cost them anything. — "What'll we
do now?" asked Kare. "Don't know," said Schorschi. "You know?"
he asked Sepp. "Nope. Don't know." — "Movies?" offered Kare.
"I've seen them all," said Schorschi. He had seen all the current
detective and wild west films. "Movies are out." — "If it were night
now," said Bene. "If it were night," echoed the others. They had
hopes of some kind for the evening. They moved, bent forward,
hands in their jacket pockets, elbows stuck out to the side, with
tired shoulders like men after heavy work, out of the stadium. The
Golden Horde. "Where's the dog," screamed Heinz. While he was
fighting, Heinz had let go of the string. The little stray dog had run
off. It had disappeared in the crowd of people. "Dammit," said
Heinz, "I need the dog tonight." He turned angrily on his companions. "You could have watched him, you snotnoses. That dog was
worth ten dollars." — "Could have watched him yourself, nigger
bastard, rotten." They began scuffling again.

Washington was standing under the shower in the stadium's
locker rooms. The cold jet of water sobered him. His heart
twitched. For an instant he couldn't get his breath. Acrid sweat ran
off him with the water. He was still in good shape. His body was still
in good shape. He stretched his muscles, filled his chest. Muscles
and chest were all right. He felt his sexual parts. They were good,
they were all right. But the heart? But the respiratory system? They
worried him. They were not all right. And then that arthritis! He
might not be able to stay active much longer. On the field he

121

wouldn't be able to stay active much longer. At home and in bed he'd go on being active for a long time yet. What could he do? What could he do for himself, for Carla, for the child, and maybe also for the little boy, Heinz? He had showered enough. He dried off. He could get out of the service, sell the horizonblue sedan, work another year as an athlete, and then maybe open a bar in Paris. He could open his bar in Paris: Washington's Inn. He'd have to talk with Carla. He could live with Carla in Paris without anyone bothering her about the life she led. They could open the bar in Paris, they could hang out his sign, could light it up with brightly colored bulbs, his sign NOBODY IS UNWELCOME. In Paris they would be happy; they would all be happy. Washington whistled a tune. He was happy. Whistling, he left the shower room.

Dr. Frahm was washing up. He stood in the washroom of the Schulte Clinic and washed his hands. 'In innocence old Pontius Pilate a lovely feeling,' he washed his hands with a good soap and scrubbed his fingers with a rough brush. He ran the bristles of the brush under his fingernails. He thought, 'no infection, that's the main thing,' he thought, 'have to cut my nails again already, Semmelweis, they're making a movie about him now, read about it in the paper, wonder if they'll show a case of metritis, wouldn't be such a bad idea, closeup shot, could be a deterrent, deter people from all kinds of things, nobody'll ever film my life, that's all right with me.' He said: "It's impossible. Sorry, Frau Carla, but it can't be done." Carla stayed close by him, she stood beside the basin over which he was scrubbing his fingers under the powerful jet of water emerging from the nickel faucet. Carla looked at the nickel faucet, she looked at the water, she looked at the soapsuds, at the doctor's hands, which the soap, the brush, and the warm water had turned lobster red. She thought, 'butcher's hands, real butcher's hands.' She said: "But Herr Doktor, you just can't do that." Her voice sounded uncertain and strained. The doctor said: "There's nothing wrong with you. You're pregnant. Probably in your third month. That's all." Carla felt nausea coming on. It was the revolting, choking nausea pregnant women have. She thought, 'why is this the way we come into the world?' She could have punched herself in the abdomen, in this abdomen that was swelling, growing like a pumpkin. She thought, 'I've got to talk to him, but I can't talk to him now.' She said: "But in your office you said I should come here." The doctor said: "I didn't say anything. Listen, the father wants to have the child. So there's nothing I can do." She thought, 'he was here, that black scoundrel was here, he's spoiled the doctor on me, now Frahm doesn't want to do it, now he doesn't want to do it, and after all those things I gave him.' She regretted having given the doctor so much coffee, cigarettes, and schnapps. She felt more and more nauseous. She had to hold on to the basin. She thought, 'I'm going to have to throw up, I'll vomit all over his hands, all over his revolting, red, butcher's hands, all the places these hands reach on you, fingernails always clipped short, reach right into where you live.' She said: "But I don't want it! Do you understand, I don't want it!" She choked and burst out crying. 'She'll be sick in a minute,' thought Frahm. 'She looks pasty.' He pushed a chair over to her. "Sit down." He thought, 'I hope she doesn't get hysterical on top of everything, I'd really be sitting in the bramble patch if I got rid of it for her.' Since he had touched the chair, he had to lather his hands up once more. 'Give her a little encouragement,' he thought, 'always helps 'em, they cry it out of their system and afterwards they're happy mothers.' He said: "Now be reasonable. You friend is a good fellow. I'm telling you, he'll be a dandy father. He'll take care of you and the child. You just wait and see how pretty the baby turns out. Just let me know in time; I'll handle the birth for you. We do it painlessly. You won't feel a thing, and afterwards you've got the baby." — 'I'll lay it on her breast,' he thought, 'hope she'll love it, doesn't look that way, poor thing, still in the dark and hated already, but if the father insists, what can I do? The father really ought to know what life is like.' She thought, 'that scoundrel Washington, that scoundrel Frahm, those two scoundrels thought this up together, and it could be the end of me.' She said: "I'll go to somebody else." She thought, 'to whom? Frau Welz is sure to know someone, the whores are sure to know someone, I should have given the whores the cigarettes and the coffee.' — "You will not do that," said Frahm. "Now stop it, Frau Carla. That's much more dangerous than you think. Afterwards, nobody will be able to help you. You think I scrub my paws here for the fun of it? Or because it's revolting to me? I stopped being revolted long ago." He felt a bad mood coming on. The woman was holding him up; he couldn't help her. She thought, 'I am going to vomit all over his hands, that'd be something fine for him, something fine on his butcher hands, that'd give him something to scrub.' — "The whole thing's not so tragic," said Frahm. 'It is death,' thought Carla.

'It's outrageous,' thought Frau Behrend. What awful luck she had! Here she had gone out to have a peaceful, cozy chat with the ladies in the Domcafé, and her lost daughter had disturbed and troubled her, there had been no peaceful, cozy chat, just disgrace and lostness, disgrace of the present times, and lostness in disorder, mazes, and moral abysses, and while such unpleasant things were happening to her and she was having a brush with disgrace— couldn't she have stayed home? in the attic it would have been peaceful, cozier, Carla wouldn't have come to the attic—, a visitor from America had been there, a relative, the son of Wilhelm who had sent her packages. What awful luck! The grocery shopkeeper told her about it. She had waved Frau Behrend into the shop. The Kirsch boy had been there. He had spoken about the packages. And the shopkeeper, that malevolent, gossipmongering shrew—oh, Frau Behrend could tell by looking at her, she knew how things stood— of course she had blabbed everything, had told him about Carla and about her Negro, had surely told everything Frau Behrend had told

her, and over there in America they were so strict with their
Negroes THE RACE DISGRACED, ARYAN CERTIFICATION, Negro or Jew,
it was the same, that Carla could do such a thing, nothing like that
had ever occurred in her family, their Aryan papers had been
flawless, and now this disgrace! "He's waiting for you in the
Bräuhaus," said the shopkeeper. In the Bräuhaus? That was nothing
but an excuse, evasion, rejection. The Kirsch boy came all the way
from America to visit Frau Behrend, to see his German relative,
and then he says she should come to the Bräuhaus. That just wasn't
true! The shopkeeper knew it! She begrudged her her rich American relative. All Americans were rich. All white Americans were
rich. The shopkeeper had begrudged her the food packages back
then. The Kirsch boy had surely already gone, had gone back,
disappointed, to the wealth and the respectability of America.
Suddenly, Frau Behrend put all the blame for the Kirsch boy's
disappearance on Carla. The Kirsch boy had fled before this immor-
ality, he had run away from the disgrace and the depravity of it. He
had shrunk back before Carla's depravity and disgrace. With the
wealth of America, he had renounced the old family, fallen into
disgrace and depravity in Germany. It was Carla's fault; it was all her
fault. The shopkeeper had been right to talk about it. The shopkeeper was a good woman. The shopkeeper was one of the respectable people. Frau Behrend would have told about it, too, if she had
known such a disgraceful thing about someone. She leaned far over
the counter. Her bosom brushed against the bell jar, under which a
Mainzer cheese was slowly melting into a puddle. Frau Behrend
whispered: "You told him?" — "Told him what?" asked the shopkeeper. She propped her arms at her sides and gave Frau Behrend a
defiant look. She thought, 'you watch out, if you want to keep
getting your sugar from me.' Frau Behrend whispered: "About
Carla." The shopkeeper directed her stern, indignant look at Frau
Behrend, the look that had already subdued many a customer, poor
customers, rationcard customers, ordinary customers. 'Don't you

start thinking it couldn't happen again, FARMERS' ASSOCIATION OPPOSES NEW PLANTING, UNIONS CONSIDER CONTROLS ON KEY FOODSTUFFS.' The shopkeeper said: "What are you thinking, Frau Behrend, me do such a thing?" Frau Behrend straightened back up. She thought, 'she told him, of course she told him.' The shop-keeper raised the bell jar; the decay was already well advanced; a putrid stench filled the room.

Philipp was thinking about the bridge across the Oder. It was a bridge under glass. The train rolled across the bridge as if through a glass tunnel. The passengers paled. Light fell into the tunnel as if filtered through milk; the sun turned into a pale moon. Philipp called out: "Now we're under the bell jar!" Philipp's mother sighed: "We're back in the East." The bridge across the Oder was for Philipp's mother the transition from the West to the East. She hated the East. She sighed because she had to live in the East, far from the sparkle of the capital or from the Fasching festivities of the Southwest. To Philipp, the East meant a child's paradise; it meant wintry pleasures, the cat by the stove, apples baking in the oven; it meant peace, it meant snow, it meant lovely, gentle, silent, cold snow outside the window. Philipp loved the winter. Dr. Behude was trying hard to construct a bell of optimism and summery pleasures over Philipp. 'He'll never be able to lead me back, he'll never be able to change me.' Philipp lay on the patient's couch in Behude's darkened consulting room. He rode again and again across the Oder. Again and again he sat in a train beneath the bell of the bridge in a pale, altered light. His mother wept, but Philipp was riding into his child's paradise, traveling into the cold, into peace, into snow. Behude said: "It's a lovely summer day. You're on vaca-tion. You're lying in a meadow. You have nothing to do. You are completely relaxed." Behude stood on the darkened room, inclined like a gentle dream figure over the couch where Philipp lay. The dream figure had gently laid its hand on Philipp's forehead. Philipp

126

lay on the doctor's couch, taut with suppressed laughter and irritation. Here kindly, good Behude was trying so hard, using up the little energy he had thinking up vacations. Philipp cared nothing for lovely summer days. He had no vacation. He had never had a vacation in his life. Life never gave Philipp a vacation. That was one way to look at it. Philipp was always wanting to do something. He was always thinking about a great task that he would begin and that would utterly exhaust him. In his thoughts, he was preparing for this task, which both attracted and alarmed him. He could rightly say his work never let go of him; it tormented and delighted him wherever he walked, wherever he stood, even while he slept; he felt called to do this work; but never or only very seldom did he actually do anything; he didn't even try. And from that perspective, his life had been one long vacation, a poorly spent vacation, a vacation with bad weather, in bad lodgings, in bad company, a vacation with too little money. "You are lying in a meadow—" He wasn't lying in any meadow. He was lying on the patient's couch in Behude's office. He was not insane. How many madmen, how many hysterics and neurotics had lain on this relaxing couch before him? Always Behude had fantasized lovely vacation days for his patients: vacation from madness, vacation from delusions, vacation from fear, vacation from addiction, vacation from conflicts. Philipp thought, 'should I dream? I won't dream Behude's dream, Behude looks to find at the core of our being a normal office worker, I hate meadows, why should I lie in a meadow? I never lie in meadows, nature seems sinister to me, nature is disturbing, a storm disturbs by altering the electrical tension on the skin and in the nerves, there is nothing more evil than nature, only snow is beautiful, the quiet the friendly the gentlyfalling snow.' Behude said: "You are now completely relaxed. You are resting. You are happy. No worries can reach you. No heavy thoughts weigh on you. You feel really good. You are drowsy. You are dreaming. You are dreaming only pleasant dreams." Behude moved away from Philipp on tiptoe. He stepped

127

into the adjacent room, which had not been darkened, into the room for the less subtle psychiatric methods Behude employed only reluctantly. Control panels and electrostatic machines here would have alarmed Emilia, who was terrified of doctors and considered them all sadists. Behude sat down at his desk and took Philipp's sheet from the patient files. He was thinking about Emilia. He thought, 'they're not a normal married couple, but they are a married couple, in fact I consider their marriage quite indestructible, even though it seems at first glance more a perversion than a marriage, it was perverse of Philipp and of Emilia to get themselves into a marriage, but the very fact that neither one of them is suited for marriage binds them together, I'd like to exert psychotherapeutic influence on them together, mutual cure of each through the other, but for what? what do I want to cure them of? they are happy the way they are, once I had cured them, Philipp would take a job with a newspaper and Emilia would sleep with other men, would the therapy have been worthwhile? I ought to get more exercise, I think too much about Emilia's infantile charms, she won't sleep with me, until she's cured she'll sleep only with Philipp, Emilia and Philipp allow themselves the perversity of a normal marriage with jealousy commitment and faithfulness.'

Emilia recognized Edwin right away. She knew that this man with the lovely black hat, who had something of an old English lord about him, something of an old vulture, and something of an old pimp, was one of Philipp's poets. Then she recalled a photograph of Edwin that Philipp had tacked up on the wall of his workroom for a while, over the stack of white, unused paper. Emilia thought, 'so that's Edwin, the great prize-winning author, Philipp would like to be someone like Edwin, maybe he will be, I hope that and I fear it, will Philipp look like Edwin then? so old? so distinguished? I think he'll look less distinguished, he'll look less like an English lord and less like a vulture, too, he might look like an old pimp, poets used

128

to look different, I don't want Philipp to be successful, if he were successful, he might leave me, but I do want him to be successful, he'd have to be successful enough for us to go away and always have money, but if we came into money that way, then Philipp would have the money, I don't want Philipp to have the money, I want to have the money.' Emilia knew herself quite well. She knew that she would give Philipp, if she did manage to sell one of her houses after all, that she'd then give Philipp plenty of spending money, but that she would always disrupt his desperate attempts to work and to write his long-planned book. 'I would stop at nothing, I'd be bad like never before, I would give him not one hour of peace, poor Philipp, he's so good.' Often she was overcome with emotion when she thought of Philipp. She wondered whether she should try to make Edwin's acquaintance. It was an opportunity that Messalina would not have passed up. 'She would have tried to drag him off to her party, poor Edwin.' Emilia wouldn't take Edwin to any parties. But she thought it would astonish Philipp if she could tell him that she had met Edwin. Edwin was rummaging about among the antiques in Frau de Voss's shop. He was looking at miniatures. He had fine, long hands, with thick hair at the base of the wrists. He was looking at the miniatures through a magnifying glass, which gave his face even more the look of a vulture. Frau de Voss showed Edwin a rosewood madonna. The madonna had belonged to Philipp. Emilia had sold it to Frau de Voss. Edwin looked at the madonna through the magnifying glass. He asked the price of the little madonna. Frau de Voss whispered the price. Emilia was not supposed to hear the price. 'I'm sure she's jacked it up tremendously,' thought Emilia. Edwin set the lovely rosewood sculpture back on the table. Emilia thought, 'he's stingy.' Frau de Voss turned, disappointed in Edwin, to Emilia: "What have you brought, my child?" She always called Emilia my child. Frau de Voss met customers who wanted to sell something with the patronizing tone of a former lady in waiting and the sternness of a schoolteacher. Emilia stammered a little. She was ashamed to open the ridiculous Scottish plaid in front of Edwin. Then she thought 'why am I ashamed? if he has more money than Philipp, it's because he was lucky.' She handed Frau de Voss a cup. It was made in Berlin. The cup was gilt inside and displayed a miniature likeness of Frederick the Great on the outside. Frau de Voss took the cup and set it on her secretary desk. Emilia reflected 'she won't haggle with me now, she has to show her friendly face now because Edwin is here, only afterwards will she show me her true face.' Edwin found nothing among the antiques that interested him. Everything in this shop was second rate. The little madonna was too expensive. Edwin knew the prices. He was no collector, but from time to time he bought an antique object he liked. He had come into Frau de Voss's shop out of boredom. Here in this city he had suddenly been bored. When one walked in the afternoon through its streets, the city was neither particularly rich in tradition nor mysterious. It was ordinary, a city with ordinary people. Perhaps Edwin would describe the afternoon in this city in his diary. The book was to appear after his death. It was to contain the truth. In the light of truth, the afternoon in this city would no longer be ordinary. Edwin picked up Emilia's cup. He looked at the image of Frederick the Great. He liked the cup. 'A handsome face,' thought Edwin, 'spirit and sadness, his poetry, his wars, and his politics were rubbish, but he put up with Voltaire, and Voltaire wrote quite nasty things about him.' He inquired about the price of the cup. Frau de Voss made an embarrassed gesture toward Emilia and tried to draw Edwin into a kind of alcove at the back of the shop. Emilia thought, 'she's mad now, if I find out what Edwin pays, she'll have a hard time getting me to take what she wants to give me for it.' The dealer's embarrassment amused Emilia. She thought, 'funny, that Edwin is so keen on the things Philipp likes.' Edwin saw through the dealer's game. It didn't interest him. But he didn't go with Frau de Voss into the alcove. He set the cup back on the secretary; as if suddenly repulsed by it, he set it back on the secretary. He turned to go.

Emilia considered taking the cup and offering it to Edwin on the street. But she thought, 'that's begging, and it would sour old de Voss on me for good, now she'll give me very little for it, if only because she's mad, but Edwin didn't notice me at all, he didn't notice me any more than you'd notice an old, ugly chair, I hate literary people, they're so arrogant.' Edwin thought, outside on the street, 'she was poor, she was afraid of the dealer, I could have helped the young woman, but I didn't help her, why didn't I? that would be worth examining.' Edwin will mention the cup and Emilia in his diary. It will happen in the light of truth. In the light of truth, Edwin will examine whether on this afternoon he was a good or an evil person. In any case, the light of truth will transfigure Edwin, Emilia, and Frederick the Great.

No transfiguration, no enlightenment, no light of truth. Where was Philipp lying? In the darkened room. 'He has me dream, little dreamdoctor little psychotherapist, sits in the next room and fills out my file card, my dream card, little psychobureaucrat, making entries: Philipp is dreaming, dreaming of meadows vacation and summery happiness, forget about the meadows, I'm visiting Frau Holle, she shakes the snow out of her quilts the cool gentle the silentmerry the peaceful snow, the cozy tiled stove, a cat stretches and purrs, the baking apples sputter in the oven, I'm dressing puppets for the theater, I'm dressing them up for my little stage on the bench by the stove, it's nice to play theater, but the most important thing is getting the puppets all ready, one puppet will be dressed like Emilia, one puppet like the little American girl with the green eyes, she could play Don Gil, Don Gil of the green trousers, jaunty green trousers green eyes fresh lively SANELLA: ALWAYS FRESH a dagger in your hand, my little lover boy, or are you the boy who set out to learn to be afraid? to be a boy you're missing one little thing, too bad for your girlfriends, but you can learn to be afraid, how should Emilia be dressed? she is Ophelia the-poor-child-

131

dragged-down-by-her-melodies-to-a-muddy-death, when I was four-
teen I recited Hamlet to myself, to-die-to-sleep-perchance-to-
dream adolescent pain, now I'm dreaming for little Behude, should
I show him my Hamlet? he always expects something indecent
erotic confessions, would like to be a little substitute father con-
fessor, I still know my Hamlet, I have a good memory, for everything back then I have an outstanding memory, the lake in front of
our house, it was frozen solid from October till Easter, the farmers
rode across the lake on their wooden sleds hauled the heavy trees
out of the forests felled giants, Eva, her pirouettes on the ice, the
crispcold sun, Eva went without stockings for me, it excited me, her
mother was outraged, was afraid she'd get ovaritis, didn't say so of
course, thought we didn't know what that was, forgot about the
encyclopedia, she looked like a mother hen cluck-cluck-cluck,
Emilia won't go on the ice, thinks sports are silly, laughed herself to
death when Behude told her she should play tennis, Emilia runs
around the city Leni-Levi-runs-around-drunk-nightly: where'd I
hear that? in the prehistoric age on the Kurfürstendamm, later the
SA came marching, cats are supposed to see the world differently
than we do: only brown or yellow, Emilia sees a secondhand dealer's
city a filthcolored city with filthy dealers, she's hunting for money,
her demon crouches on her back, she lugs her English-lord-travel-
ing-plaid to the junk dealers goes into their cellars descends to the
snakes frogs and amphibians, Hercules slew the Hydra, Emilia's
Hydra has more than nine heads, it has three hundred sixty-five
heads a year, three hundred sixty-five times up against the monster
of having no money, she sells what we have in our home, lets the
amphibians fondle her, it disgusts her, but she gets money together,
then she gets drunk on it, stands in the standup bar like all the
drunks, always just one more glass, "here's to you, neighbor," the
other drunks think she's a hooker, "no business out on the street
today?" — "no business" — "with this weather" — "with this
weather" — "how 'bout it?" — " 'bout what?" — "us two" — "no

can do" — "are you?" — "yep" — "life's a shit" — "have a drink,"
soon she'll look like Messalina, smaller, frailer, but still like Messalina the same boozer's face the big pores and blotchy skin, Messalina lures Emilia to her parties, wants to throw her to Alexander
the archdukewomansdream or the jaunty fathers, wonders why
Emilia doesn't come, Emilia isn't interested in orgies she's not
interested in Messalina's desperate friends, Emilia is desperate herself doesn't need any other despair, she says she runs around the city
for me so I can write my book, hates me for it when she comes
home, if I had written anything she would tear it up, Emilia my
Ophelia: O-pale-Ophélia-belle-comme-la-neige, I love you but
'twere better we did part, you'll go to the bottom even without me,
you'll be slain by your houses, you've long since been buried beneath your houses, all that's left of you is a small frail raging
drunken ghost of despair, my fault? yes, my guilt, everyman's guilt,
old guilt, ancestral guilt, guilt from way back, when she rages she
screams I'm a Communist, did it come to that? it did not come to
that, I could have been an author, I could have been a Communist,
all miscarried, in the Romanisches Café Kisch said "comrade" to
me, I said "Herr Kisch," I liked him: Kisch racing reporter where
was he racing to? I abhor violence, I abhor oppression, is that
Communism? I don't know, the social sciences: Hegel Marx dialectics marxist-materialist dialectics—never grasped it, Communist by
sentiment: always senselessly outraged on the side of the poor,
Spartacus Jesus Thomas Münzer Max Hölz, what did they want? to
be good, what happened? people killed each other, did I fight in
Spain? the bell tolled not for me, I dodged my way through the
dictatorship, I hated but quietly, I hated but in my room, I whispered but with likeminded people, Burckhardt said with people like
himself you could never make a state, sounds good, but with people
like that you can never bring down a state either, no hope, none for
me any more, Behude said there was hope for me, lines from Rilke:
and-in-the-East-a-solitary-church, blurred, no path, the East inside

133

me: childhood landscape, my recherche-du-temps-perdu, seek-and-ye-shall-find, odors, the baked apples, sounds, the crackling fur of the cat, the crunch of the runners of the wooden sled on the lake, and dancing her pirouettes barelegged alone on the ice, Eva: snow peace sleep—.'

Sleep, but no return home, no turn inward, a fall, a being felled. Like a heavy stone into water, massive, insentient, Alexander in his apartment plummeted into sleep. In the man who played the archduke there lived no dream. He had thrown himself, without undressing, onto a sofa; the night before, the tribadic Alfredo had lain here; there was no lust in Alexander. He was just tired. He was fed up. Fed up with the archduke role. Fed up with cranking out the archduke's inane lines. Fed up with borrowed heroism. What did he do in the war? He played. He was exempted. What did he play? Iron-Cross-flier-heroes. He luckily escaped four crash landings, while his less lucky enemies and rivals lay smashed to bits in the dust. He had never sat in an airborne plane. He was even afraid when he had to use any form of transportation. When the bombs fell, he was tucked away in the Hotel-Adlon-Diplomat-Bunker. That was a bunker for fine people. Soldiers on leave were not let in. The bunker had two stories. Alexander sat on the second: the war was far away. After the attack, Hitler Youths were clearing the rubble from the streets. They boys were looking for people buried in the rubble. They asked Alexander for his autograph. They asked Alexander the hero, Alexander the bold. They mistook Alexander for his shadow. It made him dizzy. Who was he: A daredevil-loyal-sentimental-bold-virile-hero? He was fed up with it. He was tired. He was heroed out. He was like a drawn capon: plump and hollow. His face wore a look of stupidity: the makeup was gone, it was empty. His mouth stood open, and from between the sparkling white rows of jacket crowns came a snoring of staleness and nausea, of sluggish digestion and slack metabolism. One hundred sixty pounds of human meat lay on the sofa, they weren't hanging on the butcher's hook yet, but for that moment when the wit was turned off, the stream of clever patter and wittiness which in his body had taken over the functions of the soul, Alexander was no more than butcher's meat, one hundred sixty pounds of it. Hillegonda came toddling into the room. She had heard the car with Alexander drive up, and for a while she got up the courage to let go of Emmi's hand and walk alone into the world full of sin. Hillegonda wanted to ask Alexander whether God was really angry, whether God was angry with Hillegonda, with Alexander, and with Messalina. God wasn't angry with Emmi. But maybe that was a lie. "Daddy, is Emmi-dear allowed to tell lies?" The child received no answer. Maybe Emmi was the very one God was angry with. Emmi was always summoned before God. Even very early, when the day was dawning, she had to go into God's dark courtrooms. Alexander, too, had been summoned once. He had been summoned about his taxes. He had been afraid. He had called out: "these figures aren't right!" Were Emmi's figures maybe not right? The child was in torment. She would have liked to stand better in God's eyes. It could be, after all, that God's ill temper wasn't directed at Hillegonda at all. But her father said nothing. He lay there like a dead man. Only the rattling, the snoring that emerged from his open mouth showed that he was alive. Hillegonda heard Emmi call. She had to go back to Emmi's hand. Emmi was summoned again. Again she had to kneel down, kneel on tiles, on cold, hard tiles, she had to go before God and bow down in the dust.

The Heiliggeistkirche gave its name to Heiliggeist Square, Heiliggeist Hospital, and Heiliggeist tavern. The tavern had a bad reputation. Where had they gotten to? Back when Josef was little, the market folk had met in the tavern. The market folk came riding into the city with horse and wagon, and Josef helped them unhitch and hitch up the horses. Back then, the old quarter around the

Heiliggeistkirche had been the heart of the city. Later the city's center had shifted. The old area died. The market died. The square, the houses, the hospital, the church were bombed in the war, long after they had died. Ruins remained. Never would anyone have the money to rebuild these ruins. The area had become an underworld hangout. Petty thieves met here, shabby pimps, cheap hookers. Where had they gotten to? This had been Josef's home turf, where he had played, where he had worked as a boy, the church where he took his First Holy Communion. Where had they gotten to? They sat in the tavern. The tavern was full, full of noise; heavy, warm air made up of fumes, stench, and smoke filled the room, swirled in the room like gas in a sagging balloon. Where had the market folk gone? The market folk were dead. They lay in their graves in their village graveyards beside the white churches. Their horses, which Josef harnessed, had gone to the glue factory. Josef and Odysseus were drinking schnapps. Odysseus called the schnapps gin. The schnapps was Steinhäger. It was a rotgut imitation Steinhäger. In the music case on Josef's lap, a choir sang she-was-a-nice-girl. How did they get here? What were they doing here? Little Josef had gone begging for milk. The farmer's wife had filled his pitcher with milk. Josef had run across the square and fallen down. The pitcher had broken. The milk had run out on the ground. Josef's mother slapped Josef. She slapped him hard on the ears. Life for the poor is hard; they always make their life even harder. She-was-a-nice-girl. What were they doing here? They settled accounts. Odysseus paid Josef. He took out his wallet. The Greeks hadn't been able to cheat him. Odysseus gave Josef fifty marks: great, splendid King Odysseus. Josef looked at the bill, peering through his glasses. He folded the money, laid it carefully between the pages of a dirty memo book and stuck the book into the breast pocket of his porter's jacket. The tourist trade had paid off once again. It was agreed that Josef would accompany Odysseus until evening, that he would carry the music case for him until

Odysseus disappeared in the night with a girl. She-was-a-nice-girl.
Great Odysseus. He looked into the fog of sweat, uncleanliness,
bratwurst smoke, tobacco wisps, alcohol fumes, piss odor, onion
juice, and stale breath. He waved Susanne over. Susanne was a
blossom of Guerlain scent in a garbage dump. She wanted to sit in
the dump. Today she wanted to sit right in the garbage dump where
she belonged. She was disappointed in the fine people. Damned
disgusting stingy pigs. Alexander had invited her over, the famous
Alexander. Who believed her? Nobody. Had he come to her, had
he chosen her from the flock of girls, he, whom women dream of?
Who believed it? Had she slept with Alexander? A grunting, YOU
TOO CAN EXPERIENCE ARCHDUKE AMOUR, the pigs had swilled, they
had swilled like pigs. And then? No god to reveal himself. No
Alexander to embrace her. No hero to rescue her. Women. Susanne had been beaten. Women had beaten her. And after that?
Kisses caresses touches hands on her thighs. Women had kissed
caressed touched her, women's hands lay hot and dry on her thighs.
And Alexander? Extinguished languiddull puffyeyed, eyes dead
glassy staring. Did the eyes see anything? did they perceive anything? Where did Alexander laugh and love? where did he serve
women, embrace and exalt them? At the Thalia Palace on the
corner of Schillerplatz and Goethestrasse, five showings daily.
Where did Alexander snore? where did he hang inanimate over an
armchair, where was he so much hanging meat? At home when he
had invited girls over. What present did they give Susanne after this
night? They forgot to give her anything. Susanne thought, 'after
Alexander a nigger, I'm not queer, I'm good and healthy.' She
sauntered languidly, a cigarette in her hand, over to Odysseus. The
perfume scent from Messalina's bottle accompanied her through the
heavy stenchsteaming air of the place like an isolated and isolating,
in a different way heavy, differently steaming cloud. Susanne
pushed Josef and the singing case on down the bench worn smooth
by many backsides and scrubbed to a smooth sheen. She crowded

137

the case and the old man aside like two dead objects, and the old man was the more worthless thing. The case you could sell. Josef you couldn't sell any more. Susanne was Circe and the Sirens, she was that in this moment, she had just then become it, and maybe she was Nausicaa, too. Nobody in the place noticed that there were others inside Susanne's skin, age-old beings; Susanne didn't know who all she was, Circe, the Sirens, and maybe Nausicaa; the foolish woman thought she was Susanne, and Odysseus had no idea what ladies faced him in the person of this girl. Young skin stretched smooth around Susanne's arm. Odysseus felt the pulse, he felt the blood coursing through this arm across the back of his neck. The arm was cool and freckled, a boyish arm, yet the hand that touched Odysseus's chest after slipping around his neck was warm, feminine, and sexy, she-was-a-nice-girl —

She loved jewels. The ruby is fire flame, the diamond is water the well the swelling wave, the sapphire air and sky, and the green emerald is earth, the green of greengrowing earth, the green of meadows and forests. Emilia loved the sparkling radiance, she loved the iridescent splendor of the cold gems, the warm gold, the eyes of gods and souls of animals in the colored stones, the fairy tales of the Orient, the diadem on the brow of the sacred elephant, AGA KHAN RECEIVES HIS WEIGHT IN JEWELS, TRIBUTE FROM HIS FOLLOWERS, INDUSTRIAL DIAMONDS NEEDED FOR WAR EFFORT. It was not the cave that Aladdin found. No magic lamp burned here. Herr Schellack, the jeweler, said: "No." His imposing chin was powdered smooth. He had a face like a sack of flour. Had Emilia possessed cute little Aladdin's magic lamp, the sack would have burst, an evil spirit, guardian of the treasures, would have vanished. What would Emilia have done? She would have filled the plaid with gold and precious stones. Don't worry, you jewelers, there is no magic; there are pistols and blackjacks, but Emilia will not use them, and you do have your alarm systems, which won't protect you from the devil, though, when he comes to get you. Herr Schellack looked benignly at Kay, a promising customer, a young American, maybe Rockefeller's granddaughter. She was looking at corals and garnets. The old jewelry lay on a bed of velvet. He told about the families that had owned it, the women who had worn it, he recalled the poverty that had necessitated its sale, they were little Maupassant stories he was recounting, but Kay wasn't listening, she was thinking not of jewelry chests hidden in the dresser beneath the linen, not of miserliness inheritances and recklessness, not of the necks of beautiful women, not of their full arms, their elegant wrists, not of the once well-kept hands, the manicured fingernails, not of the hunger that devours the bread in the baker's window with its eyes, she thought, 'how lovely the chain is, how that bracelet sparkles, how the ring twinkles, how the necklace shines.' Moonpale, pearls, enamel, and diamond roses fitted together, the necklace lay before Schellack, the powdered figure, and again he said, again facing her, the benign glow that had shone for Kay was extinguished, switched off, once again a switched off frosted light bulb: "No." Herr Schellack did not want to buy the necklace. He said it was grandmother jewelry. It was grandmother jewelry, geheimer Kommerzienrat jewelry; grandmother cut, grandmother setting, fashionable back in the eighties. And the diamond roses? "Worthless! Worthless!" Herr Schellack raised his short arms, his fat hands, hands like two plump quail; it was a gesture that led one to fear that Herr Schellack would try to fly, he would try, out of sheer regret and disappointment, to fly away. Was Emilia listening to him? She was not listening to him. She wasn't even looking at him. His gestures were lost on her. She was thinking, 'how nice she is, she is very nice, she is a really nice girl, she is the nice girl I might have become, she's happy that it's all such a lovely red, red like wine red like blood red like young lips, that it twinkles and sparkles so, she hasn't considered yet that she won't get a thing for the jewelry if she has to sell it someday, I know, I know what's up, I'm an old hand at this business, I love the

139

colorful stones but I'd never buy myself any, they're an unsafe investment, too dependent on what's fashionable, only diamonds give you some security, the newest cut to suit nouveau riche tastes triumphs, and gold of course, pure gold, tucking that away makes sense, as long as I have gold and diamonds I don't need to work, I don't want to be wakened by the alarm clock, I want never to say: "I'm sorry, Mr. Manager, I'm sorry, Mr. Foreman, Sir, I missed the streetcar," I would have missed the streetcar if I ever had to say that, the car of my life, never! never! never! and you, my lovely and nice Miss, you with your corals and garnets, Herr Schellack will make you pay a lot for the little rings and little crosses, for the little chains and the pendants, but go to him sometime, my sweet, come on and offer him that same little ring, that same chain, go ahead, offer them to him, he'll tell you that your pretty garnets and corals are worth nothing, nothing at all, then you'll learn, then you'll know, you innocent lamb, you shameless thing from America.' Emilia picked up her necklace off the counter. Herr Schellack said with a languid smile: "I'm sorry, Madam." He thought she would leave. He thought 'such a shame, my clientele reduced to this, her grand-mother bought those pieces from my father, she'll have paid two thousand marks for them, two thousand in gold.' But Emilia didn't leave. She was looking for freedom. For a moment, at least, she wanted to be free. She wanted to act freely, to perform one free act that was not dictated by any force or any necessity or any intention beyond the intention to be free; yet this was no intention either, it was a feeling, and the feeling was just there, quite unintentionally. She went to Kay and said: "Forget the corals and garnets. They're red and pretty. But these pearls and diamonds are prettier; even if Herr Schellack claims they're too old fashioned. I'll give them to you, Miss. I'll give them to you, dear, because you're nice." She was free. A tremendous rush of happiness coursed through Emilia. She was free. Her happiness would not last. But for the moment she was free. She was freeing herself, she was freeing herself of pearls and diamonds. At first, her voice had wavered. But now she exulted. She had dared to do it, she was free. She put the jewelry on Kay, she fastened the chain at the back of her neck. And Kay, too, was free, she was a free person, less consciously so than Emilia, and thus perhaps all the more naturally free, she stepped up to the mirror, looked at herself with the jewels around her neck for a long while, ignoring Schellack, who stood openmouthed trying to protest but unable to find the words, and said: "Yes. It is splendid! The pearls, the diamonds, the necklace. It's gorgeous!" She turned to Emilia and looked at her with her green eyes. Kay was wholly at ease, while Emilia was rather excited. But both girls had the glorious sensation that they were rebelling, they felt the wonderful joy of rebelling against reason and convention. "You have to take something from me, too," said Kay. "I don't have any jewelry. Maybe you'd take my hat." She took the hat from her head, it was a peaked traveling hat with a bright feather, and put it on Emilia. Emilia laughed, looked into the mirror and called out in delight: "Now I look like Till Eulenspiegel. Just like Till Eulenspiegel." She tilted the hat back, thought, 'drunk, looks drunk, but I swear, I haven't had a drop yet today, Philipp wouldn't believe it.' She ran to Kay. She hugged Kay, she kissed Kay, and as she touched Kay's lips, she thought, 'glorious, that's the flavor of the prairie' —

— 'just like a wild west movie,' thought Messalina. She hadn't found Susanne in her apartment, but they had told her she could find her in the tavern on Heiliggeist Square. 'Just like a wild west movie, but we're not making them any more, artless banging around.' She strode self-assuredly into the haze, into the stinking, vile aura of the place where folks used to drink a pint before going out to watch the witchburning on the market square. Messalina was shy. You could still see it on the picture that showed her as a communicant, in a white dress, a candle in her hand. But even then, when this picture was taken, in the studio of one of the last

141

photographers who still wore velvet jackets and big black butterfly bow ties and who called out "nice and friendly, please" (Messalina had not made a friendly face: it was shy, but already defiance and violence were there, battling against the shyness), even back then she had wanted not to be shy, not to play this role, not to be pressed against the wall, and it was the day of Communion, the initial point of her growth, her menstrual bleeding began, and she grew and increased in vice and vulgarity and mass of flesh, she became a depraved, vulgar monument, wherever she set foot, she was a monument that evoked alarm or rapture: who knew that she had remained shy? Dr. Behude knew it. But Dr. Behude was even more shy than Messalina, and since he had never compensated for his shyness in mammoth proportions as she had, he didn't dare, out of shyness, to tell Messalina that she was shy, and yet just that, had Behude said it, would have been a magic word, a monument-shattering word, and Messalina would have returned to the shy, pure state of before her First Holy Communion. Everyone looked at Messalina, the little hookers and the little pimps, the little thieves in unison, and even the little police officer who, known to everyone as a cop, sat here in disguise: Messalina intimidated them all. Only Susanne was not intimidated. Susanne thought, 'that scum, if she ruins this nigger on me.' She wanted to think 'then I'll scratch, bite, punch, and kick,' but she didn't think it, she wasn't intimidated, but she was afraid, she was afraid of Messalina's blows, for she had felt Messalina's blows. Susanne got up. She said: "Just a minute, Jimmy." Two clouds of the same perfume, Guerlain Paris, united, held their own against sweat, piss, onion, wurst broth, against beer fumes and tobacco smoke. Susanne was asked to come to Alexander's that evening, and she thought, 'I'd be pretty stupid if I did, a bad deal, but what if Alexander did sleep with me? yes, he'll sleep, but not with me, he can't any more, and if he could, who'd believe I did, and if nobody believes me, then I'd rather have that

142

nigger on my ass, he can, even though I'm not really out to get that, but those unsatisfied females? count me out, FIRST LEGION WARNS AGAINST COUNT ME OUT SLOGAN, MINISTER OF JUSTICE SAYS ANYONE WHO WON'T DEFEND WIFE AND CHILD IS NO MAN.' Yet Susanne found it improper to turn down the invitation of a lady, a lady of society, a superlady of a monumentality Susanne vaguely sensed. She said she would come, of course, gladly, she was honored and delighted, and she thought, 'don't hold your breath waiting, kiss my ass, but kiss it from a distance, I want to be left in peace, you think you're better than me? no way do I want to be what you are.' Messalina had looked around the place. She had spotted Susanne's empty seat next to Odysseus, and she said: "Bring along your black friend if you want." She thought, 'he might be something for the queers.' Susanne was about to answer, about to find an excuse, about to say that she had nothing to do with the Negro, or she could go ahead and accept for her Jimmy or Joe, it really didn't matter, she wasn't going anyway, when there arose a loud shouting and scuffling. Odysseus had been robbed, his money had disappeared, gone were the dollars and the German bills, the music case played Jimmy's-Boogie-Woogie, King Odysseus was offended, he was insulted, he had been outfoxed, he the fox, outfoxed, he grabbed the man nearest him, took hold of a pimp or a thief or the little police officer, accused him, shook him, "look at the gorilla, King Kong, fucker, throw him out, fucking nigger, get him out," the pack leapt up, the herd won out, camaraderie was victorious, THE GOOD OF THE COMMUNITY COMES BEFORE THE GOOD OF THE INDIVIDUAL, they fell on him, they took beer glasses, chair legs, fixed blades, they fell upon great Odysseus, the battle crashed, raged, jolted, Odysseus was in enemy territory, he was fighting for his life, the table tipped over, Josef held the music case, he held it over his head, he held Jimmy's-Boogie-Woogie over his head like a shield, the notes rattled, the syncopation hissed, it was like in the trenches, there was

143

the drumfire again, the Chemin des Dames, the Argonne Forest, yet Josef did not participate in the battle, he was atoning, he did not kill, he drifted on the waves of a far-off river, fled with Odysseus, who had fought his way free, bathed in the music of the river of a far-off continent, Jimmy's-Boogie-Woogie. Messalina stood alone, inwardly timid and outwardly a monument, amid the turmoil. Nothing happened to her. The battle moved around the monument. No one offended Messalina. She stood in the middle of the place like a universally respected landmark that belonged there. But Susanne followed her new friend. It would have been smart not to do that. It would have been smart to stay. It might even have been smart to go with Messalina. But since Susanne was Circe and the Sirens and maybe Nausicaa, too, she had to follow Odysseus. She had to follow him against all reason. She was entangled with Odysseus. She hadn't really wanted that at all. She hadn't been able to resist, she had been dumb, and now she was being foolish. Odysseus and Josef ran across Heiliggeist Square. Susanne ran after them. She followed Jimmy's-Boogie-Woogie.

The bells of the Heiliggeistkirche were ringing. Emmi and Hillegonda knelt on the tiles. It smelled in the church of old incense and fresh mortar. Hillegonda was cold. She was cold with her bare knees on the cold tiles. Emmi made the sign of the Cross and-forgive-us-our-sins. Hillegonda thought, 'what ever is my sin? if only someone would tell me, ach, Emmi, I'm afraid.' And Emmi prayed: "Lord, Thou hast destroyed this city, and Thou shalt destroy it again, for they do not obey Thee and do not heed Thy word, and their cries are an abomination to Thine ears." Hillegonda heard shrill voices from outside, and it was as if stones were being thrown against the door of the church. "Emmi, do you hear that? Emmi, what is it? They're going to hurt us, Emmi!" — "It's the devil, child. The devil is on the loose. Just pray! Oh-Lord-deliver-us!"

They lay behind rubble and stones from where the church had been hit by a bomb. The mob was moving in on them, Susanne thought, 'what am I getting myself into? I'm crazy to get myself into this, but yesterday at Alexander's they made me crazy, and now I'm getting myself into this.' Jimmy's-Boogie-Woogie. "Money," said Odysseus. He needed capital. He was in a war. He was back in the old war White against Black. The war was being fought here, too. He needed money to fight the war. "Money! Quick!" Odysseus took hold of Josef. Josef thought, 'it's like at Chemin des Dames, the black man is not the devil, he is the traveler I killed, he is the Turk or Senegalese I killed on my trip in France.' Josef did not resist. He just froze. Before his old eyes the landscape of his childhood was again transformed into a European battlefield with non-European combatants, foreign travelers trying to kill or getting killed. Josef clutched tightly to the case. The case was his job. He had been paid to carry the case. He had to hold onto it. Jimmy's-Boogie-Woogie —

They stood facing each other, friends? enemies? husband and wife? they stood facing each other in Carla's apartment, in Frau Welz's whore's quarters, in a world of licentiousness and despair, they screamed at one another, and Frau Welz left the witch's kitchen, the stove with the churning vapors, stole down the corridor and hissed through the slightly ajar doors of the girls' rooms, where they were getting themselves ready, naked, in panties, in greasy dressing gowns, startled at their toilet, putting on beauty for the evening, not yet fully formed, only halfpowdered faces, they heard the madam's hissing, the salacious delight in her voice that something evil was happening: "Now he's beating her, that nigger. Now he's hitting her. Now he's showing her. I've been wondering a long time why he doesn't show her." Washington wasn't hitting her. Plates and cups hit his chest, the shards lay at his feet: the

145

shards of his happiness? He thought, 'I can leave, if I take my cap and leave, this will all be behind me, maybe I'll forget it, it will never have happened.' Carla screamed, her face was tear-swollen: "You ruined the doctor on me. You sneak! You went to see Frahm. You think I want to have your bastard? You think I want to have him? They'd point their fingers at me. I don't want your America. Your dirty black America. I'm staying here. I'm staying here with-out your bastard, even if it kills me, I'm staying!" What held him back? Why didn't he take his cap? Why didn't he leave? Maybe it was stubbornness. Maybe it was blindness. Maybe it was convic-tion, maybe faith in mankind. Washington heard what Carla screamed, but he didn't believe her. He did not want to dissolve the bond that was now threatening to tear, the bond between white and black, he wanted to tie it tighter with a child, he wanted to provide an example, he had faith in the possibility of this example, and maybe, too, his faith would claim martyrs. For a moment, he really thought about hitting Carla. It is always despair that wants to lash out, but his faith overcame his despair. Washington took Carla in his arms. He held her firmly in his strong arms. Carla thrashed about in his arms like a fish in the fisherman's hand. Washington said: "But we love each other, why shouldn't we see this through? Why shouldn't we make it? We've just got to always love each other. When all the others call us names: we have to keep on loving. Even when we're very old, we've got to love each other."

Odysseus hit with a stone—or a stone that the mob had thrown hit—against Josef's forehead. Odysseus tore the money, the bill that he had given Josef, King Odysseus, out of the porter's memo book, out of the worn notebook in which Josef had recorded the errands he ran and his earnings. Odysseus ran. He ran around the church. The mob gave pursuit. They saw Josef lying on the ground and saw blood on his forehead. "The nigger has killed old Josef!" The square swarmed with figures that emerged from cellars, shacks, and ruins, everyone in the quarter had known him, old Josef, little Josef, he had played here, he had worked here, he had gone to war, he had worked again, and now he had been murdered: he had been murdered for his pay. They stood around him: a gray wall of poor and old people. From the music case beside Josef rose a Negro spiritual. Marian Anderson sang, a lovely, full, and soft voice, a vox humana, a vox angelica, voice of a dark angel; it was as if the voice were trying to make amends to the slain man. 'I have to get out,' thought Susanne, 'I have to get out of here fast, I have to get out before the cops come, the MPs will come, and patrol cars will come.' She pressed her right hand against her blouse, where she felt the money that she had taken out of Odysseus's pocket. 'Why ever did I do it,' she thought, 'I've never done anything like that, they made me bad, those pigs at Alexander's made me bad, I wanted revenge, I wanted to take revenge on the pigs, but you always take your revenge on the wrong ones.' Susanne strode through the gray wall of the old and the poor, which opened before her. The old and the poor let Susanne pass. They blamed her in part for what had happened, a woman was always there when misfortune struck, but they were no psychologists and no criminologists, they did not think, 'cherchez la femme,' they thought, 'she, too, is poor, she, too, will grow old, she is one of us.' Only after the wall had closed again behind Susanne did a kid shout "Ami-whore!" A couple of women made the sign of the Cross. A priest came and bent over Josef. The priest put his ear to Josef's chest. The priest was gray-haired and his face was tired. He said: "He's still breathing." From the hospital came four lay brothers with a stretcher. The lay brothers looked poor and like foiled plotters in a classical drama. They laid Josef on the stretcher. They carried the stretcher over into the Heiliggeist Hospital. The priest followed the stretcher. Behind the priest walked Emmi. She pulled Hillegonda along behind her. Emmi and Hillegonda were allowed to walk into the hospital. It was probably thought that they belonged with Josef, and then the sirens of the

147

patrol cars and the military police were heard. From all sides the sirens approached the square.

It was that moment, that hour of the evening, when cyclists whisk through the streets and defy death. It was the time when twilight falls, the time when shifts change, when shops close, the hour when workers return home, the hour when night workers swarm into place. The police sirens shrieked. The squad cars rushed through the traffic. The blue lights lent their racing a ghostly glow: danger-boding St. Elmo's fire of the city. Philipp loved this hour. In Paris, it was the heure bleue, the hour of reverie, a span of relative freedom, the moment of being free from day and night. The people had been released from their workshops and businesses, and they were not yet captive to the demands of habit and obligations to the family. The world hung suspended. Everything appeared possible. For a while everything appeared possible. But perhaps Philipp was imagining this, Philipp who stood apart, who was not returning from any work to any family. On the heels of imagination would come disappointment. Philipp was accustomed to disappointments; he did not fear them. The evening glow wrought a transfiguration. The sky burned in southerly colors. It was an Etna sky, a sky like that above the old theater in Taormina, a blaze like that above the temples in Agrigento. Classical antiquity had arisen and smiled a greeting over the city. The contours of the buildings stood like a clean brushstroke against this sky, and the sandstone facade of the Jesuit church Philipp was walking past had the grace of a dancer, it was a part of old Italy, it was humane, wise, and of a carnivalesque gaiety. But where had the humanity and wisdom and, in the end, gaiety led? The Abendecho shouted out the day's bad tidings RE-TIREE CHOSE DEATH, SOVIETS FACE A BRICK WALL, ANOTHER DIPLO-MAT DISAPPEARS, GERMAN REMILITARIZATION AMENDMENTS COM-ING, EXPLOSION GAVE GLIMPSE OF HELL. How earnest and how dumb that was! A diplomat had gone over to the other side, he had gone

148

over to the enemy of his government, TREASON OUT OF IDEALISM. The official world was still striving to think in hollow phrases, in slogans long since devoid of any conceptual basis. They saw fixed, immutable fronts, staked off plots of earth, boundaries, territories, sovereignties, they saw in man a member of a soccer team who was supposed to play his life long for the team that he had joined by birth. They were mistaken: the front was not here and not there and not only at the boundary stake over there. The front was omnipresent, whether visible or invisible, and life was constantly changing its position relative to the billion points of the front. The front cut through the countries, it divided families, it ran through the individual: two souls, yes, two souls dwelt within each breast, and sometimes the heart beat with the one and sometimes with the other soul. Philipp was no more quickly swayed than others; on the contrary, he was a loner. But even he could have changed his mind about the state of the world with his every step, and more than a thousand times a day. 'Do I have the whole picture,' he thought, 'do I know the politicians' calculations? the diplomats' secrets? I'm happy when one flees to the other side and mixes the cards up a bit, then the big wheels will have that feeling we have, that feeling of helplessness, can I still understand science? do I know the latest formulation of its view of life, can I read it?' Everyone walking, cycling, riding out there in the street, making plans, worrying, or enjoying the evening, every one of them was constantly being lied to and cheated, and the augurs who lied to and cheated them were no less blind than the simple folk. Philipp laughed about the stupidity of political propaganda. He laughed about it, although he knew that it could cost him his life. But the others in the street? Were they laughing, too? Had the laughter stuck in their throats? Did they, in contrast to Philipp, have no time to laugh? They did not realize how bad the feed was that was strewn before them, how cheaply they were to be bought. 'I'm more or less immune to seductions,' reflected Philipp, 'and yet, sometimes I'll hear a word here I like, and sometimes a call from the other side that sounds even better, I always play the ridiculous roles, I'm the old tolerant one, I'm for listening to every opinion, if you're going to listen to opinions at all, but now the earnest people are getting all excited on both sides and shouting at me that my very tolerance promotes intolerance, they are hostile brothers, both of them intolerant to the core, each with a grudge against the other, and able to agree only in vilifying my weak attempt to remain impartial, and each one of them hates me because I won't join him and bark at the other, I don't want to play on any team, not even in hemisphere soccer, I want to stay on my own.' There was still hope in the world: CAUTIOUS FEELERS, NO WAR BEFORE FALL —

The teachers from Massachusetts walked through the city two by two, like a school class. The class was on its way to the Amerika-Haus. It was enjoying a nice evening out. The teachers wanted to hear Edwin's lecture and see something of the city's life beforehand. They didn't see much. They saw as little of this city's life as the city saw of the teachers' lives. Nothing. Miss Wescott had taken charge. She strode at the head of the class. She led her colleagues according to the city map in her traveler's handbook. She led them surely and without detours. Miss Wescott was in a bad mood. Kay had disappeared. She had gone out of the hotel in the afternoon to look at shop windows. She had not returned at the appointed hour. Miss Wescott blamed herself. She shouldn't have let Kay go out alone into this foreign city. Who were these people? Were they not enemies? Could they be trusted? Miss Wescott had left a message at the hotel that Kay should take a taxi and ride to the Amerika-Haus immediately. Miss Wescott did not understand Miss Burnett. Miss Burnett said Kay had probably met someone. Was Kay capable of such a thing? She was young and inexperienced. It couldn't be. Miss Burnett said: "She'll have met someone who entertains her better than we can."—"How can you be so calm about it?"—"I'm

150

not jealous." Miss Wescott pressed her lips together. This Burnett woman was immoral. And Kay was simply misbehaving. That's all there was to it. Kay had gotten lost or lost track of the time. The teachers were walking across the large square, a park designed by Hitler, that had been planned as national socialism's memorial grove. Miss Wescott drew the group's attention to the square's significance. In the grass were some birds. Miss Burnett thought, 'we don't understand any more than the birds of what old Wescott is chattering, the birds are here by coincidence, we're here by coincidence, and maybe even the Nazis were here only by coincidence, Hitler was a coincidence, his policies were a ghastly and dumb coincidence, maybe the world is one ghastly and dumb coincidence of God, nobody knows why we're here, the birds will fly off again and we'll walk on, I hope Kay doesn't get involved in anything dumb, it would be dumb if she got involved in something dumb, I couldn't tell Wescott, she'd go crazy, but Kay attracts seducers, she can't help it, she attracts them as birds do the hunter or the dog.' — "What's the matter with you?" Miss Wescott asked Miss Burnett. Miss Wescott was put out; Miss Burnett was not listening to her. It seemed to Miss Wescott that Burnett had the face of a ravenous hunting dog. "I'm just looking at the birds," said Miss Burnett. "Since when have you been interested in birds?" asked Miss Wescott. "I'm interested in us," said Miss Burnett. "Those are sparrows," said Miss Wescott, "ordinary sparrows. You would do better to pay attention to world history." — "It's the same thing," said Miss Burnett, "it's all a matter of sparrows. You, too, are just a sparrow, my dear Wescott, and our little sparrow, Kay, is just now falling out of the nest." — "I don't understand you," said Miss Wescott sharply, "I am not a bird."

Philipp walked into the hall of the old castle, in which the state had set up a wine taproom to promote the sale of locally produced wine. The hall was much frequented at this hour. The officials of the countless ministries and state offices tanked up a little good cheer before they went home, home to their wives, to their heart-less children, to their unlovingly warmed-up supper. It was a world of men. There were few women there. Only two female reporters were there. But they weren't real women. They belonged to the Abendecho. They used the wine to extinguish the fire of their headlines. Philipp was thinking that he ought to go home, ought to go see Emilia. But he wanted to go see Edwin, too, even though his encounter with Edwin had gone so awkwardly. 'If I don't go to Emilia now, I can't go home at all tonight,' thought Philipp. He knew that Emilia would get drunk if she didn't find him home in the evening. He thought, 'I'd get drunk, too, alone in our apartment with all those animals, I'd get drunk then if I got drunk at all, I stopped getting drunk long ago.' The wine they had in the old castle was good. But Philipp didn't care for wine any more either. He was very gifted at enjoying, but he had lost his desire for almost all kinds of enjoyment. He was quite determined to go to Emilia. Emilia was like Dr. Jekyll and Mr. Hyde in Stevenson's story. Philipp loved Dr. Jekyll, a charming and goodhearted Emilia, but he hated and feared the repulsive Mr. Hyde, an Emilia of the late evening and the night, who was a savage drunkard and venomous Xanthippe. If Philipp went home now, he would still find the dear Dr. Jekyll, but should he attend Edwin's lecture, the terrible Mr. Hyde would be waiting for him. Philipp pondered whether he couldn't lead his life with Emilia differently, whether he couldn't arrange it quite differently. 'It's my fault if she's unhappy, why don't I make her happy?' He thought about moving out of the house on Fuchsstrasse, out of the dilapidated mansion that depressed Emilia so. He thought, 'we could move into one of her unmarketable country houses, the houses are occupied by tenants, the tenants won't leave, fine, then we'll build ourselves a shack on the lawn, others have done it, too.' He knew that he wouldn't build anything, no shack, no house in the country. Emilia wouldn't move away from

Fuchsstrasse. She needed the atmosphere of the family feuding, the ever-present financial disaster before her eyes. And Philipp would never move to the country, either. He needed the city, even if in the city he was poor. He read gardening books sometimes and imagined he would find peace in raising plants. He knew it was an illusion. He thought, 'in the country, in the shack we built, if we did build it, we would be at each other's throats, in the city we still love each other, we just act as if we don't.' He paid for the wine. Unfortunately, he had overlooked the city editor of the Neues Blatt at the Abendecho ladies' table. The editor reproached Philipp for not doing the interview. He expected that Philipp now would at least go to Edwin's lecture and report on it for the Neues Blatt. "You go do it," said Philipp. "Nah, not that crap," the editor answered, "that's what I got you for. You'll have to do me that favor after all." — "Will you give me cab fare?" Philipp asked. "Write it down with your expenses," said the editor. "Right away," said Philipp. The editor took a ten mark note from his pocket and handed it to Philipp. "We'll settle up afterwards," he said. 'So I've stooped that far,' thought Philipp, 'I'm selling myself and Edwin.'

Alarmed by the brawl on the Heiliggeist Square, bewildered and accompanied by the police sirens, Messalina hurried into the quiet bar of the hotel. Messalina was so charged with tension that she thought she was going to burst here in the silence. 'Isn't anyone here?' she thought. Being alone was terrible. Messalina had fled from the hooker joint back into the precincts of what she considered to be good society, the good society on whose fringes she liked to maraud. Messalina never completely parted company with the well-mannered class. She gave up nothing. She wanted to have something extra. The company of the well-mannered class was a foothold; from there, she could fraternize with the unmannered, strike up a temporary fraternity of the senses with that social stratum she considered to be the proletariat. Little did she know!

153

She need only have asked Philipp. Philipp would have lamented eloquently about how puritanically minded the proletariat was. Philipp was not a particularly dissolute person. Messalina took him for a monk. But that was something else. Philipp often lamented: "A puritanical century is dawning!" He would refer, rather unclearly, to Flaubert, who had regretted the extinction of the joy girl. The joy girl had died out. Philipp felt the puritanism of the working class was unfortunate. Philipp would have been very much for the abolition of private property, but he would have been decidedly against a restriction of joy. By the way, he drew a distinction between joy and sorrow girls; he included among the latter all prevalent forms of prostitution. 'What barbarous people,' thought Messalina, 'they're hitting each other.' In Messalina's house, beating was performed only in an aesthetically proper manner, according to deliberate ritual. Messalina looked around. The bar seemed in fact to be empty. But no, in the farthest corner sat two girls: Emilia and the little American with the green eyes. Messalina stood on her tiptoes. The large monument that she was wavered precariously. She wanted to sneak up on the little ones. The girls were drinking, laughing, they embraced and kissed. What was going on here? What kind of a funny hat did Emilia have on? She had never worn a hat. Like most insecure people, Messalina liked to believe that others were plotting against her, that they had secrets they kept from her. The little green-eyed American was disconcerting. Green eyes had talked with Philipp, and now she caught her exchanging embraces and kisses, they were little girls' boarding school kisses, with Emilia. Who was this charming little one? Where had Philipp and Emilia picked her up? 'Maybe they'll come to my party after all, then we'll see,' thought Messalina. But then she saw Edwin and she returned to her feet. Maybe she could win Edwin over. Edwin was the bigger, though less appetizing fish. Edwin entered the bar with quick strides and hurried up to the counter. He whispered something to the bartender. The bartender poured cognac for Edwin into

154

a large wine glass. Edwin emptied the glass. He had stage fright, lecture fright. He combated his agitation with cognac. In front of the hotel the consulate car was already waiting. Edwin was a prisoner of his promise. A horrendous evening! Why had he ever let himself in for this? Vanity! Vanity! Vanity of the sages. Why hadn't he stayed in his retreat, the cozy apartment crammed full with books and antiques? Envy of the actors' fame, envy of the applause heaped upon the protagonist had driven him out. Edwin scorned the actors, the protagonists, and the crowd off of whom they lived and with whom they lived. But, ah, it was seductive, the applause, the crowd, the youth, the disciples, they were alluring and seductive when one had sat as long as Edwin had at a desk, striving in solitude for cognition and beauty, but also for recognition. There was that hideous society columnist, that stairway woman again, this sex colossus, she was staring at him, he had to flee. And Kay cried out to Emilia: "There's Edwin! Don't you see him? Come on! I've got to get to his lecture. Where's that note from Wescott? Come on along! I had almost forgotten!" Emilia gave Kay a suddenly angry look: "Spare me your Edwin! I despise literary people, these cardboard dolls! I'm not going anywhere!" — "But he's a poet," shouted Kay, "how can you say such a thing!" — "Philipp is a poet, too," said Emilia. "Who's this Philipp?" Kay asked. "My husband," said Emilia. 'She's crazy,' thought Kay, 'what does she want? she's crazy, why, she's not even married, she can't expect me to stay sitting here, I'm already quite drunk, I have enough crazy females in my tour group, but she is charming, this crazy little German.' She called out: "See you again later!" She blew Emilia a kiss, a last fleeting gesture. She whirled over to Edwin. She had been drinking whiskey; now she would talk to Edwin; she would ask him for his autograph; she didn't have Edwin's book in her hand any more, where was it? where could she have left it? but Edwin could write the autograph on the bartender's note pad. But Edwin was already hurrying away. Kay ran after him. Emilia thought, 'it serves me right, now here comes Messalina, too.' Messalina stood staring indignantly after Edwin and Kay. Now what was going on? Why were they charging off? Had they been plotting against Messalina? Emilia would have to explain it to her. But Emilia had disappeared, too, she had disappeared through a hidden door. On the table beside the empty glasses lay only the comical hat that Emilia had had on. It lay like a scrap of disappointment. 'It's witchcraft,' thought Messalina, 'it's pure witchcraft, I'm all alone in the world.' She stumbled up to the bar, for the moment a broken woman. "A triple," she called out. "What shall it be, Madam," asked the bartender. "Oh, anything. I'm tired." She was really tired. She hadn't been this tired in a long time. All of a sudden she was awfully tired. But she mustn't be tired. She still had to go to the lecture, she still had so much left to arrange for the party. She reached for the tall glass as the schnapps splashed waterbright over the edge. She yawned.

The day was tired. The evening light in the sky, the setting sun, shone into the horizonblue sedan, and for a moment the light blinded Carla and Washington. The light blinded, but it also purified and transfigured. Carla's and Washington's faces were il-luminated. Only after a while did Washington flip down the visors. They were riding slowly along the riverbank. Yesterday, Carla would still have dreamt that they would go riding like this on Riverside Drive in New York or on the Golden Gate in California. Now her heart had calmed down. She was not riding towards a magazine-dream apartment with reclining chairs, television set, and mechan-ical kitchen. It had been a dream. A dream that had tormented Carla because she had, in her innermost heart, always feared she wouldn't reach that dreamland. The burden of this yearning was now taken from her. In her room, she had felt utterly beaten. When Washington led her to the car, she had been nothing more than a sack on his arm, a heavy sack with some kind of dead stuffing. Now

she was set free. She was set free, not from the child, but from the
dreams of idle bliss in life, of cheating fate by means of a dial you
could turn. She believed again. She believed Washington. They
rode along the river, and Carla believed in the Seine. The Seine
was not as broad as the Mississippi, it was not as far away as the
Colorado. On the Seine, they would both be at home. They would
both become French if need be, she, a German, would become a
Frenchwoman, and Washington, a black American, would become
a Frenchman. The French were happy when someone decided to
live in their country. Carla and Washington would open their place,
Washington's Inn, the tavern where nobody was unwelcome. A car
passed them. Christopher and Ezra were sitting in the car.
Christopher was happy. In an antique shop, he had bought a cup
made in Berlin, a cup with the portrait of a great Prussian king. He
would take the cup along to the Seine. In the hotel on the Seine,
he would make a present of it to Henriette. Henriette would be
happy about the cup with the portrait of the Prussian king.
Henriette was a Prussian, even if she was an American now. 'All
these nationalities are nonsense,' thought Christopher, 'we should
put an end to them, of course everybody is proud of his home town,
I'm proud of Needles on the Colorado, but I still wouldn't kill
anybody over it.' — 'If there's no other way, I'll kill him,' thought
Ezra, 'I'll take a rock and kill him and then into the car fast, the dog
has to be in the car already, he won't get the dollars, that Kraut, if
Christopher just steps on the gas fast and hard enough.' Ezra's little
forehead had been full of worried furrows for hours. Christopher
had given Ezra the ten dollars. "So now you won't get lost," he had
joked, "or if you do get lost, you'll find me again with the help of
the ten dollars." — "Yeah, sure," Ezra had said. The matter didn't
seem to interest him any more. Indifferently, he had stuck the ten
dollars into his pocket. "Will we get to the Bräuhaus on time?"
asked Ezra. "Whatever do you want in the Bräuhaus?" Christopher
wanted to know. "You're constantly asking whether we'll be there

157

on time." — "Just wondering," said Ezra. He couldn't let on that something was up. Christopher would be against it. "But once we've gotten to the bridge, we'll turn back," Ezra persisted. "Of course we'll turn back then. Why shouldn't we turn back?" Christopher wanted to get in a quick look at the bridge which, according to the traveler's handbook, offered one a romantic view of the river valley. Christopher found Germany beautiful.

Behude had his choice of three stand-up bars. From the outside they all looked the same. They were the same improvised struc-tures, they had the same bottles in the window, the same prices written on the blackboard. The one bar belonged to an Italian, the next to an old Nazi, and the third to an old hooker. Behude chose the old Nazi's bar. Emilia sometimes drank a glass in the old Nazi's place. It was masochistic of her. Behude leaned his bicycle against the crumbling pressboard wall of the bar. The old Nazi had flabby cheeks, and dark glasses hid his eyes. Emilia was not there. 'I should have gone to the old hooker's place after all,' thought Behude, but now there he was at the old Nazi's. Behude asked for a vodka. He thought, 'if he doesn't have any vodka, I can leave again.' The old Nazi had vodka. 'Actually, I'm more the type for mineral water,' thought Behude, 'athlete, shouldn't have become a psychiatrist, ruins you.' He drank the vodka and shuddered. Behude didn't like alcohol. But from time to time he drank it out of spite. He drank after his office hours. He thought 'and-the-purse-is-empty-and-slack.' It was a student song. Behude hadn't sung it. He hadn't sung student songs at all. But the purse was empty and slack. He himself was empty, slack, he, Dr. Behude, after every day's office hours he was empty and slack. And so was his purse. Two patients had pressed Behude for money again. Behude couldn't turn them down. He was treating them, after all, for their inability to cope with life. 'This Nazi is empty and slack, too,' he thought. He ordered another vodka. "It's going to start again soon, now," said the Nazi. "What's that?" asked Behude. "That old chingbababoom," said the Nazi. He made as if he were hitting a bass drum. 'The current is with them again,' thought Behude, 'whatever happens, it'll drift them to the top.' He drank the second vodka and shuddered again. He paid. He thought, 'if only I had gone to the old hooker's place,' but there wasn't enough money left for the old hooker.

Emilia stood in the old hooker's stand-up bar. She had wanted to go home. She hadn't wanted to arrive home drunk, because then Philipp would shout at her or sometimes even cry. Philipp was hysterical lately. It was crazy of him to be worried on Emilia's account. "I can hold my liquor all right," said Emilia. She knew of the bisection into Dr. Jekyll and Mr. Hyde that Philipp made with her. She would have liked to come home to him as Dr. Jekyll, as the kindly and good doctor. Then she would have told Philipp there was still some of the money from the loan office, some of the money from the King Frederick cup, some of the money from the prayer rug left. They'd be able to pay the light bill again. She would have told Philipp about the jewelry she had given away. Philipp would have understood. He also would have understood why, as she had put the necklace on the green-eyed American girl, she had felt so free. But on the whole, it had been annoying. Philipp would tell her right away: "you should have run away right then. You should have put the necklace on her and then run away." Philipp was a psychologist. That was wonderful and that was annoying. You couldn't hide anything from Philipp. It was better to tell him everything. 'Why didn't I run away? because her mouth tasted so good, because it tasted so fresh and free like the prairie, do I have a thing for girls? no I do not have a thing for girls, but maybe I would have flirted a little with her like with a cute little sister, caresses, kisses, and come-on-in-and-say-good-night, she felt like it, too, that stupid Edwin, every personal relationship is stupid, if I had run off I would have felt good, I should never have spoken to that American girl, I

159

hate her now!' But this time her woes hadn't driven Emilia to the old hooker's place. Emilia would have resisted the urge to stop at the old hooker's. But she had been seduced. Just back of the hotel, she had come across the stray dog with its string dragging behind. "You poor thing," she had called, "you could get run over." She had lured the dog over. The dog caught the scent of Emilia's other animals, and immediately he made it clear that he was looking for a permanent position; for him, Emilia was a good person, and his nose did not deceive him. Emilia saw that the dog was hungry. She had led him into the old hooker's bar and bought him a wurst. Since she was already in the bar, Emilia drank a kirsch. She drank the strong, stone-bitter Kirschwasser. She drank it out of bitterness with life and because of the day's bitterness, the bitterness of the jewelry episode, bitterness with Philipp, and the bitterness of the Fuchsstrasse house. The old hooker was friendly, but bitter, too. Emilia drank with the old hooker. Emilia bought the old hooker drinks. The old hooker was like a frozen jet of water. She had a big hat on that was like the crest of water turned solid atop a fountain, and then she was wearing jet-studded gloves. The jet on the gloves tinkled like ice with every movement of her hands; it tinkled like little pieces of ice being shaken in a tumbler. Emilia admired the old hooker. 'When I'm as old as she is, I won't look nearly as good, I won't look half as good, I won't have a stand-up bar either, I'll have left my money in her stand-up bar, she's kept her money together, she's never bought her drinks herself, always had men buy her drinks, I'll never stop buying my drinks myself.' The dog wagged his tail. He was very smart. He didn't look it, but he was smart. He sensed that this human being that was now looking after him could be stirred. He would rule this woman. The prospects for ruling were much more favorable here than with the children, who were unpredictable, capricious gods. The new goddess was a good goddess. The dog was, like the psychiatrist Behude, of the opinion that Emilia was a good person. Emilia will not disappoint the dog. Already she is determined to take him home with her. "You stay with your auntie," she said. "Yeah, boy, good fellow, I know, we're together for good."

In the Italian's stand-up bar, Richard was leaning over the counter. Where had he gotten to? He had just walked in there. The door had stood open. He had thought the place was a drugstore. He had thought, 'maybe there's a girl there, it would be nice if, on my first evening in Germany, I had a German girl.' Now he found himself on a battlefield. Bottles, glasses, and corkscrews became bastions and advancing tanks, cigarette packs and matchboxes were air squadrons. The Italian proprietor of the stand-up bar was a furious strategist. He showed the young American flier how Europe had to be defended. From the successful defense, he moved on to the attack and wiped out the East. "Just take a couple of bombs," he shouted. "Take a couple of bombs and victory is yours!" Richard was drinking vermouth. He was surprised that the vermouth tasted bitter. It tasted like bitter sugar water. 'Maybe the guy's right,' thought Richard, 'it's so simple, a couple of bombs, maybe he's right, why hasn't Truman thought of that? a couple of bombs, why is the Pentagon doing things differently?' But then Richard remembered something; he remembered something from history class or from the newspapers he had read or from the speeches he had heard. He said: "But Hitler already did that, the Japanese already did that: just attack, just attack overnight—" — "Hitler was right," said the Italian. "Hitler was a great man!" — "No," said Richard, "he was a detestable man." Richard grew pale, because he was embarrassed to be arguing and because he was annoyed. He hadn't come here to argue. He couldn't argue; he didn't know what was going on here. Maybe people here saw things completely differently. But he hadn't come here to deny his American principles, either, the principles he was so proud of. "I'm not here to do what Hitler did," he said. "We will never do what Hitler did." — "You'll have

161

to," said the Italian. Furious, he swept the bastions, the tanks, and the air squadrons into a pile. Richard broke off the conversation. "I've got to go to the Bräuhaus," he said. He thought, 'you lose your footing completely here.'

The warrior who hadn't wanted to be a warrior, the killer who hadn't wanted to kill, the smitten man who had dreamed of a more leisurely death, he lay on the hard bed in the Heiliggeist Hospital, he lay in a whitewashed room, in a monk's cell, he lay beneath a cross with the crucified Christ on it, a candle burned at his head, a priest knelt beside him, behind the priest knelt a woman with a much sterner face than the man of God, representative of a merciless religion that regarded even dying as a sin, so hardened was her heart, a little girl stood before him and stared at him, and more and more police officers crowded into the narrow room like stage extras. In the street the police sirens wailed. The quarter was being searched. The German police and the American military police were searching for the great Odysseus. The angel of death had long since laid his hand on Josef. What did the sirens matter to him? What did he care about the police of two nations and two continents? When Josef was working, he had avoided the police. The police never brought anything good. They brought induction notices or late payment warnings. It was best if nobody asked for Josef. If someone called for him, they wanted something from him; they always wanted something unpleasant from him. Now his dying was causing a commotion throughout the city. The old porter hadn't wanted that. He came to again. He said: "It was the traveler." He didn't say it as an accusation. He was glad that it had been the traveler. The debt was repaid. The priest pronounced the absolution. Emmi crossed herself and murmured her forgive-us-our-sins. She was a grim little prayer wheel. Hillegonda reflected: there was an old man; he looked kindly; he was dead; death looked kindly; death wasn't fearsome at all; it was kindly and quiet; but

Emmi thought the old man had died in sin and sins had to be forgiven him; Emmi didn't seem at all sure that the old man would be forgiven his sins; God had not yet determined to forgive them; at best he would pardon them out of mercy; God was very stern; there was no right before God; there was nothing you could say on your behalf, everything was a sin; but if everything was a sin, then it didn't make any difference what you did; when Hillegonda was bad, then that was a sin, but when she was good, then it was still a sin; and why had the man lived to be so old if he was a sinner; why hadn't God already punished him before, if he was a sinner; and why did the old man look so kindly? so you could hide the fact that you were a sinner; you couldn't tell by looking who anyone was; you couldn't trust anyone. And again mistrust stirred within Hillegonda against Emmi: could you trust Emmi, pious praying Emmi, was not her piety a mask hiding the devil? If only Hillegonda had been able to talk with her father about it, but her father was so dumb, he said there were no devils, maybe he thought there wasn't a God, either: oh how little he knew Emmi—the devil existed. You were always at his mercy. The many policemen: now were they God's policeman or the devil's policemen? They came for the old man in order to punish him; God wanted to punish him and the devil wanted to punish him. It was the same thing in the end. There was no way out for the dead old man. He couldn't hide. He couldn't defend himself. He couldn't run away any more. Hillegonda felt sorry for the old man. It wasn't his fault at all. Hillegonda stepped up to the dead Josef and kissed his hand. She kissed the hand that had carried so many suitcases, a shriveled hand with furrows filled with dirt, filled with filth, filled with war and life. The priest asked: "You're his grand-daughter?" Hillegonda burst into tears. She buried her head in the priest's cassock and sobbed bitterly. Emmi broke off her prayer and said peevishly: "She is the child of actors, Father. Lying, deception, and comedy are in her blood. Punish the child, save her soul!" But before the alarmed priest, who stopped stroking Hillegonda's head,

163

could answer the nursemaid, a voice came from beneath Josef's hospital bed and bier. Odysseus's music case, put out of the way under the bed and silent for a while, was speaking again. This time it spoke with an English voice, soft, quiet, lilting, a lovely, a learned, a somewhat affected Oxford voice, the voice of a philologist, and it called attention to Edwin's importance and to his lecture in the Amerika-Haus. The voice depicted it as a stroke of luck for Germany that Mr. Edwin, a crusader of the spirit, had come to the city to testify on behalf of spirit, tradition, of the immortality of spirit, of the old Europe, which, the voice quoted Jakob Burckhardt, had been shaken in its social and spiritual order ever since the days of the French Revolution and was in a state of constant twitching and trembling. Was Edwin come to banish the shaking, to order the disorder and, in the name of tradition, to be sure, to set up new tablets of a new law? The priest, who was thinking back over Josef's life, who was moved by the unrest the old porter's death had brought about in the parish, and who was strangely touched by the dour piety of the nursemaid, by her stone face utterly devoid of warmth, of joy, and stirred by the sobbing of the little girl, whose tears fell onto the lap of the priest's robe, the cleric listened with half an ear to the English voice, the voice from the music case under the dead man's bed, and he had the feeling that the voice was speaking of a false prophet.

Schnakenbach, the sleeper, the dismissed trade school teacher, the insufficiently learned Einstein, had spent the afternoon in the reading room of the American Library. He had dragged himself half asleep to the Amerika-Haus and had, as if watched over by a guardian angel, once more escaped the streetcars, the automobiles, and the cyclists. In the reading room of the library, he had stacked up all the available chemical and pharmacological publications around him. He wanted to read up on the latest developments in American research; he wanted to see how far they had advanced in

164

great America in producing sleep-inhibiting substances. In America there seemed to be a lot of narcoleptics. The Americans were deeply absorbed in the problem of staying awake. Schnakenbach learned from them. He took notes. He wrote and sketched in a minuscule hand formulas and structures; he calculated; he paid attention to the levels of the molecules; he bore in mind that there were compounds that rotated to the right and ones that rotated to the left, and that he had to find out whether his life, this part of life in general, this self-aware conglomeration of chemical forces that was he, Schnakenbach, for a while, until he was put back into the big retort, rotated to the left or to the right. While pondering this question, he was overcome by his enemy, his affliction, sleep. They knew Schnakenbach in the reading room. They didn't disturb his sleep; they did not wrest him from the clutches of his enemy. The librarian had a strange clientele. The reading room exercised an enormous attraction on the homeless, those who came in to get warm, oddballs, and nature people. The nature people came in barefoot, wrapped in handwoven linen, with long hair and unruly beard. They asked for works on witches and evil eyes, cookbooks for vegetarian dishes, pamphlets on life after death and on the practices of Indian fakirs, or they immersed themselves in the latest publications on astrophysics. They were cosmological spirits and munched on roots and nuts. The librarian said: "I keep expecting one to wash his feet here; but they never wash." The American Library was a splendid institution. Use of it was completely free of charge. The library was open to one and all, it was almost Washington's Inn, almost the place that the Negro and American citizen Washington Price was going to open in Paris, the place in which nobody is unwelcome.

Schnakenbach was asleep. While he slept, the building's large lecture hall filled up. Many people came to hear Edwin speak. Students came, young workers came, a couple of artists came

165

wearing full beards for existential reasons and did not take off their berets, there came the philosophy class from the Catholic seminary, peasant faces that tended to spirituality, sternness, or simplicity, there came two streetcar conductors, a mayor, and a court official among whose clients were literary people, which was how he had got sidetracked into this, and there also came very many well-dressed and well-fed people. Edwin's lecture was a social event. The well-dressed people had jobs in radio or in film, or they worked in the advertising business, those who weren't fortunate enough to be a representative of the people, a high ministry official, even a minister himself, or an occupation officer and consular agent. They all were interested in Europe's spirit. The merchants of the city seemed to be less interested in the spirit of Europe; they had sent no one to represent them. But the fashion designers had shown up, effeminate, fragrant gentlemen who had brought along their show models, well-built girls whom one could leave in their hands without a second thought. Behude had sat down by the priests. It was the gesture of a colleague. He thought, 'we can lend psychiatric and spiritual support whenever it's needed, nothing can happen.' Messalina and Alexander were holding court. They stood near the podium and were illuminated by the flashbulbs of the press photographers. Jack was with them. He had on a pair of rumpled American officer's summer uniform pants and a brightly striped sweater. His hair was unkempt and he looked as if he had just now, alarmed by a ringing bell, jumped out of bed. Beside him, Hänschen, his friend, a flaxen blond, slightly made-up sixteen-year-old in a confirmation day suit, was on his best behavior. He looked with cold, waterypale eyes over at the fashion designers and their models, Hänschen, little Jack, Jack be nimble, he was the lucky Hans of the fairy tale: he knew where to get what. Now Alfredo, the sculptress, appeared too. Her strained, tired, disappointed face, the angular face of a cat from the pyramid inscriptions, was reddened, as if she had been slapping herself to summon up both courage and fresh color for the evening. Compared with Messalina, Alfredo looked so delicate and small that you wished Messalina might pick Alfredo up in her arms so she could see everything. Alexander was being congratulated. A couple of pompous asses and a couple of boot-lickers congratulated him. They hoped to get onto the flashlit photos and into the newspapers: ALEXANDER CONVERSING WITH PIPPIN THE SHORT, FEDERAL GOVERNMENT CONSIDERS KULTUR-PFENNIG, ENDOWS ACADEMY. They talked about the ARCHDUKE AMOURS, BETTER FILMS IN THE NEW GERMANY, THE SCRIPT MAKES THE DIFFERENCE, POETS TO THE FILM FRONT. "It's supposed to be such a wonderful film," gushed a lady whose husband edited the Gerichtskurier, VAMPIRE IN WOMAN'S CLOTHING, and in so doing, earned enough money to let his wife buy her clothes from the effeminate fashion designers. "It's junk," said Alexander. "How clever you always are," warbled the lady. 'Of course,' she thought, 'of course it's junk, but why does he say it so loud? is it supposed to be something other than junk? then it is sure to be serious and boring junk,' NEO-REALISM NO LONGER IN DEMAND. The teachers from Massachusetts sat in the front row. They had their note pads in their hands. They took the people standing in the flashes of light to be great authorities on the spirit of Europe. They had had the good fortune not to see any of Alexander's films. "It's a very interesting evening," said Miss Wescott. "A circus," said Miss Burnett. They both kept an eye on the broad entrance doorway to see whether Kay would finally arrive. They were both very concerned about Kay. Edwin was led in through a small, separate door and up to the podium. The photographers knelt down like sharpshooters and fired off their flashes. Edwin bowed. His eyes were closed. He was putting off the moment when he would have to look out into his audience. He was a little dizzy. He believed he wouldn't be able to speak a word, not even make a sound. He was sweating. He was sweating with fright, but he was also sweating with happiness. So many people had come to hear him! His name had found acceptance in the world. He didn't want to overrate that. But the people came to hear his words. Edwin had devoted his life to strivings of the spirit, and now he could pass that spirit on: disciples received him in every city, the spirit would not die. Edwin laid his manuscript on the lectern. He adjusted the lamp. He cleared his throat. But once more the broad door was opened, and Philipp and Kay ran down the stairs that led into the hall. Philipp had run into Kay outside the door. The usher hadn't wanted to let them in, but Philipp had whisked out his press card from the Neues Blatt like a charm and the attendant had let them through. Philipp and Kay sat down on a couple of folding chairs off the auditorium that are reserved at theater performances for the fireman and the policeman. At Edwin's lecture, there was no fireman and no policeman. Miss Wescott poked Miss Burnett: "Do you see that?" she whispered. "It's that German poet, I don't know his name," said Miss Burnett. "She's been running around with him." Miss Wescott was outraged. "As long as that's all she's done," said Miss Burnett caustically. "It's just awful," gasped Miss Wescott. She was about to jump up and go to Kay; she had the feeling that somebody should call the police. But Edwin cleared his throat again, and silence settled over the hall. Edwin wanted to begin with Greek and Latin antiquity, he wanted to mention Christianity, the connection of biblical tradition with classicism, he wanted to speak of the Renaissance and direct both praise and criticism at the French rationalism of the eighteenth century, but unfortunately, instead of words, only noise reached his listeners, a gurgling and crackling and rasping like the sounds of county fair noisemakers. Edwin, at the lectern, didn't notice at first that the hall's loudspeaker system was malfunctioning. He sensed disquiet in the room and a climate unfavorable to spiritual concentration. He spoke a few words more about the importance of the peninsula that extends from the Eurasian continent, when he was interrupted by foot shuffling and shouts to speak louder and more clearly. Edwin felt like a tightrope walker who realizes halfway

168

across the rope that he can go neither forward nor backward. What did the people want? Had they come to make fun of him? He fell silent and held tight to the lectern. It was a rebellion. Technology was rebelling against spirit, technology, that impudent, degenerate, prank-loving, nonchalant offspring of the spirit. A couple of eager helpers leapt forward to adjust the microphones. But the problem was in the building's loudspeaker system. 'I'm helpless,' thought Edwin, 'we're helpless, I counted on this stupid and evil speech funnel, could I have come and stood before them without this invention that now is making me ridiculous? no, I wouldn't have dared, we're no longer people, not whole people, never could I have spoken, like Demosthenes, directly to them, I need tin and wire that press my voice and my thoughts as if through a sieve.' Messalina asked: "Do you see Philipp" — "Yes," said Alexander, "I've got to talk to him about that manuscript. He still won't have any ideas." — "Hogwash," said Messalina, "he never writes anything anyway. But the girl. The cute one. An American. He's seducing her. What do you say now?" — "Nothing," said Alexander. He yawned. He would fall asleep. Let Philipp seduce whomever he felt like. 'He must be good and potent,' thought Alexander. "Idiot," whispered Messalina. The crackling in the building's loudspeaker system could also be heard in the reading room, and it had wakened Schnakenbach. He, too, had wanted to go to Edwin's lecture, he, too, was interested in Europe's spirit. He saw that it was already late and that the lecture had already begun. He staggered to his feet and tottered into the hall. Somebody or other thought Schnakenbach was the custodian, who had probably been asleep in the basement, and handed him the microphone by mistake. Schnakenbach suddenly saw himself in front of an audience; he believed, dazed with sleep as he was, that he was in front of the class he had taught before he had had to give up his position as trade school teacher, and so he shouted into the microphone the great worry that filled him: "Don't sleep! Wake up! It's time!"

169

It was time. Heinz was watching the square between the Bräuhaus and the Negro soldiers' club. There were a lot of police on the square; there were far too many police on the square. The military police guard in front of the club had been reinforced. The military policemen were especially tall, especially well built Negroes. They looked like Caesar's Nubian legionnaires. Heinz still didn't know how he should pull it off. The best thing would be to take the dollars and run into the ruins. The American boy wouldn't find him in the ruins. 'But what if he wants to see the dog? of course he'll want to see the dog before he forks over the cash.' It was dumb that the dog had run away. That could jeopardize the whole deal. But the joke would be on Heinz if he backed out of the deal now, just because the dog had split. Heinz had hidden himself well. He was standing in the entrance to the Broadway Bar. The bar was closed. The entrance was dark. The owner of the bar had chosen to flee to the real Broadway. In the New World there was security. In the Old World you might die. In the New World you might die, too, but you died in greater security. The owner of the Broadway Bar had left fears, debts, darkness, and naked girls behind him in Europe. He had also left graves behind, a big grave, in which his slain relatives lay. The pictures of the naked girls were pasted up in the darkness of the entryway, forgotten and abandoned on the dirty wall. The girls smiled mischievously and held little veils in front of their private parts. "Ami whores" — an outraged citizen had written that. The girls smiled, they stayed mischievous, mischievously they held the little veils in front. A nationalist had painted "Germany awaken" on the wall. The girls smiled. Heinz pissed against the wall. Susanne walked past the dark entrance to the bar. She thought, 'these pigs piss everywhere.' Susanne walked up to the Negro soldiers' club. The black military police checked Susanne's identification card. They held the card in their gleamingly white gloved hands. The card was in order. A patrol jeep of the white military police pulled up in front of the club. The white police shouted a

170

message to their black companions. The white police didn't look as elegant as the black ones. Next to the black policemen, they looked shabby. Susanne disappeared through the door of the club. One of the white policemen thought, 'those niggers have the prettiest girls.'

In the club a German band was playing. The club was poor. An American band had been too expensive. Now a German band was playing, and the German band was pretty good, too. It was Obermusikmeister Behrend's band. The band played all the jazz pieces, and once in a while they played the Hohenfriedberger March or the Spanish Waltz by Waldteufel. The black soldiers liked the march a lot. They liked Waldteufel less. Kapellmeister Behrend was content. He enjoyed playing in the American army's club houses. He felt that he was well paid. He was happy. Vlasta made him happy. He looked over at Vlasta, who sat at a small table next to the band. Vlasta was bent over her sewing. Once in a while she looked up, and Vlasta and Herr Behrend smiled at each other. They had a secret: they had gone against the world and succeeded; they had, each of them, gone against his own surroundings and its views, and they had burst the circle of prejudice that tried to pen them in. The Obermusikmeister in the German Wehrmacht had met and loved the little Czech girl in the Protectorate of Bohemia-Moravia. Lots of men slept with girls. But they despised the girls they slept with. Only a few loved the girl they slept with. The Obermusikmeister loved Vlasta. At first he had resisted this love. He had thought, 'what do I want with this Czech girl?' But then he had loved her, and love had transformed him. It had transformed not just him, it had transformed the girl, too; the girl, too, had become a new person. When they began hunting the German Wehrmacht in Prague like deer in season, Vlasta had hidden Herr Behrend in her trunk, and later she fled with him out of Czechoslovakia. Vlasta had left everything behind; she had even left her fatherland behind;

and Herr Behrend had left much behind; he had left behind the whole of his life thus far: they both felt released, they were free, they were happy. Before, they wouldn't have believed it was possible to be so free and so happy. The band played Dixieland. Under the Musikmeister's baton, it played one of the first jazz compositions, German and romantic in the manner of Der Freischütz.

Susanne found the band dull. The palefaced idiots were keeping too leisurely a tempo. The band was not playing what Susanne called dizzy music. She wanted to whirl, she wanted frenzy; she wanted to let herself go in whirling and frenzy. It was dumb that all Negroes looked alike. Who could tell them apart? You could end up leaving with the wrong one. Susanne had on a dress of striped silk. She wore it like a shirt over bare skin. She could have had any man. Every man in the hall would have gone off with her. Susanne was looking for Odysseus. She had stolen money from him, but since she was Circe and the Sirens and maybe Nausicaa, too, she had to go back to him and couldn't leave him in peace. She had stolen his money, but she would not betray him. She would never betray him; she would never tell that he had killed Josef. She didn't know whether Odysseus had killed Josef with the stone, but she thought so. Susanne wasn't sorry that Josef had died, 'we all have to die.' But she did regret that Odysseus hadn't killed someone else. He should have killed Alexander or Messalina. But whomever he had killed: Susanne had to stick with him, 'we have to stick together against the pigs.' Susanne hated the world, at whose hands she felt rejected and abused. Susanne loved anyone who turned against this hateful world, who struck a hole in its cold, inhuman order. Susanne was loyal. She was a dependable companion. You could depend on Susanne. No need to worry about the police.

Heinz pressed himself against the wall with the naked girls. A German policeman sauntered past the entrance of the bar. The German and the American police were like wasps stirred up out of their nest tonight. A Negro had done in a taxi driver or a porter. Heinz wasn't sure exactly. In the old part of town they were talking about it. Some thought it had been a taxi driver, the others said a porter. 'But a porter doesn't have any money,' thought Heinz. He peered out of the corridor and saw Washington's horizonblue sedan pull up to the Negro club. Washington and Carla got out. Heinz was surprised. Washington and Carla hadn't been in the club for a long time. Carla hadn't wanted to go any more. She had refused to be in the same place with the tarts who frequented the club. If Washington and Carla were going to the club again, something must have happened. Heinz didn't know what could have happened, but it must have been significant. It troubled him. Did the couple want to go to America? Should he go along? Should he not go along? Did he even want to go? He didn't know. Right now he wanted most of all to go home, get in bed, and think about whether he should go to America. Maybe he would have sat in bed and cried. And maybe he would have just read Old Shatterhand and eaten chocolate. Could you trust Karl May? Washington said the only Indians around any more were in Hollywood. Should he go home? Should he go to bed? Should he think about all these problems? Then the car that looked so much like an airplane drove into the square. The parking attendant waved the car into a space. Christopher and Ezra got out. Ezra looked around. So he had come. He wanted to make a deal. Heinz couldn't back out now. He couldn't go home to bed now. It would have been cowardly to back out of the deal now. Christopher walked into the Bräuhaus. Ezra walked slowly behind Christopher. He kept looking around. Heinz thought, 'shall I give him a sign?' But he reflected, 'no, it's still too early, his father, the old Ami, has to sit down to his beer first.'

'What a young fellow he is, what a young Ami,' thought the Fräulein, 'it's his first night in Germany, and we've met already.' The Fräulein was pretty. She had dark curls and white teeth. The

173

Fräulein had let Richard strike up a conversation with her on the main avenue. She had seen that Richard felt like striking up a conversation with a girl and that he was too shy to do it. The Fräulein had made it easy for Richard. The Fräulein had placed herself right in his way. Richard noticed that she was making it easy for him. He liked her, but he thought, 'what if she's sick?' They had warned him in America. In America, they warned the soldiers going abroad about the Fräuleins. But he thought, 'well, I don't want anything from her anyway, and besides, maybe she isn't sick at all.' She wasn't sick. She wasn't a streetwalker either. Richard had been lucky. The Fräulein sold socks in the department store by the station. The department store earned money on the socks. The Fräulein earned little. That little bit she turned over to the family. But she didn't feel like sitting home nights, listening to the radio music that her father determined: little-glowworm-glimmer-glimmer, the eternal deadly boring request hour, the most tenacious legacy of the Pan-German Empire. Her father read, while the glowworm glimmered, the paper. He said: "In Hitler's day, it was different! There was zip in it." The mother nodded. She thought about the old, burnt-out apartment; there had been zip there; there had been zip in the flames. She thought about her constantly guarded and then burned-up dowry. She could not forget the linen chest of the dowry, but she dared not contradict the father: the father was a doorman at the Vereinsbank, a respected man. After the socks and after the glowworm music, the Fräulein was looking for some merriment. The Fräulein wanted to live. She wanted her own life. She did not want to repeat her parents' life. Her parents' life was not worth emulating. Her parents had failed. They were poor. They were unmerry, unhappy, sullen. They sat sullenly in a dismal room with dismally cheerful music. The Fräulein wanted a different life, a different joy, if it was to be, a different pain. The Fräulein preferred the American boys to the German boys. The American boys didn't remind her of her dismal home. They didn't

174

remind the Fräulein of everything she knew all too well: the endless restrictions, the endless struggle to make ends meet, the cramped quarters, the racist resentfulness, the national malaise, the moral discomfort. Around the American boys there was fresh air, the air of the wide world; the enchantment of the distance from which they came made them more attractive. The American boys were friendly, childlike, and uncomplicated. They weren't as burdened with fate, fear, doubts, past, and hopelessness as the German boys. And the Fräulein also knew how much a clerk in a department store earns; she knew the privations he suffered to be able to buy himself a suit, a suit in mass-produced bad taste, in which he looked unhappy. Someday the Fräulein would marry an overworked, disillusioned, badly dressed man. The Fräulein wanted to forget that today. She would have liked to go dancing. But Richard wanted to go to the Bräuhaus. The Bräuhaus was fun, too. So they'd go to the Bräuhaus. But in the Bräuhaus they were playing the glowworm music, too.

The halls were overflowing. The community of people and peoples, the much lauded, often sung about Gemütlichkeit of the Bräuhaus was raging. From large kegs flowed and foamed the beer; it flowed and foamed in an uninterrupted stream; the tappers never turned the spigots off; they held the liter steins under the flow, snatched them back out of the beer, and no sooner did they cut them off from the liquid than they were holding the next stein under the stream. Not a drop was lost. The waitresses lugged eight, ten, a dozen steins to the tables. The festival of the god Gambrinus was being celebrated. They clinked steins, they drank up, they set steins back down on the table, they waited for a refill. The Oberländer band was playing. They were old gentlemen in short leather pants that showed their hairy, reddened knees. The band played glowworm, it played once-a-boy-a-rose-did-see, and everyone in the hall sang along, they linked arms, they stood up, they got up

175

on the beer benches, they raised their steins and bellowed, each syllable drawn out long and with feeling, rose-upon-the-hill-ill-side. They sat down again. They drank again. Fathers drank, mothers drank, little children drank; old men stood around the washtub and looked for beer dregs left in the steins, which they thirstily, greedily swallowed. People were talking about the taxi driver murder. It was Josef's death they were talking about; but Rumor had turned the porter into a taxi driver. A porter seemed to Rumor too poor a victim for a murder. The general mood was not favorable toward the Americans. People grumbled, people griped; people had things to complain about. Beer raises national consciousness in Germany. In other lands wine, in some maybe whiskey, stimulates national pride. In Germany, beer is the stuff that arouses the love of fatherland: a dull, unilluminating intoxication. The individual members of the occupation force who had wandered into the witches' cauldron that was the Bräuhaus met with an amiable, neighborly reception. Many Americans loved the Bräuhaus. They found it splendid and gemütlich. They found it even more splendid and more gemütlich than anything they had read or heard about it. The Oberländer band played the Badenweiler March, the dead Führer's favorite march. You just needed to buy the band a round of beer, and they played the march that accompanied Hitler's entrance into the National Socialist meeting halls. The march was the music of recent and fateful history. The hall rose from the benches like a single swelling breast of enthusiasm. Those weren't Nazis standing up there. They were beer drinkers. The mood alone had made everyone get up. It was all just fun! Why be so serious? why think of things past, buried, forgotten? The Americans, too, were swept along with the general mood. The Americans, too, stood up. The Americans, too, hummed the Führer's march, pounded out the beat with feet and fists. American soldiers and men who had survived being German soldiers embraced. It was a warm, purely human brotherhood, without political intentions or diplomatic motives.

176

FRATERNIZATION PROHIBITED FRATERNIZATION PERMITTED GOOD
NEIGHBOR WEEK Christopher found it wonderful. He thought, 'why
is Henriette so against it? why can't she forget? she should see this
here, it's wonderful, these are terrific people. Ezra watched the
band, he watched the people. His forehead was even more
wrinkled; now it was really narrow, really small. He could have
screamed! He was in a deep, dark forest. Every man here was a tree.
Every tree was an oak. And every oak was a giant, the evil giant of
the fairy tale, a giant with a club. Ezra sensed that he wouldn't be
able to stand being in this forest very long. He wouldn't be able to
keep down his fear much longer. If the boy with the dog didn't come
soon, Ezra would scream. He would scream and run away. Frau
Behrend squeezed down the rows. She was looking for Richard, her
young American relative, the son of the package sender, you never
knew, a bad time might come again. CONFLICT ESCALATES relatives
had to stick together. How dumb of the boy to have her come to the
Bräuhaus! At nearly every table there was an American. They sat
there like our soldiers, almost like the soldiers of the Wehrmacht;
only their posture was worse, they sat there comfortably and not
smartly. 'Too much freedom and they go to seed,' thought Frau
Behrend. She went up to young Americans: "Is that you, Richard?
I'm your Aunt Behrend!" She met with incomprehension or laughter. Some called out: "have a seat, lady," and slid their beer steins
over to her. One fat fellow, nearly a keg himself, smacked her on the
bottom. 'This is what they call soldiers, it was only their trucks and
their planes that won the war.' Frau Behrend hurried on. She had to
find Richard! Richard couldn't be allowed to report back home
what the venomous grocery shopkeeper had told him. Frau Behrend
had to find Richard. She saw him sitting with a girl, a blackcurled,
very cute little strumpet. The two of them were drinking from the
same stein. The girl's left hand lay on the young man's right. Frau
Behrend thought, 'is that him? that could be him, he's the right
age, but that can't be him, that couldn't possibly be him, he

177

wouldn't make an appointment with his aunt and then bring his strumpet along.' Richard noticed that the woman was watching him. He was alarmed. He thought, 'that must be her, the woman with the fish face is the aunt with the Negro daughter, I'm not curious, I don't want to force myself on anybody.' He turned to his girl, he took the Fräulein in his arms and kissed her. The Fräulein thought, 'I have to watch out, he's not as shy as I thought, I was afraid he wouldn't kiss me until we said goodnight.' The Fräulein's lips tasted of beer. Richard's lips tasted of beer, too. The beer was very good. 'It's not him,' thought Frau Behrend, 'he would never behave like that, even if he did grow up in America, he would never behave like that.' She sat down on a bench and hesitantly ordered a beer. The beer was an unnecessary expenditure. Frau Behrend didn't care for beer. But she was thirsty, and she was also too exhausted to take on the waitress, to take on the whole hall and not order anything.

Carla and Washington had gone to the Negro club to celebrate the future, the future in which nobody is unwelcome any more. On this evening, they believed in the future. They believed that they would experience that future, the future in which nobody, no matter who he was or how he lived, would be unwelcome. Carla had an ear for music. Even before she saw him, she had recognized, in his way of playing jazz, her father, the old Freischütz conductor. Just yesterday, Carla would have been embarrassed to encounter the Musikmeister in a Negro club, and she would have been mortified to have him see her there with Washington. Now the meeting touched her differently. During a break in the music, Carla said hello to her father. Herr Behrend was glad to see Carla. He was a little embarrassed, but he fought back the embarrassment and introduced Carla to Vlasta. Vlasta was embarrassed, too. All three of them were embarrassed. But they had no bad thoughts about each other. "That's my boyfriend sitting there," Carla said. She pointed to

178

Washington. "We're going to Paris," she said. The Musikmeister had almost gone to Paris once. In the war, he was supposed to be transferred to Paris. But he got transferred to Prague. Herr Behrend wondered, 'is it right for Carla to love a Negro?' He didn't dare answer the question. The Negro must have been a good person if Carla was living with him. For an instant, the poison of doubt stirred in all of them. They thought, 'we associate with each other because we've all come down so far.' But because they felt merry this evening they had the strength to push aside their doubts, to kill those nagging feelings. They remained friendly and loved each other. Herr Behrend said: "Now you'll be amazed. You'll see, your father can play hot, too, real hot jazz." He stepped back onto the stage. Carla smiled. Vlasta smiled, too. Poor father. He imagined he could play real jazz. The blacks were the only ones who could play real jazz. Herr Behrend's band started to rattle the cymbals and beat the drums. Then the trumpets joined in. It was loud and it was beautiful, too. Susanne had found Odysseus. He had risked coming to the club. On account of her, he had risked coming out of his hiding place, past the police and into the club, Susanne had known that Odysseus would come; they had arranged it with a word, with a shout, and he had come. Susanne, who was Circe and the Sirens and maybe Nausicaa, too, held Odysseus in her embrace. To the Musikmeister's hot tune they glided like a single body across the dance floor, like a fourfooted, writhing snake. They both were excited. Everything they had experienced today had excited them. Odysseus had had to flee, Odysseus had had to hide, they had not caught him, the great, crafty Odysseus had evaded the bloodhounds, he had beguiled Susanne Circe the Sirens, or they had beguiled him, and maybe he had conquered Nausicaa. If that wasn't exciting . . . It was exciting. It excited them both. Everybody watched the snake with four legs, the so lithely writhing snake, in admiration. Never would they let go this embrace. The snake had four legs and two heads, one white and one black face, but never

179

would the heads turn against one another, never the tongues loose
venom upon the other: they would never betray each other, the
snake was a single being against the world.

He was not Red Snake, he was Deerslayer. The redhaired American boy was Red Snake. Deerslayer was stalking Red Snake. Heinz
had climbed into the ruins of an office building. From the stump of
the blasted-out wall, he could look into the Bräuhaus hall. The
prairie swayed. Herds of buffalo moved through the grass. The light
of the hall chandeliers, lamps suspended from huge wagon wheels,
diffused through the vapors of people and beer as if through a fog.
Heinz couldn't make out anybody. Deerslayer had to leave the blue
mountains. He would have to steal his way across the prairie. He
ducked under tables and benches. There he came across an enemy
he had not expected to find here. Astonishingly, Frau Behrend was
sitting in the Bräuhaus and drinking beer. Heinz didn't like his
grandmother. Frau Behrend wanted to put Heinz in a reform school.
Frau Behrend was a dangerous woman. What was she doing in the
Bräuhaus? Was she there every evening? Or was she just there today,
to spy on Heinz? Did she suspect that he was on the warpath? Heinz
couldn't let himself be seen. But he was tempted to play a trick on
Frau Behrend. It was a test of courage. He couldn't back out of it.
The band was playing Mister-fox-you-stole-the-fat-goose. The hall
was on its feet again. Everyone had linked arms and was singing the
song. Frau Behrend's arms were taken by two fat, bald businessmen,
and she sang better-give-it-back. Heinz wanted to pour out Frau
Behrend's beer. He crowded in behind Frau Behrend and the fat,
bald businessmen. But once he was standing right behind Frau
Behrend, Heinz was afraid to take the stein and pour the beer out.
He just took the full glass of schnapps standing next to the stein and
poured the schnapps into the beer. Then he slipped away. Once
again he was Deerslayer, looking for Red Snake.

Ezra was sweating. He was shaking. He thought he was going to suffocate. His father, too, had become a giant, one of the German giants in the enchanted German forest. Christopher stood beside the others and sang if-you-don't-I'll-get-my-gun-and-shoot-you-in-your-tracks. He didn't know the words, he couldn't pronounce them, but he tried to sing them, and from time to time his German neighbor helped him, poked him and sang the words, separating the syllables distinctly and instructively shoot-you-in-your-tracks, and Christopher nodded and laughed and raised his beer stein to his neighbor, and then Christopher and his neighbor ordered wurst and radishes, and together they ate wurst and radishes, and Christopher had no idea that his child was afraid. Deerslayer had found them. He caught Red Snake's eye and signaled to him. This was it. Ezra couldn't avoid the fight. The German boy was the opponent chosen for him by the giants of the forest. Against him he had to measure himself. Against him he had to fight. If he defeated the German boy, he had defeated the forest. "I'm going to the car," said Ezra. Christopher said: "What do you want with the car? Stay here." — "I'd rather sit in the car," said Ezra. "You come soon, too. We've got to drive home. We've got to drive home really quick." Christopher thought, 'Ezra is right, he doesn't like it, this is no place for a boy, he's still too little. I'll drink up my beer and then I'll drive him to the hotel, after all, I can come back if I want to go on drinking beer, once Ezra is asleep I can come back and go on drinking beer.' He liked it. He liked the Bräuhaus a lot. He liked thinking that he would come back and go on drinking beer.

Rumor reached Frau Behrend. A Negro had committed murder, Negroes were criminals, the police sirens shrieked, they were looking for the Negro. "It's scandalous," said Frau Behrend. "They're like wild animals. They're like wild, vicious animals. You can tell just by looking at them. Boy, I could tell you a story or two." The businessman to her left secretly suspected her of drinking his schnapps. He thought, 'well will you look at that, the old lady, perky as you please, drinks my schnapps behind my back and acts as if nothing happened.' But he found that Frau Behrend had a respectable attitude. So what if she did drink the schnapps, she had a respectable attitude, he would order her another one. Frau Behrend thought, 'I couldn't tell them, I couldn't get the words out of my mouth, but if I could—.' She pictured the businessmen's astonishment and their outrage. She thought, 'the father with a foreign strumpet and the daughter with a Negro.' And the American nephew? The nephew had sneaked off. He had made a fool of her. He hadn't shown up in the Bräuhaus. Frau Behrend grimly took a long drink from her stein. You never knew with these foreigners. With these stoneware steins you couldn't see how much you had left. Could she really have finished her beer already? It was true; the hall, the music, the people, the singing, the excitement, the annoyance, the crimes of the Negroes—everything made you thirsty. The other businessman, too, thought Frau Behrend's attitude was good. Her stein was empty. He would treat her to another beer. The woman still looked pretty good. But above all, she had the right attitude. That was the main thing. What were the Negroes doing here? It was a disgrace! The businessmen had no black customers.

"Where is the dog?" asked Ezra, "I want to see it." Red Snake wanted to see the dog. Deerslayer had been afraid of that. The whole thing could be ruined because the damned dog split. Heinz had to stall for time. He said: "Come with me into this building. Then I will show you the dog." The children faced each other stiffly and with dignity. They spoke with each other as if they had learned the sentences out of a travel phrase book for refined people. Heinz led Ezra into the destroyed office building. He climbed onto the stump of wall. Ezra followed him. He wasn't surprised that Heinz was leading him into a ruin. Ezra, too, wanted to stall for time. He, too, still had no definite plan. He was worried whether Christopher would come to the car in time. He had to come to the car in time and drive off quickly. Everything depended on Christopher driving off in time. They sat on the stump of wall and looked into the hall of the Bräuhaus. For a while, they found each other quite pleasant. 'We could make a slingshot and shoot rocks in the window, rocks into the prairie, rocks at the buffalo,' thought Heinz. 'From out here the giants don't look so frightening,' thought Ezra. 'There's no point in dragging it out any longer,' thought Heinz. He was insane with fear. He shouldn't have gotten himself into this to begin with. But now that he had gotten himself into it, he had to go through with it. He asked: "Do you have the ten dollars with you?" Ezra nodded. He thought, 'now here goes, I've got to win.' He said: "If I show you the money, then will you call the dog?" Heinz nodded. He edged a little toward the edge of the wall. From there he could jump down easily. Once he had grabbed the money, he could jump down. He could jump onto a lower wall and then run through the ruins to Bäckergasse. The American boy would not follow him. He would fall down in the ruins. He would lose time and never be able to catch him on Bäckergasse. Ezra said: "Once you've called him, can I take the dog into the Bräuhaus and show him to my father?" He thought, 'once I have the dog, we've got to leave, Christopher will have to drive off then.' Heinz said: "First you have to give me the ten dollars." He thought, 'you show whatever you want, I'll show you, but good.' Ezra said: "First my father has to see the dog." — "You don't even have the money," screamed Heinz. "I have the money, but I can only give it to you when my father has seen the dog." — 'Sly dog,' thought Heinz. This guy was clever. Red Snake was cleverer than Heinz had thought. "You don't get the dog until I have the money." — "Then there's nothing we can do," said Ezra. His voice quivered. Heinz screamed again: "You don't have the money!" He was close to tears. "I do have it!" shouted Ezra. His

183

voice cracked. "Then show me it! Show me, stupid dog, dog, stupid, show me it if you've got it!" Heinz couldn't stand the tension any longer. He dropped the refined tone and grabbed Ezra. Ezra shoved him back. The boys wrestled. They wrestled on the ruined wall, and under the movements of their bitter wrestling, under the jolts of their furious blows, it began to crumble. The mortar, parched and brittle from the heat of the fire, trickled out of the gaps between the bricks, and the wall caved in, along with the fighting boys. They screamed. They screamed for help. They screamed in German and English for help. The policemen on the square heard the screams. The German policemen heard the screams and the American military policemen heard the screams. The Negro policemen heard the screams, too. The siren of the American police jeep shrilled. The sirens of the German patrol cars answered.

The screams of the sirens came into the Bräuhaus hall and ignited the beer spirits. Rumor, almighty weaver of mischief, Rumor raised her head anew and proclaimed her tale. The Negroes had committed a new crime. They had lured a child into the ruins and slain him. The police were at the scene of the crime. The child's maimed body had been found. The voice of the people joined Rumor. Rumor and the voice of the people spoke in chorus: "How long are we going to put up with this?" For many, the Negro club was an annoyance. For many, the girls, the women who spent time with Negroes, were an annoyance. The Negroes in uniform, their club, their girls, weren't they a black symbol of defeat, of the shame of being defeated, weren't they the badge of humiliation and disgrace? For one instant more, the crowd hesitated. There was no leader, no Führer. A couple of boys were the first to move. They all followed, followed with red faces, breathing heavily and excited. Christopher was just going to his car. He asked: "What's happening? Why are they all running?" The man with whom Christopher had eaten radish said: "The niggers have killed a child. Your nig-

184

gers!" He stood up and gave Christopher a challenging look. Christopher called: "Ezra!" He ran with the crowd onto the square and called "Ezra!" His call was drowned out in the road of the excited voices. He couldn't get through to his car. He thought, 'why aren't there any police on the square?' The entrance to the Negro club was unguarded. Behind the big windowpanes shone red drapes. There was music. Herr Behrend's band was playing Hallelujah. "Enough of this nigger music," screamed the voice of the people. "Enough, enough," shouted Frau Behrend. The two bald businessmen were supporting her. Frau Behrend was tottering a little, but her attitude was impeccable. They had to support her. They had to support that good attitude. In a riot, you never know who throws the first stone. The one who throws the first stone doesn't know why he does it, that is, unless he had been paid to do it. But someone does throw the first stone. Then the other stones follow quickly and easily. The windows of the Negro club broke under the stones.

'Everything breaks down,' thought Philipp, 'we can't communicate any more, Edwin isn't talking, it's the loudspeaker speaking, even Edwin uses loudspeaker language, or the loudspeakers, these dangerous robots, are holding Edwin captive, too: his word is pressed through their tin mouth, it becomes loudspeaker language, the global idiom that everyone knows and no one understands.' Every time Philipp heard a lecture, he had to think of Chaplin. Every speaker reminded him of Charlie Chaplin. He was, in his way, a Chaplin. In the most earnest and grave lecture, Philipp had to laugh about Chaplin. Chaplin tried to articulate thoughts, to pass on insights, to speak friendly and wise words into the microphone, but the friendly and wise words tumbled like fanfare blasts, like a pack of lies and demagogic slogans, out of the loudspeaker funnels. The good Chaplin at the microphone heard only his words, he heard the friendly and wise words that he spoke into the audio filter, he heard his thoughts, he listened to the reverberations of his soul, but he didn't hear the bellowing of the amplifiers, he didn't catch their simplifications and their stupid imperatives. At the end of his address, Chaplin believed he had led his audience to reflection and contemplation, and made them smile. He was pained and surprised when the people sprang to their feet, shouted Heil, and began hitting each other. Edwin's listeners would not hit each other. They were asleep. The people who might have brawled were asleep. The ones who weren't asleep wouldn't brawl. It was the gentle ones who weren't asleep. With another Chaplin, the wild ones wouldn't have slept and the gentle ones would have nodded off. Then the wild ones would have ungently woken the peaceable ones. At Edwin's lecture, no one would be wakened. The lecture would have no consequences at all. The first to fall asleep was Schnakenbach. Behude had led him away from the microphones. He had sat Schnakenbach down between himself and the philoso- phy class of the Catholic seminary. He thought, 'neither they nor I can help him, we can't reach him.' Did Schnakenbach even exist? To Schnakenbach the hall, the lecturing poet, and his listeners were a chemico-physical process that had not attained proper reac- tion. Schnakenbach's view of the world was inhuman. It was wholly abstract. His teacher training had imparted to Schnakenbach a world view that was, on the outside, still intact, the world view of classical physics, in which everything nicely followed laws of causality, and in which God lived, smiled about but tolerated, in a kind of rest home. And Schnakenbach, too, could have settled down in this world. His classmates settled down. They died in the war and were survived by wives and children. Schnakenbach didn't want to go to war. He was unmarried. He began to reflect, and he decided that the world view he had been taught no longer fit. Above all, he discovered that there were already scholars who knew and proclaimed that this world view didn't fit. Schnakenbach, in order to evade the barracks, swallowed sleep-depriving pills and studied Einstein, Planck, de Broglie, Jeans, Schrödinger, and Jordan. Now he was looking into a world in which God's rest home was gone. Either there was no God, or God was dead as Nietzsche had claimed or, this too was possible and as old as it was new, God was everywhere, yet formless, no bearded God the Father, and the whole of mankind's father complex from the Prophets to Freud proved to be a self-tormenting error on the part of homo sapiens, God was a formula, an abstraction, maybe God was Einstein's general theory of gravity, the feat of balance in an ever expanding universe. Wherever Schnakenbach was, he was the center and the circle, he was the beginning and the end, but he was nothing special, everyone was center and circle, beginning and end, so was every speck, the grain of sleep in his eye, the generous helping he got from the sandman, was also a composite thing, a microcosm in itself with atom suns and satellites, Schnakenbach saw a microphysical world, filled to bursting with the tiniest of things, and, in fact, it did burst, it burst continually, exploded into the distance, escaped into the indescribable, the final infinity of space. Schnakenbach the sleeper was in constant motion and change; he received and emitted forces; from the most distant parts of the cosmos they came to him and left him, they traveled faster than the speed of light and traveled for billions of light years, it depended on how you looked at it, it couldn't be explained, it might be noted down in a couple of figures, maybe you could write it on the torn-off wrapper of a packet of pills, maybe you needed an electronic brain to find even an approximate figure, the true sum would remain unknown, maybe man's reign had ended. Edwin spoke of the summa theologiae of Scholasticism. "Veni creator spiritus, come creator spirit, remain creator spirit, only in the spirit are we." Edwin called out the great names Homer, Virgil, Dante, Goethe. He invoked the palaces and the ruins, the cathedrals and the schools. He spoke of Augustine, Anselm, Thomas, Pascal. He mentioned Kierkegaard, that Christianity was just a glow any more,

187

and yet, said Edwin, this glow, perhaps the final twilight glow of tired Europe, was the only warming light in the world. The fashion designers were asleep. Their models were asleep. Alexander, the actor who played archdukes, was asleep. His mouth hung open; emptiness streamed in and out. Messalina was fighting with sleep. She thought of Philipp and the charming green-eyed girl, and whether she might not be able to interest Edwin in the party after all. Miss Wescott copied down things she didn't understand but considered profound. Miss Burnett thought, 'I'm hungry, whenever I hear a lecture I get terribly hungry, there must be something the matter with me: I don't feel uplifted, I feel hungry.' Alfredo, the delicate, aging lesbian, had rested her cheek against Hänschen's confirmation day suit and was dreaming something terribly indecent. Hänschen thought, 'I wonder if she has any money.' He was a little adding machine; but he was still inexperienced, otherwise he must have known that poor Alfredo had no money. He would have pulled the arm she was leaning on out from under her. Hänschen was callous. Jack tried to take note of everything Edwin said. Jack was a parrot. He liked to repeat things. But the speech was too long. It was tiring and confusing. Jack could concentrate only for a little while at a time. He had worries. He was thinking about Hänschen. Hänschen was already asking for money again. But Jack had no money either. The whiskey she had drunk with Emilia had left Kay dopey. She didn't understand her poet. What he said was lovely and wise; but it must have been too elevated, Kay didn't understand it. Dr. Kaiser probably would have understood it. She sat uncomfortably on her fire department seat and leaned against the arm of the German poet who sat on the hard police chair. She thought, 'maybe the German poet is easier to understand, he wouldn't be as smart as Edwin, but maybe he has more heart, the German poets dream, they sing of the forest and of love.' Philipp thought, 'they're asleep, and yet there is greatness in his lecture, wasn't the madman right to want to wake us? he is one of Behude's patients, what Edwin is trying to do moves me, I admire him, now I admire him, his lecture is a futile invocation, surely he, too, senses how futile the invocation is, maybe that's what moves me, Edwin is one of those moving, helpless, tormented visionaries, he doesn't tell us what he sees, what he sees is terrible, he tries to draw a veil across his face, only sometimes does he lift the veil before the horror, maybe there is no horror, maybe there is nothing behind the veil, he's just talking to himself, and maybe he's talking to me, maybe to the priests, a colloquy of augurs, the others are asleep.' He pressed his arm more firmly around Kay. She was not asleep. She warmed him. She was warm, fresh life. Again and again, Philipp was aware of Kay's freer existence. It wasn't the girl, it was the freedom that he found seductive. He looked at her jewelry, a moonpale necklace of pearls, enamel, and diamond roses. 'It doesn't suit her,' he thought, 'where could she have gotten it, maybe she inherited it, she shouldn't wear jewelry, this old jewelry robs her of some of her freshness, maybe she should wear coral.' The necklace looked familiar to him, but he didn't recognize it as Emilia's. Philipp had no sense for jewels and no memory for their form and shape, and besides, he avoided looking at Emilia's treasures; he knew that the stones, the pearls, and the gold coaxed forth tears, tears that oppressed him; Emilia had to sell her jewelry, she cried while she carried it to the jeweler's, and Philipp, too, lived on the profits from the gems and the tears. It was one of the calamities of his existence that, were he alone, without Emilia, he could live much more simply and support himself, but since he loved Emilia and lived with her, shared board and bed with her, he robbed her of what she owned and was, like a bird to a stick, glued to the luxury Bohème of the Kommerzienrat inheritance, and could no longer move his natural wings for the little flights that were meant for him and that would have given him sustenance. It was a bondage, love bondage, shackles of eros, but the course of that life had led into a dependence on the bad management of a fortune reduced to rubble, that was a different bondage, an unwelcome one, that weighed heavily upon his feelings of love. 'I will never be free again,' thought Philipp, 'I've sought freedom my whole life long, but I've lost my way.' Edwin mentioned freedom. The European spirit, he said, was the future of freedom, or freedom would have no more future in the world. Here Edwin addressed a pronouncement by an American poet completely unknown to his audience, Gertrude Stein, of whom it is said that Hemingway learned to write from her. Edwin had an equal dislike of both Gertrude Stein and Hemingway, he thought of them as literary types, boulevardiers, second-rate minds, and they in turn repaid his lack of respect amply and called him an epigone and sublime imitator of the great and dead poetry of the great and dead centuries. As pigeons on the grass, said Edwin, quoting Stein, so something written by her had stuck with him after all, although he was thinking less of pigeons on grass than of pigeons on the Piazza San Marco in Venice, as pigeons on the grass, that is how certain modern minds regarded people, while they strove to expose that which was senseless and apparently coinciden-tal in human existence, to portray man as free of God, then to leave him fluttering about free in the void, senseless, valueless, free, and menaced by snares, prey to the butcher, but proud of this imagined freedom that leads to nothing but misery, this freedom from God and divine origin. And yet, said Edwin, every pigeon knows its dovecote, and every bird is in God's hand. The priests pricked up their ears. Was Edwin working their fields? Was he nothing but a lay preacher? Miss Wescott stopped writing everything down. Hadn't she heard what Edwin was saying now once before? Weren't they similar thoughts that Miss Burnett had expressed on the National Socialists' square, hadn't she, too, compared people with pigeons or with birds, and depicted their existence as coincidental and imper-iled? Miss Wescott gave Miss Burnett a surprised glance. Was the thought that man felt endangered and an object of coincidence so widespread that the admired poet and her much less admired fellow

teacher could articulate it almost simultaneously? That confused
Miss Wescott. She was no pigeon, nor any other bird. She was a
person, a teacher, she had a job for which she had prepared and was
constantly continuing to prepare, she had her duties, and she tried
to fulfill them. Miss Wescott found that Miss Burnett looked hungry; a curiously hungry expression was on Miss Burnett's face, as
though the world, as though Edwin's illuminations had made her
terribly hungry. Philipp thought, 'now he's coming to Goethe, it's
almost German the way Edwin is citing Goethe now, the law-by-
which-we-took-our-places, and he, like Goethe, seeks freedom in
this law: he did not find it.' Edwin had spoken his last word. The
loudspeakers crunched and crackled. They went on crunching and
crackling after Edwin had finished, and the wordless crunching and
crackling in their toothless mouths jolted the audience back from
sleep, dreams, and wandering thoughts.

The stones, the stones they had thrown, the tinkling glass, the
falling splinters, alarmed the crowd. The older ones felt reminded of
something; they felt reminded of another blindness, of an earlier
street action, of other splinters. With splinters it had started back
then, and with splinters it had ended. The splinters it ended with
had been the splinters of their own windows. "Stop it! We're going
to have to pay for it," they said. "We always have to pay for it when
something gets broken." Christopher had pushed his way to the
front. He wasn't quite sure what it was all about, but he had pushed
his way to the front. He got up on a rock and shouted: "Please, be
reasonable, people!" The people didn't understand him. But since
he held his arms out so protectively, they laughed and said he was
Saint Christopher. Richard Kirsch had also run to the front. His
Fräulein had warned him: "don't pay any attention to that, don't
get involved, it's none of your business," but he had run up there
anyway. Together with Christopher, he was ready to defend America, the black America that lay behind him, the dark America

191

hiding behind broken windows and flapping red drapes. The music had stopped. The girls shrieked. They called for help, although no one was harming them. The rush of air that came in through the shattered windows settled like a paralysis over the black soldiers. It wasn't the Germans they were afraid of. The fate that pursued them, the lifelong persecution that wouldn't let them free, even in Germany, cast a gloom over them and paralyzed them. They were determined to defend themselves. They were determined to defend themselves on the floor of the club. They would fight, they would fight in their club, but the paralysis kept them from charging into the sea, into the sea of white people, into these white seas churning for miles around their little black island. The siren cars of the police moved in. You could hear their piercing shouts. You could hear whistles, shouts, and laughter. "Come," said Susanne. She knew a way out. She took Odysseus by the hand. She led him through a dark corridor, past garbage bins across a courtyard, to a low, collapsed wall. Susanne and Odysseus climbed over the wall. They groped their way through ruins and reached a deserted alley. "Quick!" said Susanne. They hurried down the alley. The sound of their steps was drowned out by the ceaseless howl of the sirens. The police shoved the crowd back. A cordon of military police took up positions in front of the club entrance. Whoever wanted to leave the club was checked. Christopher felt a small hand tugging him off his rock. There in front of him stood Ezra. His suit was torn, his hands and his face were scratched up. Behind Ezra stood a boy, a stranger; his clothes, too, were torn, his face and his hands, too, were scratched up. Ezra and Heinz had fallen on the stones of the collapsing wall. They had hurt themselves. In the first moment of fear, they had called for help. But then, when they heard the police sirens, they had helped each other up out of the rocks and fled onto Bäckergasse. From there they had made their way back to the square. They wanted nothing more to do with each other. They avoided each other's eyes. They had awakened from fairy tales and

Indian stories and were ashamed. "Don't ask," said Ezra to Christopher, "don't ask, I'd like to drive home. It's nothing. I fell." Christopher pushed through the crowd to his car. Out the club door came Washington and Carla. They walked to their car. "There he is!" shouted Frau Behrend. "Who is that?" shouted the baldheaded businessmen. Frau Behrend was silent. Was she supposed to announce her disgrace to the world? "Is it the taxi murderer?" asked the one baldhead. He licked the corners of his mouth. "There goes the taxi murderer," shouted the second baldhead. "This woman says it's the taxi murderer. She knows him!" The second baldhead's face was beaded with sweat. A new wave of rage foamed up from the crowd. The broken windows had sobered them, but once they saw human prey, their hunting instincts awoke, the frenzy of the chase, the pack's hunger for the kill. Whistles shrilled, someone shouted: "the murderer and his whore," and again the stones flew. The stones flew against the horizonblue sedan. They hit Carla and Washington, they hit Richard Kirsch who was here defending America, the America of freedom and brotherhood, by standing by the imperiled couple, the foully thrown stones hit America and Europe, they defiled the oft invoked European spirit, they injured mankind, they hit the dream of Paris, the dream of Washington's Inn, the dream NOBODY IS UNWELCOME, but they couldn't kill the dream, which is stronger than any thrown stone, and they hit a little boy who had run to the horizonblue car screaming "Mother!"

The little dog snuggled up close to Emilia. He was still afraid. He was afraid of the other dogs in the mansion on Fuchsstrasse, he was afraid of the cats and the screeching parrot, he was afraid of the cold and dead air in this house. But the animals didn't harm him. They calmed down. They had growled, howled, screeched, they had sniffed at him and then they had calmed down. They knew the new dog would stay. He was a new companion, a new colleague, let him stay. There was enough for the animals in this house to eat, even if

193

there wasn't enough for the people any more. The dog would get used to the cold and dead air, and Emilia was to him a promise of friendship and warmth. But Emilia was freezing. She had hoped that Philipp would be waiting at home for her. So far, she was still Dr. Jekyll. Dr. Jekyll wanted to be nice to Philipp. But Philipp wasn't there. He had gone away on her. He hadn't been nice to nice Dr. Jekyll. How Emilia hated this house that she would never walk out of forever! The house was a grave, but it was the grave of the living Emilia, and she couldn't leave it. How she hated the pictures that Philipp had hung up! A centaur with a naked woman on its equine back, a reconstruction of a Pompeian mural, stared at her with a mocking smile. In reality, the centaur's face was expressionless. It was as expressionless as all the faces in Pompeian pictures, but to Emilia it seemed that the centaur was mocking her. Hadn't Philipp, too, carried her off, not exactly on horseback, but young and naked he had snatched her away from her faith in possessions, away from her lovely innocent faith in the eternal right of possession, and led her into the realm of intellect, of poverty, of doubt and crises of conscience. In a dark frame hung a Piranesi etching, the remains of the old aqueduct in Rome, a reminder of decay and collapse. All around Emilia there was nothing but decay, pieces of the Kommerzienrat inheritance, dead books, dead spirit, dead art. This house was unbearable. Didn't she have friends? Didn't she have friends among the living? Couldn't she go visit Messalina and Alexander? At Messalina's there were music and drinks, at Messalina's there was dancing, at Messalina's there was forgetting. 'If I go now,' she said to herself, 'I'll come home as Mr. Hyde.' 'Fine,' she said to herself, 'Philipp is not here. If he wanted it differently, he would be here. Should I wait here for him? Am I a widow? Do I want to live like a hermit? And what if Philipp was here? Then what? Then nothing! No music, no dancing. We'd sit facing each other and be gloomy. We'd still have love, erotic despair. Why shouldn't I drink, why not be Mr. Hyde?'

Philipp led Kay out of the hall. He still saw how Edwin bowed, how long he held his face turned to the floor, closed his eyes in shame, as if the thanks he now received, the applause he had secretly envied the actors and protagonists of the day, were something visible and loathsome, come about through pure misunderstanding, a brutal precipitation that followed incomprehension, a release for the audience, who had understood nothing of Edwin's words, and who were now, with the clapping of their hands, brushing away like a bothersome cobweb the gentle and delicate tinge of his spirit, coarsened already by the loudspeakers and, by the time it reached them, already lifeless, already dead, already become dust and decay: it was a humiliation, and because he grasped it as a mockery and humiliation—a victory for hustle and bustle, for plain convention, for the inglorious business of peddling fame, and for nonspirit—the poet closed his eyes in shame. Philipp understood him. He thought, 'my unhappy brother my beloved brother my great brother.' Emilia would have said: "And my poor brother? You don't mention that." — "Certainly. Also my poor brother," Philipp would have replied, "but that is insignificant. What you call poor is the heart of the poet, around which the happiness, love, and greatness of poetic life settle, like snow around the core of an avalanche. A cold image, Emilia, but Edwin, his word, his spirit, his message, all of which had no visible effect in this hall and left behind no perceptible tremors, number among the great avalanches tumbling down into the valley of our time." — "And destroying," Emilia would have added, "and bringing cold." But Emilia was not there, she was probably at home, creating with schnapps and wine the frightful Mr. Hyde who wept over the destruction of property, whose destroyed property had made her a drunkard, and who used destruction on a small scale, the mad raging of a drunk, to fight against the great destruction of the time. Philipp led Kay out of the hall. They escaped the teachers; they gave Alexander and Messalina the slip. The nicely made up, well-dressed, and relatively well situated American teachers were left standing like poor intimidated German teachers in the lecture hall. In their notebooks they had written dead words, a list of dead words, grave markers of spirit; words that would not awaken them to any life, to any meaning. Ahead of them lay a bus ride back to the hotel, a cold snack in the hotel, letter writing to Massachusetts we-toured-a-German-city, we-heard-Edwin-speak-it-was-wonderful, ahead lay the hotel bed, and it was not much different from the bed at other places on the trip. What else was there? There were dreams. And then the disappointment with Kay; the charming, the shameless girl, she had run off with that German poet, and they didn't even know who he was and what his name was, and one should seriously consider notifying the police, but Miss Burnett was against it, and she stopped Miss Wescott short with the thought of the scandal there would be if the military police with their siren cars had to go looking for little faithless Kay. The Amerika-Haus, a National Socialist Führer structure, lay behind Philipp and Kay. The house, its symmetrical rows of windows shining out into the night, looked like certain museums do, like a colossal tomb of antiquity, like an office building where the estate of antiquity, the spirit, the heroic sagas, the gods, is administered. Kay didn't want to go with Philipp, but something in her didn't resist going with him after all, and this something swept the Kay who didn't want to go with Philipp along with it, so strong was it, and it was a yearning for romance, yearning for the unusual, yearning for experience, for doing something special, for adventure, for age, for degeneration and downfall, for sacrifice, surrender, and Iphigenia myth, it was spite, it was being tired of the tour group, it was the excitement of a foreign place, the impatience of youth, it was Emilia's whiskey, it was that she was tired of the gushing, inhibited love of the Misses Wescott and Burnett. Kay thought, 'he'll take me to his apartment, I'll see the apartment of a German poet, Dr. Kaiser will be interested in

that, maybe the German poet will seduce me, of course I'd rather
have had Edwin seduce me, but Edwin's lecture was boring, to be
honest, it was cold and boring, I'll be the only one in our tour group
who can tell people back home what it's like when a German poet
seduces you.' She leaned against Philipp's arm. The city was filled
with the screaming of police sirens. Kay thought, 'it's a jungle,
there must be a lot of crime in this city.' And Philipp thought,
'where can I go with her? I could go to Fuchsstrasse, but Emilia may
already be drunk, she is Mr. Hyde, if she's Mr. Hyde, she can't
entertain company, should I go with the American girl to the Hotel
zum Lamm? the hotel is shabby, it's depressing, that would mean
taking the little lamb to the Lamb, what do I want from her? do I
want to sleep with her? I might be able to sleep with her, for her it's
romance abroad, for her I'm something like an aging gigolo, the
poem about the Porta Nigra by Stefan George: do I feel the arrogance of the old gigolo? Kay is charming, but I'm not so keen on
that, it's not her I want, it's that other land, I want wide open
spaces, I want distant places, another horizon, I want youth, the
young land, I want to be carefree, I want the future and things
transient, I want the wind, and since I don't want anything else,
would the other be a crime?' After a couple of steps, Philipp
thought, 'I want the crime.'

They lay together, white skin, black skin, Odysseus Susanne
Circe the Sirens and maybe Nausicaa, they writhed, black skin
white skin in a small room supported flimsily by a couple of beams
and hanging almost like a little balloon over the depths, since the
foundation walls of the house had been torn away, a bomb had torn
them to one side and never would they be rebuilt. The walls of the
little room were covered with pictures of actors, the most looked-at,
the representative faces of the day looked down with their dumb
shapeliness, with their empty beauty at them, lying on their pillows, black and white, on pillows shaped like animals, like devils
and longlegged vamps, naked white and black, they lay as if on a

197

raft, in the blending swirl they lay as if on a raft, naked and beautiful and wild, they lay, innocent, on a raft sailing off into infinity.

"An infinity! But an infinity composed of the tiniest finite bits, that's the world. Our body, our form, that which we think of as ourself, is nothing but a mass of little points, the tiniest of little points. But the little points are nothing to sneeze at: they're power stations, the tiniest of tiny power stations with the greatest of power. Everything can explode! But the billions of power stations are, for the shortest instant, for our life, blown like sand into this form that we call our self. I could write out the formula for you." Leaning on Behude's arm, half asleep, Schnakenbach tottered home. His poor head looked like a plucked chicken's crown. 'It's idiotic,' thought Behude, 'but how can I answer him? it's idiocy, but maybe he's right, we don't know much about things small or large, there's no home left for us in this world that Schnakenbach wants to interpret for me with a formula, did Edwin have an interpretation? he had none, his lecture left me cold, and it only led into a cold, dark, dead-end alley.'

Edwin had withdrawn from everyone, like an old eel, he had slithered out of all invitations, he had even avoided the ride home in the consulate car; down the stairs of the Amerika-Haus, down the marble steps of the Führer building, he had slipped into the night, into the foreign city, and into adventure. A poet doesn't age. His heart beats young. He had walked into the alleys. He walked without a plan, following his nose, his big nose guided him. He found the dark alleys around the station, the parks around the courthouse, the alleys of the old part of town, the precincts of Oscar Wilde's golden adders. At this hour, Edwin was Socrates and Alcibiades. He would have liked to be Socrates in Alcibiades' form, but he was Alcibiades in Socrates' body, though erect and well dressed. They were expecting him. Bene, Kare, Schorschi, and Sepp were expecting him. They had been waiting a long time for him. They didn't see Socrates and Alcibiades. They saw an old John, an old fool, a wealthy old pansy. They didn't know that they were beautiful. They had no idea that there is such a thing as falling victim to beauty, and that the lover can love in his beloved, in the body of a coarse youth, the reflection of eternal beauty, of immortality, of the soul as Plato worshiped it. Bene, Schorschi, Kare, and Sepp hadn't read Platen either he-whose-eyes-pure-beauty-hath-beheld-is-already-in-the-grasp-of-death. They saw an elegant, rich John, a funny business they didn't even quite understand, but which, as they knew from experience, was at times profitable. Edwin saw their faces. He thought, 'they are proud and beautiful.' He did not overlook their fists, their big and brutish fists, but he kept his eyes on their faces, proud and beautiful.

It was a party without pride and beauty. Was it a party? What were they celebrating? Were they celebrating the void? They said: "We're celebrating!" But they were only giving rein to their dulled senses. They drank champagne and they let desolation prevail, they filled the vacuum of their lives with sounds, they chased their fear with midnight music and shrill laughter. It was a hideous party. There was no party atmosphere; there wasn't even an atmosphere of lust. Alexander was sleeping. He was sleeping with his mouth open. Alfredo, too, was sleeping, with pointed chin, disappointed, a little cat having bad dreams. Messalina was dancing with Jack. Jack was the reluctant loser in a freestyle wrestling match. Hänschen was talking with Emilia about business. He wanted to know whether the occupation dollar would be taken out of circulation. He wanted to buy himself scrap gold. He knew that Emilia knew something about such dealings. Little adding machine Hänschen-be-nimble purred. Emilia was drinking. She drank champagne and strong, burning gin, she drank high proof cognac and heavy Rhine Palatinate

199

Spätlese wines. She filled herself full. She drank everything she got her hands on. She constructed Mr. Hyde. She constructed him maliciously and systematically. She drank to hurt Messalina. She danced with no one. She let no one touch her. She was a chaste drunk. She poured down whatever would go down. What did she care about the other guests? She had come here to drink. She lived for herself. She was the Kommerzienrat heiress. That was enough. The heiress had been robbed; people had laid hands on her inheritance. That was enough for her. That was enough of people for her. She didn't need to know anything more about people. When she was finished drinking she would leave. She had drunk enough. The orgy didn't interest her. She left. She went home to her animals. She went home to rant and rage, home to make accusations. Philipp the coward wouldn't face up to Mr. Hyde, he would stay away from the raging, she had to rage at the superintendent, she had to scream at the bolted doors, at the doors behind which lived only cold self-interest.

He closed the door of the room, and he saw that she was cold. The ugly single room, the shabby place with its cheap, high gloss finished furniture, these tasteless, factory-made furnishings, was that the poetic dwelling, the home of the German poet? He looked at her, 'she thinks it's a flophouse.' He couldn't try to be tender with her now; he had to throw her down, like a calf in the butcher's yard, he had to throw her down, 'so she'll have something from her flophouse.' Withered. Numb. He felt old and he felt his heart growing cold. He thought, 'I don't want to become evil: no heart of stone.' He opened the window. The hotel air was stale and sour. They inhaled the night. They stood at the window of the Hotel zum Lamm and inhaled the night. Their shadow leapt onto the street. It was the shadow of love, a momentary apparition flitting by. They saw the electric sign of the écarté club flash on and the lucky clover leaf unfold. They heard the police siren cars. They heard a cry for

200

help. A shrill English voice called for help. It was only a short cry, and then the cry died. "That was Edwin's voice," said Kay. Philipp answered nothing. He thought, 'it was Edwin.' He thought, 'what a sensational story for the Neues Blatt.' Even the Abendecho would put a world famous author who got mugged on the front page. Philipp thought, 'I am a bad reporter.' He didn't move. He thought, 'can I still cry? do I still have tears? would I cry if Edwin were dead?' Kay said: "I'd like to go." She thought, 'he's poor, how poor he is, he's ashamed because he's so poor, how poor this room is, he's a poor German.' She undid the necklace, the moonpale necklace of pearls, enamel, and diamond roses, the old piece of grandmother jewelry that Emilia had given her. She laid Emilia's attempt to do a free and spontaneous deed on the windowsill. Philipp understood the gesture. He thought, 'she thinks I'm starving.' Little Kay saw the clover leaf, the flashing neon light and thought, 'that is his forest, his oak tree grove, his German forest where he strolls and composes poetry.'

Midnight strikes in the tower. The day is done. One page falls from the calendar. A new date is written. The editors yawn. The printing blocks of the morning papers are being quoined up. What had happened during the day, what had been said, lied, killed, and destroyed lay, poured in lead, like a flat cake on the trays of the makeup men. The cake was hard outside and inside it was slippery. Time had baked the cake. The newspaper people had broken the bad news into pages, misfortune, need, and crime; they had pressed screaming and lies into columns. The headlines stood, the help-lessness of the heads of state, the dismay of the scholars, the fear of mankind, the disbelief of the theologians, the reports of the acts of the desperate were ready to be multiplied, they were dipped into the bath of printer's ink. The rotary machines ran. Their cylinders pressed onto the roll of white paper the slogans of the new day, the torches of foolishness, the questions of fear, and the categorical imperatives of intimidation. Just a few hours, and tired, poor women will carry the headlines, the slogans, the torches, the fear, and the faint hope into the reader's home; freezing, irritable vendors will hang out the augurs' pronouncements for the morning on the walls of their newsstands. The news doesn't make it warmer. TENSION, CONFLICT, ESCALATION, THREAT. In the sky, the fliers drone. For now, the sirens are silent. For now, their tin mouth goes on rusting. The air raid shelters were being blown up; the air raid shelters are being rebuilt. Death is conducting war games. THREAT, ESCALATION, CONFLICT, TENSION. Come-now-gentle-slumber. Yet no one escapes his world. Dreams are heavy and disquieting. Germany lives in a field of tension, eastern world, western world, broken world, two world halves, alien and enemy to each other, Germany lives on the seam, where the seam splits open, time is precious, it is just a span, a meager span, wasted, a second to catch your breath, breathing spell on a damned battlefield.